Nerds
Who
Kill

By Mark Richard Zubro

The Tom and Scott Mysteries

A Simple Suburban Murder
Why Isn't Becky Twitchell Dead?
The Only Good Priest
The Principal Cause of Death
An Echo of Death
Rust on the Razor
Are You Nuts?
One Dead Drag Queen
Here Comes the Corpse
File Under Dead

The Paul Turner Mysteries

Sorry Now?
Political Poison
Another Dead Teenager
The Truth Can Get You Killed
Drop Dead
Sex and Murder.com
Dead Egotistical Morons

Nerds
Who
Kill

Mark Richard Zubro

St. Martin's Minotaur
New York

www.minotaurbooks.com

Library of Congress Cataloging-in-Publication Data

Zubro, Mark Richard.
      Nerds who kill / Mark Richard Zubro.—1st St. Martin's ed.
          p. cm.
      ISBN 0-312-33301-3
      EAN 978-0-312-33301-0
      1. Turner, Paul (Fictitious character)—Fiction. 2. Women authors—Crimes against—Fiction. 3. Science fiction—Authorship—Fiction. 4. Police—Illinois—Chicago—Fiction. 5. Congresses and conventions—Fiction. 6. Gay police officers—Fiction. 7.Chicago (Ill.)—Fiction. 8. Gay fathers—Fiction. 9. Gay men—Fiction. I. Title.

PS3576.U225N47 2005
813'.54—dc22
                                                                                    2005040701

First Edition: June 2005

10 9 8 7 6 5 4 3 2 1

For Barb and Jeanne, as always,
many thanks.
Thanks also to Bob Beran.
And to Kyle and Kyle—you both helped.

Nerds
Who
Kill

1

A tremendous crash woke Paul Turner out of a sound sleep. He was on his feet and out his bedroom door in seconds. Ben, his lover, was right behind him. When he got to the top of the stairs, he heard the tinkle of shattering glass. His son Brian, baseball bat in hand, emerged from his room. Paul rushed down the stairs and banged open his younger son's bedroom door. The bed was empty. He listened for a moment. The source of the noise was the kitchen. He dashed in that direction.

In the light from the hall, he saw his eleven-year-old son, Jeff's, wheelchair on its side, up against the far cabinets. Using his hands, arms, and elbows, Jeff was crawling along the floor. Paul hurried to him. Jeff looked up at his father. He said, "I'm fine. I don't need help."

Paul knelt over his son. Jeff very much needed help, but the boy had been insisting on being more independent lately. Paul hovered inches away, set to help or guide, lift or carry, as his son wished or needed.

Ben flipped on the kitchen light. The room looked as if every pot in the house was on the stove or on the floor. Strings of translucent metal criss-crossed the kitchen table. Metallic paint and silver-colored plastic shimmered in a variety of bowls, pots, and pans. Shards of a glass pitcher were strewn over half the floor. A metallic, burnt plastic smell wafted through the air. A cool breeze flowed in from the open back door.

Jeff stopped trying to right himself and breathed heavily. He saw his brother with the bat. "What's that for?" Jeff asked.

Brian said, "For bashing little brothers."

"Hah."

Jeff was in his blue *X-Men* pajamas. The two adults were in white briefs. Brian wore black silk boxer shorts and a black T-shirt.

"What were you trying to do?" Paul asked. "It's two in the morning." He shut the back door. The smell became stronger immediately. Seconds later the smoke detector began beeping. Paul turned off all the burners on the stove, removed all the pots on top of it, and then opened the door again. Ben stood on a chair and disconnected the battery. The beeping stopped. Hands on hips, Paul turned to his son.

Jeff said, "I had to make some last-minute adjustments on my costume. I was trying to heat the plastic so I could form it into the right shapes."

Paul knew his sons were excited about going to the World's Ultimate Science Fiction Convention, which was being held this weekend in Chicago. The younger boy, Jeff, had dinned whole symphonies of enthusiasm into his ears for months. Jeff wanted to wear a superhero costume. Paul thought that being confined to a wheelchair might limit his son's possibilities. Jeff had decided he was going as Charles Xavier from *X-Men* and he'd insisted on a new suit. Ben had spent hours creating a headpiece that Jeff claimed the character wore in the movies to enhance his mind control abilities.

Paul hadn't seen the movies. He knew Jeff had stacks of comic books in chronological order, carefully arranged by superhero or heroes. Most of the attachment to the wheelchair apparatus, tendrils of twisted coat hangers, plastic, glue, and aluminum foil, was on the back porch awaiting transport for the occasion.

"We could have helped you," Paul said.

"I know. I wanted to try doing it myself."

Paul said, "Wanting to try doing it yourself is a good thing. Doing it at this hour of the morning is a bad thing. And next time you want to try doing it yourself, you need to have one of us supervise."

"Dad!"

Paul held his younger son's eyes. He was not going to debate with an eleven year old. Jeff was not above trying to use his spina bifida as a ploy for getting attention or for avoiding punishments, but Paul was immune to the manipulations of his son. The kid knew his big, deep brown eyes and his disability worked well, mostly with strangers. Paul gazed silently until the boy lowered his eyes.

"Sorry," Jeff said. He glanced around at the mess. Again, he tried to get up. This time, he allowed Paul to lift him into his wheelchair, which Brian had righted. When Jeff was seated, the youngster said, "I'll clean up the mess."

Brian trudged back up to bed.

"You need some help?" Ben asked.

"I think we've got it covered," Paul said. "I'll be up in a few minutes." Ben went upstairs and brought Paul back a pair of jeans. He gave Paul a brief hug and went back up to bed.

Paul helped Jeff clean. Plastic had congealed in the bottom of two pots. They were ruined. Paul held them out for Jeff to inspect. The boy said, "That'll shoot my allowance for half a year."

"About that," Paul agreed.

Into the silence, Jeff asked, "I can still go to the convention?" His voice quavered.

Paul said, "This wasn't malicious, but it could have turned into something dangerous. There could have been a fire. You know I'm serious about you asking one of us for help."

"I know. I will."

"You can go to the convention."

"Yes!" The boy began to pump his arm up and down in triumph.

"And your consequence will commence the day after."

The boy eyed his dad. "I understand," he said softly.

"Good." Paul ruffled the boy's hair. "I'm glad you didn't try and turn this into a debate. It is far too late, and you've been trying that far too much lately. That has to stop as well."

"Okay."

Father and son cleaned together in the quiet house. When the ruined pans were trashed and everything else was back in its place, Paul said, "Show me what you were trying to do."

Jeff took his materials and spread them out on the table. He explained the complicated changes he wanted to make to the part that attached to his wheelchair. Paul said, "Do you want me to try it?"

"You could show me."

Paul began to explain the process as he put together the parts and used heat and cooling as the plastic took on another shape. When he looked up, Jeff's head was sunk on his chest. The boy was fast asleep.

Paul shut the back door, then reinstalled the battery in the smoke detector. Then he wheeled Jeff to his room and lifted him into bed. He pulled the blanket over his son. He went back to the kitchen and finished the costume. It was nearly three-thirty when he crawled into bed. Ben woke briefly. "Everything okay?" he asked.

Paul murmured, "The aliens have not landed." He snuggled close and fell asleep.

The next morning it was a struggle to get his younger son to go to school. Normally, the boy loved to attend, but his distraction by the imminent opening of the convention was nearly total.

Jeff inspected his costume where Paul had left it on the back porch. The boy declared the final shape to be "cool." Paul didn't think it looked half bad.

Paul Turner spent a full day at his job as a detective for the city of Chicago. They had a call late in their shift from the new movie complex just east of Halsted and Randolph. The case was a no-brainer. At a Friday matinee a gray-haired man in his seventies had shot the teenager sitting next to him through the head. The teenager and his friend had sat through an early movie talking, laughing, and hitting each other. During the closing credits, the man had simply pulled a gun and fired. One teen lay dead. His partner in movie dis-etiquette was on the floor. He had shit and pissed his pants and, between sobs and tears, was begging for mercy. When the police arrived, the older gentleman simply turned over his gun to the cops and said, "That's one for the good guys." Buck Fenwick, Turner's partner on the police department, had been willing to argue for justifiable homicide. As he'd succinctly put it, "What exactly about this scenario was wrong?" Making noise in theaters was right up there in Fenwick's "done wrong" pantheon, just behind Cubs relief pitchers who blew saves but ahead of criminals who disturbed his lunch.

Unfortunately, the cowards in the row behind the man-versus-teenager drama—cowards who had been unwilling to verify the older gentleman's initial complaint—were now insistent upon seeing the person who shot the gun arrested. Fenwick had grumbled, "Some witnesses don't know when they've got it good." The arrest and paperwork had put Turner behind schedule for the evening's activities. As prearranged, he met everyone down at his lover's auto shop. He looked forward to something completely different.

Brian had kept his costume a secret. Paul wondered why his older boy, Brian, had gotten so interested in the convention. Paul hadn't known the older boy was particularly interested in science fiction or superheroes. He'd grown out of

5

his *Star Wars* mania and his interest in comic books a few years ago.

When Paul entered the shop, he saw that Mrs. Talucci, their ninetysomething next-door neighbor, was present, along with Myra, the most famous lesbian mechanic in the city. The two of them would be driving to the convention together. Mrs. Talucci was attending as an elderly Tribble. With all the extra padding she'd added to her slight frame, Mrs. Talucci now looked like a medicine ball covered in fur. Paul's son Jeff had worked up a small computer-guided electrical device so that Mrs. Talucci could cause the outer layer of her costume to wiggle and a hidden microphone to give off chirpy squeaks. Turner had to admit, it was pretty effective.

They were discussing Myra's lack of a costume. She said, "Half the dykes in the hall are going to look like Xena. What's the point if you can't stand out? I've got no imagination and no creativity. I'm going to watch the spectacle. And it's going to be quite a spectacle."

Jeff asked, "Why is it going to be a spectacle?"

Myra's eyes gleamed. "I call it the Michelin tire effect."

"What's that?"

Myra leaned closer to the boy. "Most of the women in those Xena costumes should have gone on every diet on the planet years ago. They've got all this metal surrounded by a leather skirt that might be adequate protection on a vehicle, but is not going to make it on their three-hundred-pound frames."

When Paul saw Brian, he realized why his older son had been totally mum about his costume. The teenager was in a butt flap and leather harness. The bit of brown leather covered by an eighth of an inch the front of the bottom of his torso, and his butt by slightly less. A broadsword dangled from a strap on his back. He was leaning one elbow on the side of their blue van. Myra began helping him cinch up the harness on the torso underneath.

"They let you bring those things?" Paul asked.

"The sword? Yeah. You've got to get special permission, and you've got to get bonded. You also have to be at least sixteen."

Paul examined the sword in its scabbard. "Is it real?"

Brian reached over his head, took out the sword, and handed it, hilt first, to his dad. "Try it."

It took two hands to heft it. The thing was as heavy as it looked. "You sharpen this?" Paul asked.

"No, the place you rent it from says you're not supposed to do anything with it."

The hilt had a bright blue stone in the center and glittery stuff that sparkled and rubbed off on his hands. "What's the glittery stuff?" Paul asked.

Brian said, "I think the technical term is 'glittery stuff.'"

Paul gave it back to his son. "Be careful with the thing."

Brian held out a metal clasp. "I have to have this attached so it can't be drawn. Convention rules."

Paul had asked Jeff if everyone would be in costume. Jeff had said, "Usually there's just like this one big costume deal on Saturday night." His son spoke as if he were an old hand at attending conventions as opposed to the reality, which was that he found these answers on the Internet. "There's so many people attending this convention that they divided the costume competition into categories for Friday night, with the top winners in each category as finalists on Saturday night."

"Who are you supposed to be?" Myra asked Paul.

Paul was in his navy blue sport jacket, beige pants, white shirt, and tie. Turner said, "A boring police detective."

"Got that in one," Myra said.

Paul said to Brian, "Who are you supposed to be, Tarzan?"

"No. The Beastmaster." Brian was in excellent shape and the costume revealed far more muscles than Turner thought appropriate. It wasn't an obscene costume, but it was trying to be.

"This costume is appropriate," Brian said.

"It's obscene," Myra said.

Jeff came around the van from the front. He said, "Ben told him he had to wear something under the butt flap."

"I knew that," Brian said.

Jeff said, "You're not going to make him change?"

Paul was not about to fight his sixteen year old over the costume. He knew he had to pick his battles, and this wasn't one of them. Going to the convention in this get-up might fill Brian's need to try to get himself attention. The boy wasn't doing drugs, he didn't come home drunk, and he hadn't gotten a girl pregnant. He didn't come home late or try to sneak in or out. His grades were excellent and, at least for now, he'd given up trying to get a tattoo and/or a motorcycle. A costume wasn't worth a hassle.

Ben came in. He wore jeans and a black T-shirt. He and Paul kissed. Ben said, "You've seen Tarzan here?" He patted Brian on his leather shoulder strap.

"The Beastmaster," Brian corrected.

Jeff said, "Could that be a master beaster?"

Brian glared at his younger brother. "If you're implying . . ."

Jeff said, "That you're like everybody else."

Brian said, "You know far too much and are much too young."

"Am not."

"Round one for tonight is over," Paul said. "And all sexual innuendo stops right there, no matter how remote."

Both boys huffed.

Ben said, "I think Fenwick might say, 'Maybe he's trying to work undercover.'"

Mrs. Talucci said, "Fenwick would come up with a much worse and more clear pun."

"They can't all be gems," Paul said. He patted Brian on the shoulder. "I imagine you will probably be cold. If that doesn't bother you, it doesn't bother me." The weather for

March had been seasonal, which meant a butt flap, harness, and Speedo were not a lot of protection. Paul suspected Brian would be too stubborn to admit he was cold. If the kid was willing to pay the price, Paul wasn't going to bug him about it.

Ian Hume walked in. He was a reporter, a former cop, and had been Turner's first lover. Ian was covering the convention for the local gay paper, the *Gay Tribune*.

Ian said, "Nice butt flap."

Brian said, "I wore it for you."

Paul said, "No more comments about butt flaps."

Ian wore his usual slouch fedora, khaki pants, blue shirt, and subdued tie. Myra looked him up and down, and said, "And you're going disguised as Indiana Jones on dress-up day?"

"I'm going as a bored reporter who covers this kind of shit for a paper whose stringer who covers these things has the flu."

"A perfect disguise then," said Mrs. Talucci.

Ian said, "And I'm going to be there for all three days. The idiot stringer set up all these interviews ages ago. I'd rather have root-canal surgery."

Myra said, "I shall begin weeping for your plight immediately."

They used their van to tote all of the paraphernalia for Jeff's costume. He would only actually don the cumbersome headpiece during the competition. When completely assembled it stretched nearly ten feet in every direction. According to Jeff, if it had been truly realistic, it would have extended past the ceiling.

A one-hundred-foot-tall inflatable Starship *Enterprise* floated outside the Greater Chicago Hotel and Convention Center. The entry hall of the hotel had a vast atrium in the middle, a one-thousand-seat restaurant to its left, and the hotel registration desk to the right. Copious large signs on easels pointed the way to the convention.

At the convention registration desk Turner saw a number of costumed individuals, but to his surprise most people were in ordinary attire.

Ben said, "I thought I'd see odder costumes and more of them."

Jeff said, "Boy, you guys are so out of it. There's like a hundred thousand people here. It's the biggest SF convention ever. Only maybe a couple thousand will be in costume. Most everybody who's going to be doing costumes will only have them on for the contest. Can I go to the game room first? I'm supposed to meet Bertram there as soon as I'm done registering."

A crowd swept toward their small gathering.

"Who is it, Dad?" Jeff asked.

Through a gap in the milling throng, Paul saw a woman dressed in a passionate purple evening gown. She carried a two-foot-long red ostrich feather in her right hand.

Paul said, "A woman in an evening gown. She's carrying this gigantic feather-plume thing."

"A red one?"

"Yeah."

"That's Muriam Devers." Paul had heard the name. She was one of the most renowned female science fiction writers, and she trailed only J. K. Rowling for sales. Devers and her entourage swept past.

Jeff pulled himself up as high as he could in his chair and craned his neck to look. When the milling mass had passed, Jeff said, "That was cool."

Brian said, "I thought you didn't like her books."

"No, I used to like her books, just not so much anymore. But she's famous. I want to see all the famous people here at the convention."

"What's with the feather?" Ben asked.

Jeff said, "The red ostrich feather is in her first book as a big part of the main character's costume. She started wearing them to all these conventions. Then it became a big deal, like her trademark. She's always wearing one in her pictures on the book jackets."

Bertram's parents and Paul and Ben had worked out a system so that one set of parents would be present at the convention at all times. Paul and Ben would take Bertram, Jeff's best buddy in fifth grade, home tonight and monitor activities on Sunday. Bertram's parents had the day shift Saturday. Everyone would be present Saturday night.

Ian was planning to attend several panels at the convention on gay sensibility in the field. There were also several graphic novelists who were trying to start a gay group. Ian said, "I'm supposed to be interviewing some guy who just had the third volume of his great gay space-opera trilogy published."

"How are you going to find him in this throng?" Paul asked.

"He's supposed to be this heavyset guy in a white beard."

Paul said, "Find somebody with a Santa complex and you're all set."

Ian said, "I set it up to meet him at the third pillar from the left at Pierre's."

"More intrigue than I care to know about," Paul said.

Paul had to work the next day and would have preferred a quiet evening at home. He saw Brian with three people, one in a Spider-Man costume, the other two scantily clad nymphets. He understood now why the boy wanted to attend.

Paul walked around the convention. In the dealers' room he saw people hawking posters and paraphernalia. It seemed to him that every second-rate television show that had anything to do with science fiction or fantasy had at least one booth trying to sell schlock souvenirs. There was another room with rows and rows of tables where people were demonstrating how to illustrate comic books to crowds clustered three or four deep. In another large hall, hundreds of people playing board games were gathered around octagonal tables. Paul was impressed with the level of seriousness and struck by the fact that the people all seemed to be intent and at ease at the same time.

Mrs. Talucci stomped over. She was using a cane. She claimed it wasn't for getting around, it was for moving slow people out of her way. She still walked to the store every morning for her daily papers.

"Why did you come?" he asked.

She smiled at him. "Never been to one of these. Thought I'd check it out. I haven't worn a costume since Halloween of nineteen forty-five and I don't get enough silliness in my life. Thought I'd try a little of that, too." She pointed at his outfit. "Wouldn't hurt you to unbend a little."

Ben said, "I tried to talk him into wearing leather chaps and a vest."

Mrs. Talucci said, "Hot as that would undoubtedly be, this isn't a leather bar or your bedroom. I think you'd look great as one of those X-Men."

"You went to the movie?" Paul asked.

"I've got cable," Mrs. Talucci said.

Paul said, "Ben's not in costume."

"I don't do sci-fi drag," Ben said.

They got home late. Jeff burbled happily for the entire trip. He discussed at length all the things he planned to do the next day. He'd come in third place in his category of costuming—comic heroes. All those in first through fifth place in their categories would be finalists the next night at the banquet. Mrs. Talucci had come in first in the *Star Trek* subcategory. Brian had come in fifth in his. He said he figured several of the female judges and one of the male judges thought he was hot. He also said he'd gotten the phone numbers of several of the girls he'd met.

Jeff said, "Aren't you dating Jane?"

Brian said, "We aren't going steady, and how do you know about Jane?"

"It's too late for wrangling," Paul said.

"I saw a woman pinch Brian's butt," Jeff said.

"Is that something that affects you in any way?" Paul asked.

"No."

"Then it's not something you need to tell me. We don't gossip." Recently, Paul had needed to remind both sons about the tattling rule and had done some clamping down.

"My butt's fine," Brian said.

Paul said, "For which I'm sure all the females on the planet are grateful, but which I do not wish to discuss."

Brian smiled but refrained from further comment. The sixteen year old knew when to back off.

◣ 2 ◢

For Paul Turner, working on Saturdays was a pain in the ass. However, when it was your turn in the rotation, you did it. Saturdays were about the same as any other day. Original crime was rare.

The problem with weekend work was time. On the weekend his family was more likely to be around to fix something with, have a quiet moment with, to talk to, to listen to. Before he left for work, he watched the costumed aggregation of his family and neighbor assemble in the family van for the drive to the convention center.

This Saturday at Area Ten headquarters, Turner and his detective partner, Buck Fenwick, slogged though tedious follow-ups on their active cases. Most detectives had about twenty of these that they were working on at one time. Each hot new murder took precedence, then there was all the follow-up work on past cases. First thing that morning they showed pictures of possible suspects to mostly reluctant and usually unreliable eyewitnesses. After that they listened to crime lab people explain possibilities and probabilities but not certainties. Then the detectives wrote reports on all their activities.

Just after eleven a call came in reporting a dead body on one of the top floors of the Greater Chicago Hotel and Convention Center. Turner and Fenwick were in line for the next case.

Turner felt a pang of anxiety about it possibly being one of his kids. Then he remembered that they weren't staying at the hotel, and there was no word that the person who was dead had any connection to the convention. Still. The detectives hurried over.

Turner and Fenwick entered the massive complex, which was just west of the Kennedy Expressway past the Hubbard Street tunnel. While it couldn't rival McCormick Place, few venues could; it was still one of the largest hotel/convention centers in the country.

The halls to the elevators were thronged with people, several in outlandish costumes. Turner saw *X-Men* and *Star Wars* characters. He spotted at least three Hulk imitators. None of them fit the size or shape he imagined the creator of the character had envisioned. He knew his sons were somewhere in the throng. All of the revelers he saw seemed content and happy.

Fenwick pointed at the crowd. "Nobody seems out of sorts."

Turner said, "They must not know. I doubt if they're the kind of people who hear awful news and decide to party. Most people aren't."

Fenwick said, "Maybe these are revels without a cause."

Turner said, "You want the corpse count to double before we even get to the elevator?"

"You're jealous because you didn't think of it."

"I'm picturing the story of 'Fenwick and the Fatal Pun.'"

Fenwick said, "It would sell millions."

"Unfortunately, probably."

Fenwick leaned closer. "Most of these costumes are pretty ugly."

15

Turner scanned the crowd. "They look okay."

"Look closer." He pointed discreetly. "That guy is only going to win a contest if there's a category for the largest gut in a Tarzan costume. The woman next to him should not be wearing a gauzy fairy piece of chiffon; better she be covered by a canvas tent."

"You're being prejudiced about the person, not the costume."

"Just aesthetic judgments."

Turner said, "No cop has ever said the word 'aesthetic' before."

"I still get bonus points from my eighth grade teacher when I use words such as those. She was hot. I'd have done anything for her. Did I ever tell you about the outfits she wore?"

"Several million times. I'd prefer to examine a dead body than listen to the intricate details of your sexual awakening or another one of your puns. And no, I don't want to hear about punishment."

Fenwick said, "You heard the old joke about the real aliens who happened to come to Earth and land in the middle of a *Star Trek* convention."

"Do I want to?" Turner asked.

"Yes."

"Maybe later."

David Sanchez, a beat cop they had worked with before, met them at the main elevator bank. They were not about to cause an uproar by a chance remark. They ascended to the twenty-seventh floor in silence. As they exited, Fenwick said, "We're moving up in the world." Sanchez and Fenwick ignored him.

Once they were alone, Sanchez said, "We got a call at ten forty-six from the hotel. They said there was a body. When we got here, hotel security was on the scene. We moved them out and took over."

Outside the elevator, the corridor was empty. Sanchez led them out of the small elevator hall and down a long corridor that branched at the end. They turned left. At the farthest end of this second long corridor they saw a uniformed Chicago cop standing in front of an open door. Two people huddled around him.

A matronly woman in the group said, "Please, I'm with the convention. I must know what is going on. Muriam is scheduled to give the keynote address to the convention in a few hours. Right now we are supposed to go to a luncheon tea reception."

The beat cop nodded at Turner and Fenwick and said, "You need to talk to these two. They're in charge."

"I'm Oona Murkle. I'm in charge of the speakers for the luncheon and tonight's banquet and I'm a good friend of Muriam's. They won't let me into her room. She was supposed to join us over an hour ago. Can you please tell me what is going on? While the tea isn't that important, she really does need to give the speech tonight."

Turner said, "Ms. Murkle, we'll get information to you as soon as we can." She subsided. The woman equaled at least two thirds of Fenwick's bulk. She had gray hair and wore a navy blue pantsuit that shimmered and sparkled when she moved.

Fenwick asked, "Who's with hotel security?"

A man about six foot two stepped forward. He wore a well-cut light brown suit. He had brush-cut hair. "Brandon Macer." After handshakes, the two detectives and Macer entered the suite. They passed from a kitchen area into a living room. They joined a beat cop standing twenty feet away from the corpse.

Macer pointed. "That was Muriam Devers." The body had a broadsword transfixing the chest. A gush of blood had covered the weapon halfway to the hilt. Turner and Fenwick had long since given up gaping at corpses, but this one did give them pause. Fairly horrific stab wounds were more than commonplace in their line of work, but this was more grotesque than your average gangland dustup over drugs.

"Who found what?" Fenwick asked.

Macer said, "A man waiting for the elevator on this floor said he heard a scream."

Turner said, "Hell of a long way to hear a scream. Must have been awfully loud."

Fenwick said, "If somebody was ramming a sword through my chest, if I could make any kind of noise, it would be at the top of my lungs."

Macer said, "You can talk to him. The door to this suite was open."

"Nobody else reported anything?" Turner asked.

Macer said, "If they heard anything, they didn't report it. Middle of the morning on a Saturday, most people are out. A lot of the people are here with the convention. There's a full schedule of events going on with that. Our guy says he came down the hall, saw this door open, called out, stepped in, saw what there was to see, got sick, and went to his room to call. He says he didn't see anyone else in the hall. There's a fire exit at the end of the corridor. Anyone could take the stairs up or down."

They thanked him. He left. The stink from the witness being sick hit their nostrils as they moved forward to begin their examination of the murder scene. Skirting the witness's mess and being careful not to touch anything in the room, Turner and Fenwick approached the corpse. The rug on both sides of the chest cavity was black with blood. As they neared the body, Turner could see in the sword hilt a bright blue stone. His son Brian's sword had a bright blue stone. He said, "Brian's sword had the same kind of stone."

Fenwick said, "The killer would have to be pretty strong to be able to snatch it from your kid."

Turner certainly didn't think his son had committed murder, but he did feel a twinge of anxiety over the coincidence. He did not like the idea of there being a remote similarity between this weapon and the one he'd seen strapped to his son's back.

The corpse wore boots that reached her knees, a short skirt, and a leather bodice contraption that clung to her torso. To Turner it looked like she was wearing a metallic bra.

Fenwick said, "That's a Xena, Warrior Princess outfit. I think she's a little old for that."

Turner noted the sags and wrinkles on the arms and face of the corpse's slender frame. The woman had to be in her seventies at least. He saw no Michelin tire effect, as Myra had mentioned.

Turner said, "Brian always watched the show. I never got what was so interesting."

"Exactly," Fenwick said.

Turner asked, "Does Madge know you know what a Xena, Warrior Princess outfit looks like?"

"You presume I didn't buy her one as a Christmas present."

"I know you didn't," Turner said.

"How so?"

"You haven't said anything about Madge chopping your nuts off. Which she would have done had you brought her such a thing."

Fenwick said, "You're probably right."

Madge was Fenwick's wife and one of Turner's favorite people.

Turner said, "So she's in this full battle dress."

Fenwick said, "I wonder if she had time to say 'tanks for the mammaries.'"

Turner said, "Maybe when she said that she drove the killer over the edge. He decided he was never going to listen to one more hideous pun. I can certainly understand that."

"A Philistine, as are so many others," Fenwick replied.

He pointed at the corpse. "Killer must have gotten soaked in blood."

"Hard not to be," Turner said. "Did the killer bring a change of clothes or did the killer risk running out into the corridor and being seen?"

To look for bloody clothing, they organized several other uniformed cops into teams to examine every trash receptacle in the hotel.

Fenwick said, "I'm going with a crime of passion. You don't get people dressed in business suits in the Loop who also casually wear a broadsword as decoration or protection. Do you really plan to kill someone with a broadsword? It's a weapon you go to a great deal of trouble to acquire."

"Maybe the sword was hers. It could have been here already and the killer used it because it was the first thing that was handy."

Fenwick said, "Which would be an argument for crime of passion, spur of the moment."

"We'll have to find out how sharp it is," Turner said.

"What's that glittery stuff on the hilt?" Fenwick asked.

"I have been informed by those in the know that the technical term is 'glittery stuff.' I handled Brian's earlier. The glittery stuff comes off."

"Easy way to find the killer," Fenwick said.

"Unless the killer wore gloves."

"That would complicate things. So, we're looking for blood and glitter. Is it significant that there's a broken red feather deal about four feet from the body?"

Turner pointed it out to the Crime Lab team and made sure they included it as part of the evidence. Now that the immediate needs of examining the body were over, he began to inspect his surroundings. The pictures on the wall looked like average hotel art, kind of milky impressionists, designed to soothe and be faceless. The lamps were fake brass. He opened the curtains that covered the entire east wall of the suite. He got a spectacular view of midday lights in the heart of the city in a gray rain. It rivaled the view from the Ohio Street off-ramp on the Kennedy expressway. Because of the downpour, traffic was more than its usual snarl on all the streets that could be seen.

Another of the red ostrich feathers lay on the bed.

Fenwick said, "It's another one of those damn red plume deals." It was a twin to the broken one near Devers' corpse.

Turner added, "I saw her carrying one of them yesterday." He explained.

"Your kid knows this stuff?" Fenwick asked.

"That and a great deal more. It's frightening in an eleven year old."

Turner took Sanchez aside before he left. He said, "My kids and a few friends of mine are attending the convention. Could you find out where they are? Make sure they're okay?" He said nothing about the broadsword at the moment.

Sanchez said, "I'm willing to help out. I know they're your family, but that security guy said there were a hundred thousand people at this convention. I'm not sure how I'll find them."

Turner said, "Jeff's in a wheelchair. Another older-lady friend is in a Tribble costume. They'll stand out."

Bless the universality of *Star Trek*: Sanchez knew what a Tribble costume was without asking. Sanchez said he would do his best. Turner didn't mention Ian. He figured that as an ex-cop, his friend could take care of himself. He didn't want to deal with Ian switching from friend to investigative reporter, not right at this moment.

As the Crime Lab team performed its work, Turner and Fenwick examined the rest of the suite.

In the dead woman's luggage they found several pairs of pantyhose, a pair of jeans, a pantsuit, and a pair of low heels. She also had a supply of the three-foot-long red ostrich feathers.

Fenwick held one up. "Another fetish. I prefer grit to fetishes."

Turner said, "Maybe it was a gritty fetish."

Fenwick asked, "Was the feather in the other room put there by the killer as a statement, or was the damn thing just laying around, and why was it broken?"

"The killer will know," Turner said.

"Assholes always keep secrets," Fenwick said.

In the closet they found a full-length red evening gown and a matching pair of high heels. There was a blue bathrobe made of thick, fuzzy cotton. It had the hotel's logo on it. They found an iron and an ironing board. In a large economy-size Band-Aid box they found basic personal items along with prescription allergy pills. On the night stand they found books by Ursula K. LeGuin and Agatha Christie. Muriam Devers' convention schedule was in a packet on the bed. They found a sheet of paper listing her activities. She'd appeared at a signing that morning. Later this afternoon she was scheduled to be on a panel, the topic of which was "Existential Realism in the Gothic Fantasy Novel." Fenwick nudged Turner and pointed to the title. He asked, "What does this mean?"

Turner said, "That pretentiousness isn't limited to any single literary genre?"

Fenwick said, "I love it when you say 'genre.' I get all tingly inside."

"You getting 'tingly' is not a pretty concept. Besides, you're the poet in this relationship. I'm just trying to catch up with you." Turner held out his arm across the front of Devers' dark brown suitcase. "Broadsword could fit in here sideways."

"Did she bring her own death weapon?"

Turner said, "You can't just drag one of those things onto a plane. Even in your luggage it's got to be a pain in the ass to take along."

"That's if she was the one who brought it," Fenwick said.

The two detectives watched from an unobtrusive corner as the Crime Lab techs and Medical Examiner's people worked.

"Nothing's out of place," Fenwick said.

"Just the corpse," Turner said. "Other than the sword, I don't see any evidence of another person's presence. Only one glass used in the bathroom. Only one wet towel."

The ME people joined them. The ME said, "The obvious is true. Dead from the broadsword through her chest. Can't be a lot of those floating around."

"Chests or swords?" Fenwick asked.

Everybody sighed.

Turner filled the void. "You forget, this is the largest science fiction convention ever. There could be all kinds of the damn things."

"No signs of a break-in," Fenwick said. "She knew her killer?"

"Got to be," Turner said. "Or she opened her door to strangers a lot."

Fenwick said, "She couldn't have committed suicide, plunged the sword into herself or propped it up and fell onto it?"

"Done it herself?" the ME said. "I don't know. Her hands are bloody and cut, like someone tried to shred them. Normally those are defense wounds. Question is, are they real defense wounds or do they just look like defense wounds? It could be from trying to keep the sword from going in or trying to get it out. Or a neural reaction of trying to clutch the wound. Nothing under the fingernails. Her arms show no trace of a fight. No bruises or abrasions on her head or torso."

The police personnel knew that if it was not clear whether a death was a suicide or murder then the occurrence was treated as a homicide until it was clearly not a homicide.

"No suicide note," Turner said.

"The sword is heavy," the ME said. "Doesn't mean an older woman couldn't wield it, just means it would have been awkward. Whichever it was, she would have been very alive while she was being skewered."

"She couldn't have tripped?" Fenwick asked. "Maybe been fooling around with the damn thing, lost her balance, fell on it somehow, rolled onto her back?"

"Blood stains say she didn't move far after she was stabbed. She didn't go staggering around the room. There's a lot of blood within a foot or so of where she lay. She may have flopped around for a few seconds involuntarily. That would be caused by her body shutting down. Once she was skewered, she probably died pretty fast. She lost a lot of blood very quickly. She got plowed from the front and down she went."

Fenwick said, "Somebody heard a tremendous shout."

"Her vocal chords didn't get sliced. She could have screamed before she was skewered, when the stab started, or for a few seconds during. Blood rushing into her throat would have choked her too fast for it to last very long."

Turner asked, "Did you see any evidence that the killer tried to silence her?"

"We'll do some checking," the ME said. "Nothing visible to the eye says that the killer did anything like that."

Turner said, "How did the killer know someone wouldn't be just outside the room and hear what was going on? Maybe she was yelling for help. The killer seemed to be taking an awful lot of chances. Either he surprised her or he was lucky."

Fenwick said, "How strong does somebody have to be to ram a sword through an entire human body? Can't be easy."

"Ever tried to skewer somebody?" the ME asked.

"Not lately," Fenwick said.

"Not easy, even with the sharpest of swords," the assistant ME said. She held up two pieces of paper and said, "The edge of the sword split this easily. It was very sharp. The sword would need a powerful thrust behind it to skewer her like it did. Just less powerful because it was so sharp."

"Somebody reasonably strong," Fenwick said. Head nods.

A younger member of the ME's staff said, "Maybe the sword could have been hurled from across the room."

The ME glared at the speaker. She said, "Doesn't seem likely."

"You ever try to pick one of those things up?" Turner said. Head shakes. "They are heavy and unwieldy. You'd have to be incredibly strong to toss it even the slightest distance."

Fenwick pointed out, "People throw javelins."

"The balance would be all wrong for tossing it any kind of distance," Turner said. "Say the blade is as sharp as possible to penetrate someone. Could the killer grab it by the middle of the blade and throw it? He'd have to risk cutting himself pretty severely. If he threw it while holding it by the hilt, he'd have to aim directly upward and hope it came down on a probably supine and hopefully unmoving body with enough violence to penetrate all the way to the back."

"Maybe he wore gloves?" the assistant ME said.

"Nobody threw the damn thing," the ME said.

Fenwick said, "Get a grip."

The ME said, "There are never enough broadswords around when you really need them."

Fenwick said, "If the killer didn't have a change of clothes, he should be easy to spot. The guy's gotta be drenched in blood."

Turner said, "So we have a bloody somebody, a naked somebody, or someone who planned ahead. Somebody who's got a gym bag or a plastic bag that won't let moisture out. If it happened a while ago, the killer could be out of his bloody clothes and be right next door or on his way to the airport for a flight to Bombay."

They thanked the ME. She promised to get them finger-print information in a timely fashion. Turner knew the prints would only start to do good when they began lining up suspects. They needed to begin their interviews.

Sanchez reported finding all of Turner's party except Brian. They were all at various parts of the convention. All were fine and having a good time. So far the demise of the night's keynote speaker had not been broadcast.

Macer, the head of security, gave them a computer key card to get into the suite the hotel was making available for them to use for questioning.

"Pretty fancy," Fenwick said when they entered. Turner noted that the decor was similar to Devers' suite: hotel art, gray carpet, and brass lamps. Turner didn't think it was fancy or un-fancy. He was used to taking camping trips with his family. They'd spent a week in northern Ontario last summer. Mostly it was tents, and sleeping bags, and hard ground, and bugs. When they stayed in motels along the way, they were the kind that lined interstates. Turner said, "Don't you know how to tell if a hotel is pricey or not?"

"It costs a lot?"

"Without knowing the price, you can tell. The fancy ones have irons and ironing boards in the room, and the fanciest ones have those thick, fuzzy bathrobes."

"Ain't never been in a place with all that."

"Me neither, but I was told."

Fenwick plopped down on one of the easy chairs. He said, "I know where they scrimped on money. This thing has no bounce." He thumped the cushion under his butt. "This does not qualify as comfy."

"I'll call the Zagat guide."

Sanchez escorted Oona Murkle into the room. As she sat down, she said, "Something has happened. The police don't keep a presence this long unless something is very wrong. I know it's bad."

Turner said, "I'm sorry. Ms. Devers is dead."

Ms. Murkle put a hand to her throat and gave a small

gasp. "How can that be? She was so vibrant and alive. I talked with her at breakfast. She was. She was . . ." She gasped again. She began to cry. Turner found the tissue container in the bathroom, pulled out a neat handful, and put them within her reach.

Turner and Fenwick let her take as long as she needed to compose herself. Some minutes later, she asked, "What on earth happened? I know she wasn't ill. She'd have told me. Was it a heart attack?"

"She was murdered," Fenwick said.

"No." Ms. Murkle's eyes shifted from Fenwick to Turner and back. "That is not possible. She was kindness itself. Everybody loved her. She went out of her way for everybody. It was a coup for the convention to get her as the guest of honor. It's one of the reasons we had a record number of people in attendance. We got Muriam on board early. Once she was in, it was easier to get others interested. It began to snowball. Eventually everybody who's anybody wanted to be here. She only went to a select few events. When she did attend, she always had time for everyone. Her fans loved her. She always took extra time with them. Always. She was never rude. She was just . . . she was just . . ." She dabbed at her eyes. "She was my friend." She used a tissue to dab at fresh tears.

Turner and Fenwick waited patiently. When she was composed, Turner said, "We're sorry to have to ask you questions at such a difficult time, but the first few hours of a case can be vital."

She nodded.

Turner asked, "Can you remember the exact time you last saw her?"

"Let me see." She thought. "About nine. She had an enormous line of fans waiting to have their books signed. You know how some authors don't like it if fans bring more than one book? Muriam didn't mind. If you had one, some, or all of her books, she was flattered. So many authors get offended if fans want to chat. She always smiled for the photographs. She left people thinking she had all the time in the world just for them. She didn't even mind if people disturbed her for an autograph while she was having a meal. That's supposed to be forbidden. People can be so rude. But she didn't mind."

"Do you know of any problems she might have had lately?" Turner asked. "Fights or disagreements with anyone?"

"I don't know of any problems. She never fought with anyone. A large crowd of us had dessert in her suite last night after all the activities were over. It was a very informal get-together. We had room service deliver the house specialty, these most exquisite chocolate confections."

"We'll need a list of those people," Fenwick said. "We'll probably have to get all their fingerprints, too." With any luck, the results would match any the killer left.

"Did anyone act oddly at this meeting?" Turner asked. "Do something out of character? Have any disagreements?"

"Everyone was friendly and happy. The convention got off to a smashing start. Muriam was a delight. She talked about the new book she was starting."

Turner asked, "Did she ever seem suicidal, severely depressed?"

"I thought you said murder."

"We have to check all the possibilities," Turner said.

"Well, no. Last night she was talking about how happy she was. She had moods like all of us, I suppose, but she was mostly up. She wouldn't tell joke after joke at a gathering or anything like that, but she was always pleasant. I'd never dream of her committing suicide."

Turner asked, "What did she bring for her costume?"

"She didn't enter the competition. She was one of the judges. She thought costumes were kind of silly. Why ever do you ask?"

Turner said, "She was found in a Xena, Warrior Princess outfit."

Murkle's jaw dropped an inch and a half. "Xena? I didn't even know Muriam had such an interest. Wouldn't that be a little . . . young for her? I suppose age doesn't matter. Although it is odd. I never heard of her having any kind of costume, much less that."

"Would she have brought a broadsword with her?" Turner asked.

"Impossible. She was not into violence. Why do you ask about broadswords? She wasn't . . . oh, dear. How awful."

The detectives let Ms. Murkle begin to process the information provided by her own insight. Turner figured that most people thought they knew their friends fairly well. Most of the time we run in fairly standard ruts. Details about the entertaining we do for ourselves could quite often be startling to those closest to us.

After several moments, Fenwick said, "We also found a red feather plume thing near the body. Was there a particular significance to that?"

She explained what Jeff had already told Turner. Murkle added, "Over time, Muriam got sick of the silly things. She had this huge supply. For years they've been selling them in the dealers' room at all the conventions. She donates the proceeds to her favorite charities."

"So they're readily available," Turner said.

"Oh, yes. Her fans loved to see her with them. It was the only thing she'd sigh over. That's the most negative I ever saw her get, a bemused sigh. One of her series characters was so identified with the feathers that people identified her with them."

"Did she have family?" Turner asked.

"She has two grown children. I believe one lives on the east coast and one lives in France."

"Where does she live?" Turner asked.

"She has several homes. One in the upper peninsula of Michigan, one in New York, and I believe a condo in Palm Springs. And she always spends a month in Colorado in January for a vacation."

"Was she married?"

"Not currently," Murkle said. "She never spoke about her ex-husband. The divorce was years ago. I don't think they talked much. The children are far beyond the age for any custody dispute and she certainly didn't need alimony. She never remarried. She never spoke about dating anyone and I'm sure she would have mentioned to me if she was seeing someone. She never seemed very interested in personal relationships."

"Any problems with people here at the convention?" Turner asked. "Did she have any enemies?"

"Oh, no. She was the most popular person here."

Fenwick said, "You hear about jealousies between writers."

"She was involved in none of that. And this convention was far more than just writers. We have fans. Thousands and thousands of fans. This convention covers the entire spectrum of fantasy and science fiction. Movies, games, comics, everything. She may have been a big star, but she wasn't the only star. She was absolutely gracious and charming at the special dinner we gave for all the stars Thursday night. In fact everyone was charming. It was marvelous. The whole convention was a huge success." She paused. "Until now. What are we to do? Is there something I can do to help?"

Fenwick said, "We may not be able to talk to everyone who came in contact with her, but we have to try. We'll get beat cops to begin interviewing fans who stood in line to have books autographed. Could you give us a list of the people who knew her best and perhaps begin to help get them up here?"

"Certainly." They took down names as she gave them.

"Anyone else we should try and talk to?" Turner asked.

"There were so many people who knew her. None of them

are violent. None would have a reason to kill her. No one is wild, or out of control, or crazy." She paused a moment then resumed, "Of course, at these conventions there's always the loon, probably several at this convention because it's so huge."

"The loon?" Fenwick said.

"You see them at all kinds of seminars, workshops, and conventions. You know the type."

"A lot of the people here look loony to me," Fenwick said. "What's the difference?"

"You know. They just don't fit in. They're kind of odd. Always on the fringes. Never talk to anyone unless they buttonhole some poor schlub, and then they won't let them go. Or they ask inappropriate or off-the-wall questions at a panel. Or they hang around after a signing and ask an author to read their seven-hundred-page manuscript and help them get published. Or they hang around after an event and try to get close to a celebrity. We have to be careful. They usually aren't dangerous, but they do make people uncomfortable at times. We're always careful."

"Do you know any of their names?" Turner asked.

"I know I saw a couple. I don't know their names. I'll try and think of someone who would. Hotel security and convention security might have a notion. I could point them out to you if I saw them. It's such a big convention, they might be hard to find."

Turner said, "We need to know how the weapons were handled here at the convention."

"For what . . . oh. I'll get you the person in charge of that. We worked closely with hotel security. We sent out a notice to everyone who was attending the convention about what to do about weapons. Everybody who wanted to bring a weapon had to be bonded."

"What does that mean?" Fenwick asked.

"The convention had insurance, but the sword owner had to post a bond as well. We also required that everyone with a weapon had to have it wired shut so that it couldn't be drawn. Everybody who attends these things knows you are not to draw your weapon. Everyone knows that you are not to touch someone else's weapon."

Fenwick said, "People must break the rules sometimes."

Murkle said, "Less often than you might think. These people are fans. Lots of folks think that means they're kind of silly and funny. Just kind of dressed up and delusional. These are good people. Very serious people. Very committed people. They really are not violent. They are committed to worlds of fantasy that bring them comfort and enjoyment. It's mostly harmless."

"It wasn't today," Fenwick said.

"What am I going to tell everyone?" She looked at her watch. "I don't know how we're going to tell everyone. The convention can't possibly go on."

Turner said, "We'll want to round suspects up as soon as possible. For now, I'd say let everything proceed. We don't want people to leave."

Fenwick said, "Even if the festivities are canceled, many of them probably have hotel reservations until tomorrow."

Murkle frowned. "I don't know how I'm going to get through this. I've never been involved in something so awful." She took several deep breaths. "It hasn't sunk in yet. I'll need to tell the convention organizers. They're going to want to know what this is about. By the end of the day, we can make a decision on canceling all of Sunday's events. I'll begin getting people for you to question."

There was no particular reason for Murkle not to tell. Everyone would find out sooner or later. The news might shock some of the convention goers, but their getting the news sooner or later was unlikely to affect the killer. The fact of the murder wouldn't be a secret from the killer: he or she already knew Devers was dead.

Turner said, "There's no need to make a general announcement, but you can let people know."

Murkle sniffed. "The convention organizing committee deserves to know before the others."

"You might start with them. We'll send an officer with you. We can begin interviewing the people you mentioned."

They thanked her. She left.

"Okay," Fenwick said, "I'll ask. Devers wasn't into costumes or Xena. What the hell was she doing in such an outfit?"

"Not baking cookies," Turner said. "Unless warrior princesses bake cookies."

"Not that I ever saw," Fenwick said. "Speaking of cookies."

"And we were."

"All this sweetness and light about our warrior princess is enough to make me gag. She lived a saccharine-drenched life? She never kicked a puppy?"

"You've never kicked a puppy."

Fenwick said, "Yeah, but I'm not dead with a sword through my gut."

Turner said, "Okay, sweetness and light didn't get her killed. I'm open to opinions on what did."

"Gotta be sex," Fenwick said. "How can it not be? You don't get into a Xena outfit unless you're after something. Nobody just casually puts this shit on."

"Lot of costumes at the convention," Turner said.

"Yeah, but you heard Murkle. Devers wasn't into costumes. This is out of character."

"Or Murkle didn't know her as well as she thought," Turner said. "Lots of lesbians are into a Xena thing. Is there a lesbian angle to this murder?"

"Could be any number of angles," Fenwick said. "Whatever angle leads to the killer is my favorite."

Turner asked, "Is what was out of character part of what got her killed?"

"Are you saying her costume killed her? Or because of her costume, she was killed? If she'd been wearing leather chaps and a motorcycle helmet, she might not have been killed?"

"Depends on our killer."

Macer entered with a gentleman who looked to be in his mid-forties. He had a bright red face and a pot belly. A couple more years, Turner thought, and he'll be stroking out from high blood pressure. Macer said, "This is the head of weapons for the convention." Bram Stivens shook their hands.

Without preliminaries he said, "I warned them this kind of thing could happen."

"Murder?" Fenwick asked.

"Those damn swords. We had to have them. We had to be authentic. We had to be better than any other convention. Oona is a dear, sweet woman. We assigned her simple tasks. She escorted stars to different events such as the afternoon tea and the banquet. And she's a tremendous fan and so good-hearted. But she's so unrealistic. People do stupid stuff. We had to have dangerous weapons. Lots of conventions ban them and we should have, too."

"They didn't listen to you," Turner said.

"Goddamn right. We wouldn't be having this problem right now if they'd listened to me. You can have any kind of accident with real weapons. You can have any kind of loony tune trying to do something stupid."

Turner said, "We were told the people all had to be bonded and the weapons had to be fixed so they couldn't be drawn."

"Ha! As if some lock thing can prevent the crazies of the world from doing crazy things. You've got to plan for that."

"Do you have a list of who had swords?"

"I brought it with me when Oona told me." He gave it to them. Turner saw his son's name. His anxiety level rose exponentially.

The detectives dispatched beat cops to find the people on

it as soon as possible. They needed to find which swords weren't accounted for. They didn't think the killer would be stupid enough to be the only one without his original weapon.

Other than being willing to go on at great length about the failings of those who organized the convention, Bram Stivens knew nothing else of interest to them.

3

Before they started the rest of their interviews, Sanchez gave them a report. "I found Mrs. Talucci, Myra, and Jeff. I couldn't find Brian. This is a big damn convention. There's a large luncheon in full swing. Some of the seminars and panels and lectures are still going on. I stopped in at seven of them. Short of getting up in front of the room at each panel or seminar and making an announcement, I don't think we'll find him. Do you want me to do that?"

"At this point I'd like him to be found."

"The last they saw of your older boy, he was talking with what your son Jeff said 'was a real looker' of a young lady. I'll hunt some more."

"Thanks," Turner said. He knew Brian prided himself on his ability to attract young ladies. He was concerned that Brian hadn't been found yet. His deep-rooted father instinct set off tendrils of expanding worry. Brian was usually as sensible as a teenager could be. Still, he wished Brian and his sword had been accounted for.

Fenwick asked, "Any luck with witnesses on this floor?"

Sanchez said, "We found three people in their rooms at the other end of the corridor. One said he was in the shower.

The other two were kind of embarrassed. They were having sex and were too engrossed."

"They said 'engrossed'?" Fenwick asked.

Sanchez looked at his pad of paper. "That's what they said."

So far no one had seen anyone covered in blood. No one had reported any bloody clothes in trash cans anywhere in the public areas of the hotel. Turner knew that beat cops with hotel security were looking for all the people with rooms on this floor. Getting into the rooms was another matter. They wanted to hunt for bloody clothing, but a hotel room is considered the same as your home for searches. In the absence of a warrant, you didn't have to let the police in. So far, they'd found only a few of the people. Even if they were at the convention, they'd be hard to find by room number. There was no one place to make a general announcement. The cops had to wait. On the other hand, the police could prevent people from getting access to their rooms. Macer, of hotel security, was asked to screen those who got off the elevator on this floor. They'd station personnel at the elevator banks to make sure no one without a key got upstairs. They didn't have the people to screen all the hotel guests or conventioneers.

Anyone with a room on this floor would be asked to allow an inspection before being allowed in. Those who wouldn't consent would be asked to wait unless it was an emergency. Turner knew how that worked. Half the people would be claiming to have heart medicine stashed in their overnight bags just so they could look at nothing happening. Cops would accompany all the onlookers to their doors on their "emergency" runs.

The next person they interviewed was the man who called the police after hearing the scream and finding the body. Arthur Bobak wore a tuxedo. Turner thought he might be in his early thirties. He was talking on a cell phone when they brought him in. He saw Turner and Fenwick and told the person on the other end that he had to go. He wasn't under arrest so there was no question that he could use his phone. His hand shook as he clicked his phone off and put it in his pocket. He said, "I'm supposed to be the best man at a wedding. Am I going to make it?"

Turner said, "We'll take a statement and get you out of here as soon as we can." He didn't add that the finder of the body was always under suspicion. They would question him for as long as it took.

Fenwick said, "Tell us what happened."

Bobak said, "I came back up because I forgot my gift for the wedding. I know you're supposed to send them, but I always bring it with. I'll never do that again." He shook his head. "I closed my room door, turned into the little corridor with the elevator, and I had my hand out to press the button. I'll never forget that moment. It was the most awful sound I ever expect to hear."

"How long did it last?"

"Maybe ten seconds. Maybe fifteen." He wiped his hand across his forehead. "I think I'll hear it in my dreams. I guess that's what death sounds like."

Turner reflected that the detectives knew better than almost anyone other than those in the medical profession what death sounded like. Mostly there wasn't a lot of noise. Loud or soft, the finality didn't change.

Bobak was very pale. Turner hoped it wasn't his natural color. If it was, he thought the guy might join the corpse. "I knew the sound came from down this corridor. No question. I guess I'd begun to move toward it unconsciously." He shook his head. "I got to the split in the corridor. I could no longer tell which way it had come from. I walked down this way. I saw the open door. I called out. I was afraid to go in. I wasn't sure it was this room. Nobody else was in the corridor. Then I heard this kind of gurgle. As if someone had pulled the plug on a drain. I called out several times. Nobody answered. I entered.

I saw . . ." He gulped and wiped his hand across his face. After several moments, he resumed, "I got sick. I don't remember making a decision to leave the room. I found myself in the hall. I used my cell phone to call the police."

"Did you see anyone else?" Turner asked.

"No. The hallway was empty. I thought the door at the far end of the corridor might have just finished closing as I turned into this corridor."

"You called right away?" Fenwick asked.

Turner knew the fact that he didn't have blood all over himself meant that either this guy didn't do it, or he'd done the murder and then changed. Would the real killer have planned on the noise or been aware of the risk of some passerby hearing it? A fit of passion, careful planning, or sheer luck for the killer?

The fortuitous whims of chance ruled their success or failure with cases more often than Turner cared to admit.

"It might have been maybe a minute before I called. Not longer than that."

"Did you know Muriam Devers?" Turner asked.

"Is she the dead woman?"

Turner nodded.

"I sort of recognize the name. Isn't she some kind of writer? I think my wife likes her books. Didn't they make one of those children's movies out of her stuff? I think I took my kids to one of them. I didn't know her."

Once he left, Turner said, "The killer has got to be desperate, or stupid, or both."

"Maybe he was just lucky," Fenwick said.

Turner asked, "Why'd he leave the door open?"

"Incompetence? Stupidity? An accident?"

The next person from Oona Murkle's list was Muriam Devers' personal publicist, Pam Granata. She walked into the room, sat down, and began to weep. The news was obviously beginning to get out. Granata was in her early thirties. She had wispy blonde hair. When she was finally composed enough to speak, she said, "She was a saint, a veritable saint. She always took time for her fans. Always went out of her way. She was rich enough to never write again, but she did. She felt she owed it to her readers. Instead of holing up in splendid isolation in some rich condo in Paris and enjoying the international jet-set life, she would work hard at her craft. She was a regular person. She was terribly nervous before making presentations. She always wanted to say something meaningful and witty. She made an extra effort to do so. And she was a delight one on one. She would sit in the VIP lounge hour upon hour gossiping with chance acquaintances, casual friends, and colleagues."

Fenwick asked, "Is there always a VIP lounge?"

"At the bigger conventions, yes. People come and go. Sometimes there are limits on who is admitted to the lounge. There had to be some control here with so many stars and so many fans. Quite often people claimed to be a star's best friend. It happens all the time. Muriam was close to only a few people. She'd have quiet dinners with her inner circle. She avoided fights and the back-biting and quarrels of her profession."

"Was there a lot of that?"

"You can find that kind of thing with any professional group. Not with Muriam. She never once said a bad word about her colleagues. She was in a writing group with four other authors. Still, after all of her successes, she was trying to improve."

"Are any of the people in her writing group at the convention?"

"I believe three of the current members of the group are." She gave them their names. She sighed. "The five of them were an odd bunch. I never did understand it. Muriam was always singing the praises of anyone who was in her writing group. Who was in the group wasn't terribly consistent. I think the others were a bunch of no-talent hacks trying to live on her glory. Muriam didn't see it that way. Of the three who are here, you might check into Ralph Marwood the most. At first he was a sweet man, always willing to help others, but then he got real cynical. I'm not sure the cynicism had anything to do with him being in a writing group with Muriam, but there were rumors that he was unhappy."

"Were other people jealous of her?" Turner asked.

"No," Granata said, "not that they made public. I don't know of anyone."

"Did she have any quarrels, fights, difficulties with editors? A fan who stalked her?"

"No."

"Who were the people in her profession who did have fights and arguments?"

"She didn't know any of those people. She didn't need to know any of those people."

Fenwick said, "We'd like the names just to be sure."

She gave them three or four who were at the convention. When done, she said, "Those are all good people. These petty fights would not be a cause for murder. Maybe I shouldn't have given them to you."

Fenwick said, "We check everything in a murder investigation."

Turner said, "She didn't have any critics who gave her lousy reviews?"

"She didn't care about the reviews. She didn't have to care about the reviews. Her fans didn't care about the reviews. They bought her books. Each new volume brought out herds of people stampeding to the stores. Everybody loved her."

"Was she ever depressed or down?" Turner asked.

"Heavens, no. She was always upbeat and cheerful. She was one of the most patient people."

"When did you see her last?" Fenwick asked.

"We talked this morning at breakfast. Later, I waited until

her signing was finished. I kind of like to hover around. Then I had several business meetings. I was working on her next tour to a number of media outlets. Many of them sent representatives here."

"Any problems setting up her appearances?"

"No, everybody wanted her. It was a matter of scheduling and perks, you know, like tea in the green room before being interviewed. It was mostly details. There's always lots of details. I have a law degree as well as an undergraduate degree in business, minoring in negotiations."

Turner said, "You're listed as Ms. Devers' personal publicist. I'm not sure exactly what that means."

Granata said, "Muriam had a publicist at her publishing house. Those people have many authors to service. I was her personal publicist. I could give the care and attention to her career that was needed."

"And for a hefty fee," Fenwick said.

"Yes," Granata said.

Before Fenwick could get snarky about the briefness of this last response, Turner asked, "Do you know who was the last person to see her at the book signing?"

"I'm not sure. I didn't recognize any of the people waiting in line. If I remember right, the last one was in a Beastmaster costume."

Turner flinched internally at the mention of the costume, the same as his son's.

Fenwick asked, "How many people in Beastmaster costumes were there in attendance?"

"You didn't have to register your costume. A lot of people use these conventions to be as daring as possible. To wear as little as possible and call it a costume when they're being exhibitionistic. There's a whole cult of nearly naked strong guys. Tarzan for the comics and movies, Beastmaster, those kind. Some of those comic costumes can be pretty revealing. I've seen Superman costumes that were so tight they revealed everything except the expiration date and the wearer's imagination. Too many of them don't have the figure for what's exposed. It's gross."

Fenwick said, "Which isn't against the law but should be."

Turner knew Fenwick never displayed his ever expanding bulk offensively. Except for red suits and white beards once a year, he didn't draw attention to his heft.

Turner asked, "Did Ms. Devers have a broadsword?"

"Pardon?"

Turner repeated the question.

She said, "Good heavens. I can't imagine she would. Why do you ask?"

"That was the weapon used."

"How awful. What an odd thing. How strange. There must be a madman loose."

"Did you ever see her in a Xena, Warrior Princess outfit?"

"No. That's impossible. She never mentioned a costume of any kind. Was there one in her luggage?"

Fenwick said, "She was wearing one."

"That is totally out of character. Muriam was not a costume person, not that I knew of anyway."

She knew no more. After she left, Fenwick snorted, "More sweetness and light. Gag."

Turner said, "Brian was wearing a Beastmaster costume."

"You think he'd be interested in a relationship with a woman old enough to be his grandmother?"

"I sure hope not."

Fenwick said, "We could get a whole *Harold and Maude* thing going here."

Fenwick loved movie comedies, the more offbeat the better. Turner happened to like *Harold and Maude* as well. He didn't particularly think his son was a granny chaser. Then again, he wasn't sure whether or not his son was still a virgin, and he'd rather not have to find out that information. And he definitely didn't want to find it out in the middle of a murder investigation. Turner said, "I'd rather avoid familial speculation."

Fenwick said, "I'm not buying suicide."

"Certainly not from what Granata and Murkle said. On top of that it would be a hell of a thing to stab yourself with an unwieldy weapon that you had to drag here yourself."

Fenwick said, "Be a hell of a thing to stab yourself with anything."

Turner and Fenwick heard murmuring in the hall. A moment later Sanchez, the beat cop, entered. He said, "We've got another dead body."

4

Turner, Fenwick, and Sanchez hurried down one flight of stairs. A small crowd of uniformed cops was outside a door about halfway down this hall.

About thirty feet past them, a woman was being supported by Brandon Macer and a man Turner didn't recognize. She was in her early to mid-thirties. She wore a whole lot of blue body paint and very little else.

Sanchez filled them in. "The woman in blue down there, Michaela Diaz, came up to meet her boyfriend. She forgot to write her room number down, and she wasn't sure which one it was. It's not on those little plastic cards the big hotels use nowadays. You've got to remember it or write it down. She got to this door, found it open. She thought it might be the right one. Thought her boyfriend might have left it open for her convenience. She walked in and found the body and started screaming. That got the attention of a couple of passersby."

"Who's the dead guy?" Fenwick asked.

"Dennis Foublin. He is not Ms. Diaz's date. The still-living date is the guy who isn't Brandon Macer down there with her. No one reported hearing anything at all before she started screaming."

Turner and Fenwick entered the room. It was a mess. Lamps were overturned. The mattress was half off the bed. One of the legs had broken off the table. The television screen was smashed.

"This one fought," Fenwick said.

"Or the killer went berserk," Turner said. "Somebody must have heard the commotion."

Foublin's left arm was flung high, revealing a wide gaping hole just under his left armpit. There was another gaping wound on his right shoulder. Blood had gushed from both spots. He had a convention badge hanging around his neck. His throat was bruised, red, and raw in various spots. Foublin wore a purple spandex muscle T-shirt, poufy black pants tucked into black engineer boots, and a gauzy purple shirt. The gauzy shirt, now more remnant than shirt, was ripped and torn and hung nearly off his torso. There were cuts on Foublin's arms from wrist to shoulder. He lay half on the bed and half on the floor.

"These large enough to be made by a broadsword?" Fenwick asked.

"I'm not sure," Turner said, "this is only my second broadsword murder. We don't get a lot of those this century."

Fenwick said, "This broadsword shit could become all the rage. Issuing broadswords to gang bangers. Now there's a concept. Better yet, Marlon Brando in *The Godfather* wielding one to chop off various parts of recalcitrant people's bodies. I'm there."

"Pleasant as that concept might be, let's focus," Turner said. "The killer skewered this guy and then took the weapon. In Devers' murder, he leaves it there. Why not do the same thing at both?"

Fenwick said, "The killer had more time?"

"Presumably. Unless the same sword was used here first then there. One sword, two dead bodies. But I think we've got even more problems. So the killer's running around using a sword, which is kind of okay, because there's a lot of them at the convention. But if he used it at the first murder, he'd have to rinse off before he goes on his merry way. And he runs or walks around in bloody clothes? A change of clothes?"

Fenwick said, "We better check to see if anyone's broadsword is missing. It's possible the killer brought his own supply. Do we want to confiscate all of them?"

"We need to round up everyone who for sure brought one." They sent Sanchez to accomplish this task.

Turner know this group would include his son. He was uneasy about that.

Turner pointed to a corner of the room. "We've got another broken feather."

"Our killer is leaving signatures," Fenwick said. "I like that in a killer. Adds zest to the operation."

Turner said, "I'd be happy if it turned out to be a moronic affectation on the killer's part that gave him or her away."

Fenwick said, "Well, aren't you the technical one."

"Red feathers strike me as silly. I wonder what it had to do with in the book." Turner shrugged. "The bigger problem is time. Did the killer bring broken feathers with? Was there an interview with symbolic feather breaking so the victims knew why they were going to die? Or did the killer risk taking more time after the murder to arrange a message? And if they're a message, for whom is he leaving them?"

Fenwick said, "Takes only a second or two to break and drop a feather."

"If you've got one handy. If not, you've got to find one. Or you've got to remember to bring a supply. You've got to be thinking clearly. Even if it's well planned, you do something this violent, it's got to shake you up."

It was Fenwick's turn to shrug. He said, "We've seen some very cold killers. I can't believe our dead guy here wouldn't have bellowed when he was stuck. I sure as hell would have. Would someone have heard the noise with the door closed? The killer couldn't be sure no one would hear the noise of a fight."

"But the door was open," Turner pointed out.

"Which would be most likely to happen as the killer made his escape."

"You've got time to break a feather but not close the door?"

"Don't forget, we don't know when the feather was broken."

They experimented with the acoustics and various noise levels. Turner stood out in the hall. Fenwick bellowed at various levels from behind the closed door. Turner had heard Fenwick reach remarkable volume levels of bellowing. Fenwick also turned up the television and the radio to full volume.

Turner reentered the room. "I could hear plenty."

Fenwick said, "Maybe the guy didn't yell. Maybe he was too busy fighting for his life."

"What about the people above and below?" Turner asked.

Sanchez reported that no one on this floor or the ones above or below had heard anything. Silence had reigned until the body discoverer had let loose.

With his plastic gloves on, Turner picked up the man's wallet by one corner and opened it carefully. He examined the driver's license. Foublin was from Minnesota. He found a ticket for the hotel parking garage. He showed it to Fenwick. Turner said, "He drove. He didn't have the problem of transporting weapons on planes. He could just stash a heap of them in his car. If he was the one who had the weapon."

"Yeah," Fenwick said. "Was the sword his or the killer's? Did our killer come to kill him or was it done in a moment of passion?"

"We'll have to check the car, if necessary, get the forensics guys to go over it."

Fenwick said, "One murderer or two? I'd prefer one. It's easier on the paperwork."

Turner said, "I'm sure whoever did these is doing his or her best to accommodate you. We have no evidence of more than one. Can't rule it out yet. I still don't get why the door was open."

"The killer fled in a blind panic? He wanted the body discovered quickly because he's on a tight schedule? How many guesses do I get?"

Ignoring these feeble attempts at humor, Turner said, "Who died first? Was Foublin killed earlier but found later? Was this another thing the killer was leaving to chance?"

Fenwick said, "I hate it when you ignore my feeble attempts at humor and start asking questions."

"It's part of my humor management technique. I took a class."

"There is no such class."

"A twelve-step program?"

"Only in your dreams."

"For those of us who know you, they have both."

"I'd be miffed, but that's a pun waiting to be exploited."

"Can we get back to this?"

Fenwick said, "You're just jealous. Did I tell you, they're setting up a government program? They're going to pay me to not tell jokes. I'm supposed to keep it a secret."

"I'd be willing to pay half my salary in taxes to fund such a program. So would anyone who knows you. People would stampede to pay higher taxes. It could become a whole new concept in government."

"Paradise without my humor? Pah."

Turner said, "Can we get back to this?"

Fenwick said, "Unless the killings were done quite a while

apart, forensics won't be able to tell us which one happened first."

"Makes sense if we've got the sword at the Devers' scene that this one happened first. One killer. One sword. Wiped the blood off."

"It works," Fenwick said. "Now all we have to do is find out if that's what really happened."

Foublin only had the one room. They examined it carefully and worked around the Crime Lab people when they arrived. Foublin had much less in his luggage than Muriam Devers had had in hers. In the bathroom they found a shaving kit with deodorant, a razor blade, a comb, and other normal stuff. In his luggage they found underwear, socks, and the latest Barbara D'Amato novel.

They met with the Medical Examiner. Fenwick said, "I hope this kind of thing isn't catching."

The ME said, "Murder by unleashing a broadsword virus? There's a lot of twisted terrorists out there, but my guess is this wouldn't be the most efficient way to do in a large group of people."

Turner said, "From the marks on his throat I thought the convention badge we saw around his neck might have been used to strangle him."

The ME said, "Not sure yet. From the amount of blood, I'd say he was alive when he was stabbed. Could have fought while somebody tried to strangle him. Whether or not he was conscious when stabbed is another matter. We'll have to check."

Fenwick said, "Maybe he was unconscious while he was fighting."

The ME said, "Stop that. No humor. None. Zero. Zip. I don't get paid enough to listen to that crap."

Turner said, "Is there much point to strangling him after he's dead?"

"Not you, too," the ME said.

"It's catching," Turner said.

"I'll put it in my notes," Fenwick said. "Ask killer when he strangled him."

The ME muttered, "I'd say there's a shortage of good, usable broadswords in here."

Turner said, "So he was skewered in the middle of a fight."

The ME said, "More like the end of a fight. He wasn't doing much of anything but dying after he got stuck. It would be sensible to assume the wounds we see killed him, but you know us. We'll check everything at the lab and let you know. Those throat marks especially have to be checked."

Turner said, "It had to be done by someone very strong. Or it could have been two or more people. One strangling him and the other with the sword."

"A very strong person," the ME said, "or someone in the grips of an incredible passion. Certainly the former would be most likely, although you can't rule out the latter."

"Could be both," Fenwick said.

"Or could be two people," the ME said.

Turner added, "Who could be both passionate and strong."

"Any chance of it being suicide?" Fenwick asked.

The ME considered a second or two. "He could have wedged the sword firmly into something. I don't see anything in this room strong enough to hold the sword. Then he could have stood on his head backwards, stabbed himself, and removed the wedge that was holding the sword."

"I gotta ask the question," Fenwick said.

The ME said, "You're not the only one who can try to be funny. As many people laughed at my crack as they do yours."

"My crack or yours," Fenwick said.

Turner said to the room at large, "They're offering a humor management course in the department. Anybody want to sign up?"

Everybody but Fenwick and the corpse raised their hands.

Then an assistant ME, on his knees next to the corpse, accounted for the only other one present without his hand raised.

Fenwick glared at the corpse and said, "Et tu, you son of a bitch?"

Turner said, "So it wasn't suicide?"

"No," the ME said.

5

Turner and Fenwick strolled down the hall to talk with Michaela Diaz. In the room, she still had her blue makeup on, although she now wore one of the hotel's bathrobes. A young man in his mid-twenties in a pirate outfit held out his hand. "I'm Frank Cay. What's happened? Why did they take my cutlass?"

"We need to talk to Ms. Diaz," Fenwick said.

Diaz sat in a chair staring out the window. She turned at her name. "I will never forget what I saw. I will never forget those moments. I do not wish to discuss them. Please leave me alone."

Turner said, "Ms. Diaz, it would help if we could ask some basic questions. We'll try to make it as painless as possible."

Cay walked over to her and sat on the arm of the chair. He held her hand. She gazed at him then turned to the detectives and nodded her head half an inch.

Turner asked, "Did either of you know Dennis Foublin?"

"Is that the dead guy?" Cay asked.

"Yes," Turner said.

"I never heard of him," Diaz said. "I'm here to be with Frank. He wanted us to wear costumes to the convention. I came in second in my preliminary category last night. I liked the X-men character that had all that blue makeup. I thought it would be fun. I may never have fun again."

Cay said, "I'm into science fiction movies. I never heard of Foublin until I got to the convention. I saw his name as fan guest of honor. There's always some fan guest thing."

"You go to a lot of these conventions?" Turner asked.

"At least one a year since I was sixteen," Cay said.

"This is my first one," Diaz said, "and it's going to be my last."

Turner asked, "Did either of you know Muriam Devers?"

"I love her books," Diaz said. She looked from one to the other of the detectives. "Did something happen to her? Is she . . . ?" Her voice trailed off.

"She was murdered," Fenwick said.

Both detectives watched their reactions carefully. Diaz clutched Cay's hand convulsively. He leaned over and said soothing words.

When Diaz was calmer, she said, "I didn't know her personally. Her books were fantastic. I've read them since I was a kid. I always liked her women characters. They were strong." Big gulp of air. "I guess I'm not."

Cay said, "You've had a shock."

Diaz said, "I saw the movies they made out of her books that had most to do with science fiction. They were okay. Some were pretty short on action."

Everyone's a critic, sometimes at the most inopportune moments.

"Do you know anything about the red ostrich feathers she carried with her?" Turner asked.

Diaz said, "I heard it was some publicity thing she started way back when. One of the women in her first book had one as some kind of symbolic thing."

Cay said, "She always had one with her when I saw her at

conventions. It was a symbol her main character adopted."

They knew no more. They left.

The detectives met with Oona Murkle in the suite they were using for interrogations. Fenwick said, "Dennis Foublin is dead."

She clutched at her throat and gasped. "My God, what is happening? What is going on? Is there a madman on the loose?"

Turner said, "We know this is difficult for you, Ms. Murkle, but if you could answer a few more questions."

"I suppose. I can try."

"What can you tell us about Mr. Foublin?" Turner asked.

She said, "His wife is here. She's probably downstairs. I told the convention organizers about Muriam's death. Word has gotten out. I'm afraid rumors have started to spread."

They dispatched a beat cop to find Mrs. Foublin. They asked Ms. Murkle for background on Foublin.

Murkle said, "Dennis was the web master for an Internet magazine, *Science Magic*. He was also the editor and nearly the only staffer. His wife helped him with it. He wrote numerous short stories. He was a good, good man."

"But someone killed him," Fenwick said. "Someone must be upset with him. Do you have any idea who?"

She thought for several moments and finally said, "The only thing I can think of is that a few unprincipled people said he was the kind who always got almost all of his facts right."

Fenwick asked, "Wouldn't a first-rate writer want to get all of his facts right? Who said he didn't?"

"Oh, it was those Internet chat somethings. I have trouble getting online. I'm not good with computers. Dennis had a huge following. His web site received thousands of hits a month. It was a bible among the SF cognoscenti. People read him faithfully for his opinions about books, movies, anything that had anything to do with fantasy or science fiction. He had myriad interests. The committee organizing the convention thought it was a great coup when they got him as the fan guest of honor."

"Why was it a coup?" Turner asked.

"He hadn't been to one of these in a long while. He was known as a fabulously knowledgeable recluse."

"Fan guest of honor?" Fenwick asked.

"Yes. At these conventions you want to serve every segment of your public. There is almost always a fan guest of honor. They get their name prominently in the program. They get to wear a special badge, and they get to meet some of the stars. For our convention he attended the Thursday night pre-convention celebrity dinner. In person, Dennis was a very charming man. He had lots of friends."

"If he gave opinions online, couldn't that lead to some people being angry at him?"

"Yes, but I never heard of any. I never read what he wrote. I'm a fan myself, but I know what I like. I wouldn't care what he wrote."

Turner said, "And some people didn't think he had all his facts right."

"There were occasional rumors about him being slipshod or careless. Nobody bothered to challenge him. Let me give you an example of what I mean. He kept a bestseller list on his site. He claimed he got the data from bookstores. A few people claimed a disproportionate number of books he liked made it on the list."

"Did that make people angry?" Turner asked.

"It was one list on a relatively obscure site. He might have been a big fish, but the pond isn't that big. I doubt if anyone much cared. If it was the *New York Times* list or *Publishers Weekly,* people might care. Not for this. Not for murder."

Fenwick said, "It might have made a difference to someone who got on the list or made someone angry who didn't make the list because of Foublin's serendipitous way of doing it."

"I never heard of anyone protesting," Murkle said. "A few people complained about how odd it was sometimes. Not a big deal. I did my own informal checking. I found no problem. When I brought up his name to have him be the fan guest of honor, no one mentioned any problems, and I certainly wasn't going to. After all, I was the one who proposed his name. I had no proof. No one else did either, or no one brought any forward. And he does have a large following."

A woman dressed as an inmate of a harem out of the *Arabian Nights* entered. She was in her late forties. She might have been all of five feet tall and weighed about one hundred and ten.

Sanchez said, "This is Anna Foublin."

This was the toughest part of Turner's job. It never became easier. He hoped it never would. Turner said, "Mrs. Foublin, I have some bad news."

She gazed at him.

"Your husband has been murdered."

She glanced at each of them, her eyes finally resting on Murkle. "Is this true?" Mrs. Foublin asked.

Murkle nodded.

Mrs. Foublin dissolved in tears. Murkle rushed to her. Mrs. Foublin fell into her arms. After comforting her for some moments, Murkle led her to a seat. The older woman patted her arm and said soothing words. Turner produced tissues. When Mrs. Foublin was more composed, Turner got her some water to drink. He watched her swallow several gulps. "Can I see him?" she asked. "I have to see him. I don't believe this."

Turner said, "We'll go with you to identify him. Ms. Murkle may come with if you wish." The body, covered by a white sheet, was on a gurney on the twenty-sixth floor.

After they completed the unpleasant task of identification,

they returned to the interrogation suite. Turner said, "It's important that we interview Mrs. Foublin." He didn't want to order Murkle out, but he didn't want her here for the interview either.

Murkle caught on. She stood up. "If you need anything, Anna, I'll be right outside."

Mrs. Foublin, Turner, and Fenwick sat together. Mrs. Foublin kept a stack of tissues at her side.

Mrs. Foublin pulled in several deep breaths and asked, "What happened?"

Turner gave a brief description, leaving out the grisly details. When done, he said, "Mrs. Foublin, we know this is an awful time, but we need to discuss this. The first hours of a case are the most important."

She nodded.

"Do you have any idea who might have wanted to harm your husband?"

"No. He was a dear, sweet, innocent man. You know he ran a review site on the Internet?" The detectives nodded. "He always tried to say something good about the books he read. Even the ones he hated the most, he tried to find something to praise. He was always trying to be positive." She dabbed at her eyes with tissue.

"Did he know Muriam Devers?"

For an instant Turner thought he saw a look of intense distaste rush across her features.

"They met many years ago when he still went to conventions all the time. They did correspond frequently, the past few years; they exchanged tons of e-mails. He always got along with her, but they were more acquaintances than friends. He did go out of his way to praise her books. He may have genuinely liked them. I was never sure. Why do you ask? Does she have something to do with my husband being . . . ?"

She couldn't finish the sentence.

"No, ma'am," Turner said, "she's dead."

She gaped at them. She blew her nose again then burst out, "She was a hateful sow."

Turner and Fenwick had been detectives long enough to be able to conceal their intense interest.

"You just said your husband got along with her," Turner said.

"He did. I didn't. In the past few years, I've attended far more conventions than my husband. Devers was so sweet in public, but if you couldn't do her any good, she had no use for you. She always had that smile, that simpering, never-ending smile. She was always mind-numbingly cheerful. And my husband believed that crap from her. I remember years ago, he'd listen to her for hours. Always encouraging her with that 'how interesting, tell me more.' That after-dinner-dessert get-together last night in her room was awful. I had to sit there and trade hypocritical smiles with that back-stabbing bitch. I shouldn't be saying these things. I'm just so upset. I could believe that woman had something to do with Dennis's death."

Turner was very aware that they did not know which person died first. Or if either one had had anything to do with the death of the other. Turner presumed there had to be some connection between the killings. He thought it most likely that there was one murderer, but he was not going to close his mind to any possibility at this point. He doubted that Muriam Devers could best someone in a fight and heft a sword at the same time. Although she could get behind someone, strangle them just past the point of unconsciousness, and then stab them. They'd have to check.

"Did you see them together at this convention? Did they talk at the dinner Thursday or at last night's get-together in her suite?"

"I imagine they must have, but I didn't actually see them together."

Turner asked, "If she never did anything bad to your husband, how was she a back-stabbing bitch?"

"Dennis would not listen to me. He was such a sweet, dear man. He believed the best about everybody. He was friends with everyone. People begged him to review their books. We have stacks and stacks of them all over the house. We could barely donate them to libraries fast enough." She used a tissue for a moment.

Turner prompted, "And you felt differently."

"I'd heard things about her. I'm a writer, too. I knew Melissa Bentworth. She was Muriam's first editor at Galactic Books. Melissa and I knew each other in college. We've stayed friends. She's a good editor, smart, hard working. Always has solid comments to make about a writer's books. Muriam Devers got her fired."

"How'd she do that?"

"She lied. She made things up. She went to Melissa's bosses behind her back."

"Why?" Turner asked.

"I've never gotten the whole story. Melissa was never able to find out. Everything worked out for the best because Melissa founded her own small press. She's had some remarkable successes, but it took her years of hard work. I'm one of her authors."

"You've had books published?" Fenwick asked.

"My sixth came out last month. Melissa has been most kind to me over the years."

"Did Ms. Devers have any other enemies?" Turner asked.

"You hunt around the fringes of the science fiction community, you are going to find people who hated her. They might be hard to find, but they're there. She had a lot of power and clout. Nobody talked against that sweetness-and-light image, not publicly. You risked getting black-balled in this community."

"And she got away with this?" Turner asked.

"You could never accuse her of anything specific. People rushed to her defense if you made the slightest negative comment. It was amazing how she got on all the talk shows when one of her books came out. Dare to mention just that one fact and people began clamoring and protesting, accusing you of jealousy and not being a good sport. As if Muriam ever was some kind of good sport. Maybe she was on those shows because she's famous. Maybe the shows made her famous. Who else are they going to put on those shows? Some schlub who's spent twenty years slaving away at some three-volume unpublishable fantasy drivel? No. Still, it was all Muriam, all the time."

"What about the non-public part?" Turner asked.

"She had kind of an assumed clout in the community. Kind of a Wizard-of-Oz effect. She had all this power because people assumed she had all this power. People deferred to her. It didn't hurt that she was rich. Money counts. A lot of people think of writers as these saintly dweebs pouring out their hearts for their art. Hah! Trust me, they're camped out at their mailboxes desperate for those royalty checks."

"That sounds more gossipy and backbiting," Fenwick said. "That doesn't sound like a motive for murder. Sounds kind of average for almost any profession."

Mrs. Foublin said, "You let anything fester over time and watch the explosion you get. One reviewer dared to write a negative review of one of her books. He never got invited on another talk show. His editor dropped his reviews. It took the reviewer awhile to put cause and effect together."

"Who was this?" Turner asked.

"Matthew Kagan, a very nice young man."

"Is he at the convention?"

"I saw his name on the list of attendees, but I haven't seen him."

"Were there other conflicts?" Turner asked.

"Those people in that writing group of hers. They were slime incarnate. She used them like gang hitmen. It was disgraceful."

"How were they like gang hitmen?" Turner asked.

"If she wasn't able to do her dirty work, she'd get them to do it for her. She was vile and unprincipled with loyal followers who would cut their hearts out for her."

"How did they do that?"

"If she wasn't at a convention, they would be. They'd be great at innuendo. Nothing you could ever track down or prove."

"Did any of them try to do something to your husband?"

"He never thought so."

"But you did."

"Yes."

"Like what?"

"My husband's web site would be sabotaged. He always said it was probably teenagers. Ha! Why would they care? Or there'd be whispering campaigns. At some of the smaller conventions they vote to give out their own awards. Nobody is supposed to campaign for the awards. It's just not done, but somehow my husband never got an award for criticism or for his short stories. Authors Muriam was angry at never won. Either she'd win, again and again, or buddies of hers would."

"Maybe your husband's critiques or stories weren't any good," Fenwick suggested.

"They were excellent. Why Devers hated my husband, I don't know."

"But your husband didn't think she hated him," Turner said.

"No."

"Did he ever say anything bad about her?"

"Not really, but that's the way this world works a lot of the time. Everybody used the coin of hypocrisy. Certainly Muriam did. The truth and that woman were not friends."

Turner said, "Your feelings about her seem to run pretty deep."

Anna Foublin sighed. "There was jealousy, too. I'll admit it. It burned me up to see her on all those talk shows. Every single one of them. Every single time one of her books came out. Those producers on those shows have no imagination. Maybe I'm just a lesser-known hack grousing about the ways of the world, but I'm sure I'm not the only one who felt this way. She'd whine about her wrist needing a splint after a book signing. As if her poor wrist would just give out, poor thing, because she autographed so many books. While the rest of us sat with one fan who would drone on and on, she'd have these huge lines the rest of us could kill for . . . oh dear." She put her hand over her mouth.

"Do you know anybody else who felt jealousy?" Turner asked.

"No. I just assumed it existed."

Fenwick said, "You could have not watched the shows."

"I couldn't resist. It was like watching evil blossom right in front of your eyes. Like a poisonous flower all pretty and smiling and deadly and awful."

Turner said, "We found a broken red ostrich feather next to your husband's body. Do you attach any significance to that?"

"No. I know Devers paraded around with one at every public moment. She even insisted on having a bouquet of them behind her at every public appearance. A lot of birds died for that woman's sins."

Turner persisted. "But your husband had no association with the feathers."

"Certainly not. It was an absurd affectation on that woman's part."

"Did your husband have any fights with anyone?" Fenwick asked.

"No, no one. He was a good man."

"With you?" Fenwick asked.

She gave him a startled look.

Fenwick said, "We have to cover all the bases."

"I suppose you have to ask the family," she said. "What an awful thing to ask."

The detectives waited.

"We loved each other. We'd have been married twenty-five years next August. He was a good man. He had quirks. We all have quirks."

"Do you have children?"

"One. A son in the Peace Corps in South Africa. God, I'm going to have to call him. What am I going to say? This is too awful. This is too unbelievable." She wiped at her nose.

"Do you know other people who didn't like Ms. Devers?" Turner asked.

"I can give you a list of people I know. I don't think any of them is a killer. I'd hate for them to think that I pointed a finger at them."

"Someone did this to your husband. It's most likely it was someone at the convention. We know your husband got along with Ms. Devers. We need to know who didn't get along with her. We assume the deaths are connected."

"Well, I can give you a few names."

When she was done, Turner asked, "Why was Mr. Foublin in the room at this time?"

"He had to make a presentation at tonight's banquet. He was in the room making some last-minute changes to his talk."

"How long was he gone for?"

"An hour or two. He always waited until the last minute to prepare any remarks. It was just his way."

"Where were you?" Fenwick asked.

"I was sitting in the hotel lounge with some friends waiting for him."

"The whole time?" Fenwick asked.

"Yes."

"What time did you last see him?"

"About ten. He was going to stop in the dealers' room and then come up here. My friends and I ate a leisurely breakfast then passed the time on the comfy chairs in the lobby. I love watching the people."

She had an alibi.

"Did either of you have a broadsword as part of your costume?" Turner asked.

"No. Dennis wasn't into violence. He didn't like it that people brought weapons to these conventions. He thought they were dangerous. Some people tried to lead a campaign against them, but Dennis was against an outright ban. That kind of thing gets pretty absurd."

"How so?" Fenwick asked.

"Well, do you ban ray guns and laser pistols? They're all fake. He was against both the weapons and the ban. It was all silly and a little absurd, but Dennis loved that kind of thing, taking fun things and playing with them. Testing the limits of the absurd." She dabbed at her eyes.

"Did you see anyone who looked suspicious hanging around?"

"No. No one who looked like a murderer. It never even crossed my mind. Something like that doesn't, usually, does it? This is so inexplicable." She began to cry softly.

"Can we have someone sit with you?" Turner asked. "We could call someone."

"I'll talk to Oona."

Turner found Sanchez in the corridor and gave him the list of names. Turner pointed to Matthew Kagan's. "See if you can find him first." He brought Oona back into the room with him. He and Fenwick watched the two women leave together.

After they left, Fenwick said, "I love someone who hated the victim. It is one of my favorite things."

Turner said, "Raindrops on roses, whiskers on kittens,

dead victims bleeding, witnesses blabbing, those are a few of your favorite things."

"You are not to begin singing Broadway show tunes."

"You write poetry."

"Yeah, but you can't sing."

"Hey, I always say every syllable of your poetry is perfection."

"Yeah, but you never say anything about the poems themselves."

"Every single one of your syllables is flawless. It's just some are more flawless than others."

"Something can't be more flawless."

"Precisely. And I wasn't singing, I was misquoting. Besides, being able to sing Broadway show tunes is part of the gay gene."

"I thought there wasn't a gay gene."

"There isn't, but it's a handy cliché at a moment like this."

Fenwick said, "Mrs. Foublin didn't look like she had the heft to be plunging swords into people."

Turner tapped his notebook. "But we now have people who didn't like Devers. A lot more than we had earlier."

They returned to the room Foublin had been killed in. At the door, Turner said, "They each knew the killer, so they let them in, or somebody knew how to break into the modern hotel room."

"Could they have been having an affair?" Fenwick asked.

"Devers and Foublin?" Turner said. "We'll have to find out. Foublin didn't look studly and young to me, but you never know."

Fenwick said, "His wife wasn't bad looking. Why go after someone nearly twice your age?"

Turner said, "I assume there is some connection between these two murders, and between these two victims, that caused the killer to want to murder them, and I'm ready to eliminate all consideration of suicide on the part of anybody.

And I don't buy the notion of murder down here, and then Devers going up to her room and committing suicide."

Fenwick said, "I agree."

"No puns, no humor, no corpse cracks?"

"When you're right, you're right."

6

Sanchez entered with a thin, pale young man. He wore khaki pants, a blue shirt, and a navy blue blazer. Sanchez introduced him as Matthew Kagan.

Kagan said, "There's all kinds of rumors downstairs. People keep disappearing and not coming back. I don't think it's some big, clever, secret event that needs lots of planning and personnel. And nobody has an explanation for all the cops being here. They don't need this many cops to have a balloon drop." He had a tenor voice.

Turner said, "Muriam Devers and Dennis Foublin are dead."

Kagan gaped for a moment. He said, "The rumors are true."

"How well did you know them?" Turner asked.

"Devers got me fired from a reviewing job. I was starting to syndicate my science fiction reviews around the country. I didn't put it together that she was responsible until long after. The firing didn't happen the day after my negative review about her appeared. Devers was a sneaky bitch. She planned it so I'd never figure it out. She was big on secrets."

"How did you find out it was her?" Turner asked.

"I was having coffee with her first editor at Galactic Books, Melissa Bentworth. She told me what had happened to her.

I began to put two and two together. I had a friend of mine who still worked at the syndicate ask my former editor. The friend got the story. It was Devers."

"She was that concerned about one review?" Fenwick asked.

"She was concerned about everything connected with her career down to the smallest detail. She had that sweetness-and-light persona perfected. Everybody loved her except those of us that hated her."

"What didn't you like about her book?" Fenwick asked.

"The plot and the characters."

"Doesn't leave much," Fenwick said.

"She was great at settings. I don't know why people loved that book. I didn't. She's rich. I'm still scrambling. Maybe I was wrong. Her books for kids were even worse than her adult books. They were just drivel. The plot development constantly turned on everyone keeping the same silly secrets. There was no reason for the characters to keep the secrets she had them keeping."

"But they sold," Fenwick said.

Kagan agreed, "They sold tons."

"Where were you around ten today?" Turner asked.

"I was having coffee with an agent who was interested in a movie script I was working on. We were discussing options for over an hour and a half, from ten to eleven thirty."

"Did you know Dennis Foublin?" Turner asked.

"I visited his web site frequently. I thought he liked stuff a little too often. I disagreed with him on some reviews, agreed on others. I never met him."

Turner asked, "You hear any gossip about them possibly having an affair?"

"I can't imagine Muriam having an affair with anyone. Although as part of that overly sunny persona she was always giggling at handsome young men. Some might call it flirting, but I watched her. Her flirting never led to anything. She reminded me most of the character Mae West played in the movie *Myra Breckenridge*. She did a whole lot of showy posing and flirting. The Mae West character is never shown following up the invitations. Devers certainly never followed up on hers. If some guy tried to accept her apparent invitation, she shut them down real fast. She'd go so far as to pinch their butts and do this stupid simpering number. But I never saw or heard of her actually inviting someone to her room or of her giving someone her room key."

"You watched her that closely?" Turner asked.

"After she ruined one possible career for me, how could I not notice her? If you hung around enough of these conventions, she was impossible to miss."

"Nobody thought what she did was sexual harassment?" Fenwick asked.

"Who would give a rat's ass?" Kagan said. "She was in her seventies. Sometimes the butt pinching escalated to a lingering pat or, on occasion, a solid grab. If it was a forty-year-old boss with a twenty-year-old intern there'd be lawsuits flying faster than you can say hostile environment. Maybe it's part of the hypocrisy of society. She could approach the edge with younger men, hell, even go over it. I certainly never heard a rumor about harassment or lawsuits. Supposedly a previously pinched butt was an entree to her writing group. I have no idea if that was true. I live in Boise, Idaho, and wouldn't have been able to make any such meeting. Although I wouldn't have gone even then."

"Why not?"

"Writing groups? Pah! I don't have time for writing groups. They're for cowards, or people who need help with their writing. I don't need help from some snarky wannabe. You work by yourself. Not with a committee. Writing groups are utter nonsense."

"You mean, you were never invited to join one," Fenwick said.

70

"Boise doesn't have a lot of SF writers."

Turner asked, "Did Ms. Devers have fights with anyone that you know of?"

"She was involved for a long time in several science fiction organizations. I heard she could get pretty steamed up over some awfully small issues."

"Like what?" Turner asked.

"Some fairly typical stuff. Who should be in charge? Should the organization be centered in New York, Los Angeles, or somewhere more central in the country? Should they be a group dedicated to professionals already writing or should they be trying to help new authors get established?" He shook his head. "It got kind of silly, but Muriam hated any kind of change. In public Devers tried to position herself above the fight, but she was desperately working against the newbies in sneaky, underhanded ways."

"What would those be?" Fenwick asked.

"Working against candidates who might be more representative of an organization's membership. Trying to make any change to a group's by-laws require a two-thirds majority to pass."

"Sounds like a weird kind of democracy to me," Fenwick said.

Kagan said, "Didn't feel like any kind of democracy if you were on the losing end."

Fenwick said, "We heard the members of her writing group did her bidding in a lot of these negative things she perpetrated."

"They were all desperate wannabes. I hate wannabes. They hang around these conventions in droves. Frankly, I'm ready to believe she kept the members of her writing group around as sexual toys, but I have no proof for that. Studly young men? I heard most didn't hang around long in the group. I assumed they got tired of getting hit on or tired of being led on with no sex to show for their groveling. Maybe they got smart and realized their careers were going nowhere, and gave up. They were kind of a joke among those of us familiar with the situation. I don't know any of them personally."

Turner asked, "Do you know anything about a red ostrich feather connected with Ms. Devers?"

"She always had one when she appeared in public."

"What was the point?" Fenwick asked.

"She used it in publicity for her first book."

"Why?" Fenwick asked.

"It had something to do with the main character, some kind of symbol of purity and truth. What's important about the feather?"

"We found broken ones near both dead bodies. Ms. Devers had a large supply in her luggage."

"Would anybody else have a negative association with them?" Fenwick asked.

"You mean did she attack someone with one, use one to try to strangle someone? Or that someone might have attacked her because of some anti-red-ostrich-feather complex? I can't imagine. It was a harmless affectation."

They got the name of the Hollywood agent that had met with Kagan about his script and then they told him he could go.

When he was gone, Fenwick said, "We have come full circle. We've got an elderly woman who kept a group of boy toys."

"Is that progress?" Turner asked.

"When we announce it, we can see if all the feminists have a party to celebrate."

Oona Murkle, Sanchez, and Brandon Macer, the hotel security man, entered. Between the two officials was a scrawny man wearing black high-top tennis shoes. An unbuttoned and threadbare red flannel shirt covered a ragged and torn black T-shirt. Turner thought the splotches on it could be remnants of meals long forgotten. His black, ill-fitting jeans had a belt which had a foot of leather drooping past the buckle. The man might have cut his own hair with a pair of children's scissors. Clumps stuck out here and there, some parts longer than others. He wore black horn-rimmed glasses. There was no pocket protector in sight. Turner supposed this might have been a costume, but it looked like an outfit that had been slept in and worn daily for weeks. He caught an odor of too much aftershave trying to mask an unwashed body.

Sanchez said, "This guy's been asking questions of every beat cop he can get hold of." He handed them a black backpack. "This is his."

Macer said, "We had to stop him from hanging around several of the celebrities."

"Which ones?" Turner asked.

Macer gave them a list of names. Turner recognized Muriam Devers' but none of the others.

"We'll take care of it," Turner said.

Murkle beckoned Turner over to a corner of the suite out of the hearing of the others. She said, "I've seen him lurking at a number of these conventions. The name on his badge is obscured. He probably does that deliberately. It looks like Melvin or Mervin. I've seen him trying to buttonhole people. Mostly they ignore him. I did get one complaint from a male author yesterday morning." She pointed. "When I talked to him about it, he promised to stay away from people. No one else has come to me about him."

Sanchez, Murkle, and Macer left.

Turner walked up to Mervin/Melvin. The name on the convention badge was impossible to make out clearly. Turner asked, "What's your name?"

The man met Turner's eyes for a second then studied the floor.

"Melvin," he muttered.

"Melvin what?" Turner asked. He kept his voice low and non-threatening.

"Melvin Slate."

What Turner could catch of his voice was high and reedy. He might have been six foot three. He probably didn't weigh one hundred forty pounds.

Fenwick unzipped the backpack halfway. "What you got in here, Melvin?"

"You can't look at my stuff," Melvin said. As he snatched at the backpack, a bony wrist protruded from the red flannel shirt. Turner noted a black and gray metal thumb ring on the hand. The design alternated flames and pentagrams. He saw its twin on Slate's other thumb.

Turner's son Brian had considered purchasing this type of body decoration but had decided to purchase a couple CDs instead. Brian had explained several times to him, with that patient exasperation teens develop on their thirteenth birthday, that thumb rings were not automatically a sign of membership in a Satanic cult. He had insisted over and over that among most teens the iron rings were simply a personal decoration. Turner had done his own research. His data confirmed that the rings could be simple personal decoration, or they could be the sign of a person in a cult of the nastiest sort.

Fenwick pulled the backpack out of Melvin's reach, but he took his hand off the zipper. Turner knew the backpack couldn't possibly contain a broadsword. He wasn't about to risk the fact that this could be a killer quite happy to switch methods of killing and pull out a semi-automatic. All three of them sat down on the uncomfortable chairs. Melvin's eyes roved between his backpack and the hotel room painting of a Paris street in the rain.

Turner said, "Melvin, we heard that sometimes you bother people at these conventions."

Slate's eyes rarely met Turner's directly. As the distinctly emaciated man spoke, his eyes darted from carpet to painting. Slate said, "I go to a lot of conventions. I like to go to the conventions. I pay my registration fee. I can't always afford to stay at the main hotel. I have to scrimp. When I'm here, I try to talk to people. If they ask me to, I always go away."

"Are you supposed to bother people?" Fenwick asked.

"I'm allowed to ask questions. I go to lots of workshops and seminars. They like me because I always have questions. Lots of times they ask for questions, and there aren't any questions, and so I ask questions."

Turner suspected the gratitude was more in Melvin's mind than in the thoughts of the people at the seminars. Still, he felt sorry for such an obvious loser, a man who would get little more than sneers from everyone he met—at conventions, on the street, in his job. But his sympathy did not preclude him from wanting answers.

"Do you have a job?" Turner asked.

"I help at a pet shop sometimes, and I do small jobs at a library near my home."

"Where do you live?" Turner asked.

"Here in the city. I've got an apartment in Logan Square."

Turner knew that this was a dicey part of town, filled with gritty eccentrics. It also had the highest murder rate in the city.

"I live with my mom. She needs help getting around. My brothers and sisters are too busy to help. I can't always get away to these conventions because of that."

"You've been pestering the police."

"Something strange is going on. I watched people lining up for the luncheon. I don't pay for convention meals. Lots of times I don't. It's a lot of money for some goopy dead chicken." Turner couldn't dispute his analysis of banquet food.

Slate continued to mumble to the wall, floor, and ceiling. Turner noted that his long fingers twisted the rings on his fingers round and round while he was being asked questions. During his answers the fingers would lie still. "If I do go to the banquets, nobody ever wants to sit at a table I'm at. If I go early, the table stays empty. If I go at the last minute, they always say that the empty seats are saved. But later, no one is sitting there."

"Why bother the police?" Turner asked.

"This many police don't show up unless something bad has happened. I sat in the lobby and counted at least twenty. There's a lot more than that. Plainclothes like you guys. There's a buzz in the line for the luncheon. I notice things. They're buzzing about something."

"Do you know Ms. Devers or Mr. Foublin?" Turner asked.

"I downloaded every issue of Mr. Foublin's magazine. It had some of the best illustrations of any of the fan magazines. He had some good contributors. They could have been drawing for the comics. I e-mailed him sometimes at the magazine site. He'd e-mail back. He knew a million things about science fiction movies, books, comics, and magazines. You could ask him about the most obscure character, and he would know book, author, publication date. Without looking it up, he knew who Solomon Grundy was, and the dates of his first and last appearances in the comics. Everything. He was a great resource. I read all of Ms. Devers' books. I was a fan. She is a very good writer."

"Did you talk to either of them this weekend?" Turner asked.

"I tried to talk to Ms. Devers. Every time, someone got in between us."

"Who got in between you?" Turner asked.

"Different people. Usually some woman. I don't know who. I don't know why."

"You look weird," Fenwick said.

Slate's fingers now pulled the rings off both thumbs. He caressed the rings a moment, replaced them, then raised his eyes to Fenwick's. "And you're fat. That doesn't mean you shouldn't be allowed at conventions or be forbidden to get autographs or kept from talking to people."

"Did somebody forbid you?" Turner asked.

"Someone was always watching me."

"Look at how you're dressed," Fenwick said. "If you didn't want to draw attention to yourself, why didn't you show up in a costume?"

"You've seen some of the people here, and you're saying I don't look normal?"

"Look at yourself," Fenwick insisted.

Slate glanced at his attire. "I dressed up as best I could."

Turner suspected this was true. He said, "I noticed your rings."

"So what?"

"Some people associate them with some pretty dark cults."

"I'm not a member of a cult. No cult would have me."

Turner wondered what kind of life someone lived where Gothic cults didn't even want you. He asked, "You said you go to a lot of these conventions?"

"I always go to them if they're in Chicago. I get to a few around the rest of the country. It's the best way to meet people in the business so you can sell your stuff. I write some things, too."

"You tried to get close to Foublin and Devers, but you didn't interact with them?" Fenwick asked.

"No. I told you. I know everything about them I could read. There's a bunch of stuff on the Internet about both of them. I like to spend time on the net. I go to the library every day and look things up. They're very nice to me in the library. I never bother them. Sometimes I have to come back if they have a line waiting to use the computers. I go to web sites and enter chat rooms about all the writers at the conventions. I don't care about the television and movie personalities so much. They aren't real artists. Writers do the real work."

"What else did you find out about Ms. Devers and Mr. Foublin?" Turner asked.

Slate drew his feet up onto the couch. He wrapped his

arms around his long skinny legs and drew them close so his knees were inches away from his chin. "A lot of it was gossipy stuff. I bet most of it wasn't even true."

"What was it?" Turner asked.

Slate licked his lips, adjusted his glasses, and tugged at his pant legs. He said, "Ms. Devers had this reputation for being nice to everybody. But boy, she was mean. She wouldn't give me the time of day. Lots of people on the net said she was rotten."

Fenwick said, "A lot of people we talked to say they really liked her, and that she was extraordinarily kind."

"Do you really believe that's true about anybody?" Slate asked. "I bet there are some people who don't like you. Can I have my backpack?"

"No," Fenwick said.

"What did they say about Ms. Devers?" Turner asked.

"All kinds of stuff. How she tried to trample on all kinds of people on her way to the top of the bestseller lists. How she wrecked other writers' careers. How she got editors fired. She ruined some people's careers in Hollywood, too. All the fights she caused within organizations."

"Did you believe all that stuff?" Fenwick asked.

"You asked me what it said. The Internet says lots of stuff. People believe what they want to believe."

"Do you remember any names of people who didn't like her?"

"We all use screen names. Nobody uses real names. You don't have real names in chat rooms."

"What did they say about Mr. Foublin?"

"Not so much. He wasn't very famous. His web site was great. He wrote lots of stories. Most of them were about husbands and wives who had lots of marriage troubles. He'd post the stories on his site."

"Was his marriage in trouble?" Fenwick asked.

"I don't know. He just wrote lots of stories like that. Once in a while somebody on the net would make hints about his past."

"About what?" Turner asked.

"Nobody ever said. As if there was something shady that nobody could prove. I don't know what. I tried to find out."

Turner wondered if he really didn't know. He didn't picture someone confiding in Melvin, but over the Internet who knew what strangers might reveal to each other? Or totally fabricate?

"Why didn't you wear a costume to the convention?" Turner asked.

"I can't afford any of that cool-looking stuff. Lots of times I just watch. It's pretty fun just looking at the people."

"Do you have a room here at the hotel?"

"No. I commute from home. It isn't as much fun when you don't stay at the convention hotel, but it's okay."

"Do you know anything about a red ostrich feather?" Turner asked.

"Sure. It was Ms. Devers' publicity signature, a gimmick. She made sure the artist somehow worked it onto all the covers of all of her books in the Althea Morris series."

Turner asked, "Do you know the significance of the feather in the book?"

"Is this like, I'm helping the cops?"

Fenwick said, "This is like, tell us what you know before we get pissed off."

Slate glanced at Fenwick for barely a second. He wrapped his arms tighter around his legs and pulled them closer to his chest. His chin now rested on his knees.

Turner loved working with Fenwick. He enjoyed their partnership and, truth be told, their repartee and Fenwick's humor, but once in a while, he wished his partner were a little less abrupt with those who were a little more vulnerable. They were getting information. Why be a hardass? Then again, Fenwick made it easy to play good cop/bad cop. It just wasn't always necessary to go directly to that role-playing method of getting information.

Turner said, "I don't know her books. It would help if you could explain."

Melvin didn't look in Fenwick's direction. He said, "Althea Morris is one of the perfect archetypes of the new strong woman character in science fiction. She didn't need a man to rescue or complete her. Althea was popular with a lot of women but especially young girls because they identified with her. In the books, when Althea was born, her father placed a feather from a Ramble bird on her bed. It was a talisman and a symbol. It most closely resembles an ostrich feather on Earth. When Althea led the revolution at the climax of the book, her warriors all wore a red plume. The feathers meant truth and purity and good. Her fan club sells red plumes as a fundraiser. Why are they important now?"

Fenwick said, "We're not sure if they are, but they've come up in the investigation. Before you go, we need to look in your backpack. We won't take anything. A lot of people are probably going to have to get their room or their belongings inspected."

Turner imagined the backpack filled with cheap pornography, tomes on building bombs, and at least one unregistered firearm. He doubted Slate was capable of organizing himself well enough to commit a crime. He wasn't about to take any chances either. Slate looked pretty odd, as did a number of people he'd seen in the halls, but Slate didn't sound terribly nutty. Probably shy and not good with people. Then again, he wouldn't have been surprised to find a supply of red feathers.

"Can I hand the stuff to you?" Slate asked.

"No," Fenwick said.

"Isn't that unconstitutional?" Slate asked.

"We're going through everything," Fenwick said.

"One of the rumors is that Ms. Devers was killed with a broadsword. You don't think I could keep a broadsword in there, do you?"

"We'll be going through everything," Fenwick said.

"Should I call a lawyer?" Slate asked.

"Do you think you need one?" Fenwick asked.

"I don't know."

Turner said, "You're not under arrest."

"Then I want my backpack, and I want to go."

Fenwick forwent the inspection. They had no hard evidence implicating Slate. Fenwick leaned forward and held the backpack out to Slate. With his best low, grumbly snarl, he said, "Don't leave the convention." Slate reached a hand toward Fenwick as if he were putting it into the mouth of a cranky crocodile. He grabbed his possession and scuttled out the door.

Turner figured that if looking weird became their criterion for making arrests, they'd have to put handcuffs on more people than all the jails on the planet combined could hold.

When he was gone, Fenwick said, "I noticed the rings too. Do you really think a cult wouldn't have him?"

"The man is a walking picture of 'reject me.' I don't want to eliminate the possibility, no matter how remote, but I'm not ready to move the idea anywhere near the realm of probability."

Fenwick said, "You've read about the cults that require people to commit murder to get in. Maybe Melvin has a conscience and couldn't do it. Wasn't Carruthers trying to link all of his cases to cults there for a while?"

They both sighed. Randy Carruthers was the Melvin Slate of their detective squad. For months Carruthers had dinned into their heads useless facts and theories about cults. Not an iota of the information had helped any of the detectives solve a single one of their cases.

Turner said, "Isn't there something about if you don't cover your tracks for your murder, they try and kill you?"

"You would know. I tune Carruthers out."

Turner's innate courtesy often kept him listening far longer than any of the other members of the squad to Carruthers' claptrap. Turner said, "Is either of us suggesting Muriam Devers was in a cult?"

"Evil grandmothers on the loose? I'm not ready to go that far yet. That theory leaves out Foublin. Nothing about either one of them suggested cult to me." Fenwick added. "Sorry I shot my mouth off when you were asking him about the Althea character. I know it didn't help."

"He kept talking."

"Yeah."

Turner said, "Neither of us is perfect, yet."

"Let's not spread that around," Fenwick replied.

Turner said, "What about his suggestion that there was something sinister in Foublin's past?"

"Slate could suggest Foublin could flap his arms and fly to the moon. Doesn't make it so. Sigh. We'll have to ask. He was such a loser."

"I feel sorry for him," Turner said.

"Why?"

"I'll bet he doesn't have a friend. Can you imagine him having a date? His mom probably drives him nuts."

"Maybe she's a sweet lady, and he's got lots of friends. He just likes to look like an awful loser when he's at huge conventions. It's his costume or cover."

"I'm afraid I'm right."

"You probably are," Fenwick said. "I wish we could have inspected that backpack. Who knows, maybe he had one of those folding broadswords in it. You know, like the magicians use."

"I must have missed those in magic class. No, I don't want an explanation of how they work."

82

"Humor management classes and magic classes? Is this like a graduate degree?"

"Ph.D."

"Oh."

7

The next person on their list was Melissa Bentworth, the chairperson of the committee in charge of the convention. She was a tall woman in a light brown and green flowing gown that billowed as she walked. A spray of lilies was entwined with oak leaves in a garland around her head. Turner thought it looked like some kind of galactic Mother Earth Spirit costume.

She said, "Oona told the committee what happened. She looks like she's under a terrible strain. Her health hasn't been the best these past few years. Now the most ghastly rumors are running through the convention. What is going on?"

Turner confirmed the information about Devers and Foublin.

Bentworth threw back her head and gave a whoop of delight. "We said we wanted this to be the most memorable SF convention ever. I guess it's going to be, whether we like it or not."

Turner had seen a wide range of emotions when people dealt with someone's demise. This wasn't the oddest reaction he'd ever seen, but it was kind of up there on the "different" scale.

"Did you know Ms. Devers and Mr. Foublin?" Turner asked.

"Muriam and I knew each other quite well. Too well. I was up in her suite for that dessert party with the group last night. It was a happy get-together. Mr. Foublin I knew as a fan. We always have a fan guest of honor at these conventions. Usually it's some old poop who's hung around for years. His only real competition came from an elderly gentleman from Fort Lauderdale, Florida, who was actually very close to being picked. Then he went and had a heart attack and died the day before we voted. That ended any possible controversy."

"Did either of them have fights at the convention or prior to this with any of the attendees?" Fenwick asked.

"Fighting was not Muriam Devers' public persona."

"What was her private persona?" Fenwick asked.

Bentworth sighed. "Do you know how she got her start?"

The detectives shook their heads.

"It was at Galactic Books. She's still with them. They are the biggest fantasy and science fiction publisher in the world. I was her first editor there. I read her first manuscript. I was the one who saw potential in it. I was the one who believed in her. I was the one who helped her out. I was the one who offered her her first contract. I got repaid all right. I was the one she stabbed in the back. She got me fired. I was the first one whose job she trampled over on her way to the top. She didn't have a grateful bone in her body. She always had an eye out for herself. She was very, very good at watching out for herself. She never took her eye off of whatever was good for her."

"How did she get you fired?" Turner asked.

"That was sneaky. Her first book hit the top of the bestseller list. She and it were hot properties. I found out later that she felt I was holding her back, that I had been too heavy on the criticism for her first book. She's the kind of writer who thinks every sentence she writes is deathless prose and needs no revision. When she turned in her second manuscript, she didn't want me working on it. She couldn't change companies. She was under contract. We weren't going to let her out of it. She ran to each of the higher-ups in the company in turn. When she got to the CEO, he looked at the bottom line and at me. I was easy to sacrifice."

"Is that CEO at the convention?"

"His name is on the list of attendees. I haven't seen him."

Turner said, "Don't editors always make comments on writers' manuscripts?"

"Some more than others. Some writers need it more than others. Muriam needed it more than many others. Has either of you read her latest books?"

The detectives shook their heads no.

"She could have used a team of editors on those last couple, but from that first overnight success, she was too rich to be messed with. She just didn't want anyone suggesting changes in her precious prose. Some writers improve over time. She started out raw, but with tremendous potential. She's working her way to mediocre."

Fenwick said, "A number of the people we've talked to so far have said she was gentle and saintly."

"Ha! I'm not the only one she trampled on her way to the top. There are other editors, and agents, and authors. There are directors, and actors, and producers. They've made over half of her books into movies. You'd think she'd be happy with that kind of success. Everything she wrote turned to gold. Her first unedited stuff was mostly promise. Her later stuff was mostly crap. I guess that's what Hollywood likes the most."

"We heard there was mention of this dual persona on the Internet," Turner said. "How'd she have this saintly reputation if she was such an awful person?"

"She could pay for more PR than anybody. At conventions

she was saintly with her fans. They loved her. She got on the best interview shows. Did you ever see her on *Larry King Live*? Or any of the talk shows? She was a marvel. She'd talk in this soft, gentle voice. She'd dish out compliments. She was so self-effacing and humble, it made you want to puke."

"You still watched her after you were no longer her editor?" Turner said.

"And I read her books. You have to keep up with the competition in this business. I opened my own small press. It is not easy keeping it going."

"We've heard all kinds of rumors about rifts in the convention."

"Mostly silliness. We wanted this convention in Chicago. We got voted down three straight times by factions in other cities. It wasn't fair. We decided to go ahead with our own. We planned extremely well. We had stars here from movies, books, and comics. We had millions of things for fans to do, but we didn't neglect the professionals and serious writers who might attend. We had sessions on how to write books in all the distinct subgenres of science fiction and fantasy. We had strands on how to write and illustrate comics. We had editors' and agents' forums. We had script-writing seminars. We had manuscript critiques. We had one room with movies and another with old television shows—all running continuously. We've got the world premier of *World Domination,* which is supposed to be the next hot SF movie. We had more game rooms than any previous convention. We had panels of stars for fans."

"Where do you get this kind of money?" Fenwick asked.

"You start with seed money. My husband is a successful used car salesman. He's got dozens of lots all over the Midwest, four here in the Chicago metropolitan area. Once you buy and pay for a few big stars, set up your web site and get the word around at the other conventions, it just spreads. By the time we landed *World Domination,* we were already big.

87

Once the movie was on board, we became gigantic. We took out full-page ads in all the science fiction periodicals. We had links on the net with every site that would have us. We tried to meet every need. We had more and better give-away gifts in the convention packets. We went to previous conventions and had tables to sign people up. Once people started registering for the convention, we were able to use that money to parlay it into something even bigger."

"You got the Greater Chicago Hotel and Convention Center on your husband's used car business?"

"He's very successful."

Turner asked, "What do you know about red ostrich feathers?"

"I was the one who suggested to Muriam about adding the feather in the first place. I told her it would make the character stand out. The thing went from a marginal MacGuffin to a central symbol in that series of books."

"What did it symbolize?" Fenwick asked.

"Trust, truth, the triumph of good. There wasn't a lot of that connected with Muriam until tonight, and what little now exists is only because she's dead."

Turner said, "You must have really hated her."

"She ruined my career in New York."

"Where were you between ten and eleven?"

"I had a small problem with an author and the hotel. He'd originally decided to come then he'd changed his mind. We'd gotten him a fairly nice suite. Do you know Darryl Hammer?" They shook their heads. "He's the latest rage in the SF world. So he changes his mind again and decides to show up at the last minute. I want the convention to be a perfect experience for everyone. We've gotten nothing but compliments." She frowned. "Although I guess that's going to change." She shrugged. "At any rate, Darryl was starting to make a fuss. We had to do some quick rearranging. The hotel is booked, but we've got these complimentary suites. We managed to work something out for him, but it took awhile. I don't understand why people who screw up think they are entitled to a free ride. I held his hand for the hour and a half it took to talk to people and then for him to reregister and get everything straightened out."

Fenwick asked, "Who else was on the list of people who didn't like Ms. Devers?"

"I'm not sure. You might try talking to Darch Hickenberg. He's an author who Devers didn't like."

"Why didn't she like him?"

"I know one example. He's got this web site, blog. Mostly he's devoted it to long, rambling self-descriptions and long-winded diatribes against other authors. If he's got an opinion, he's going to share it."

"He had opinions about her?" Turner asked.

"He dumped on everybody and everything. Publishers, editors, other authors."

Fenwick asked, "Why did they keep publishing him?"

"Because he made whoever he was working for tons of money. A lot of people liked his blogs. They thought they were funny. Muriam didn't."

"Humor management," Fenwick muttered.

"Pardon?" Bentworth said.

"Nothing," Fenwick said.

Turner asked, "Do you know Melvin Slate?"

"Who?"

Turner described him. "Oh, yes. The loon. There's always one. At least one. I had to step between him and several of the authors. Muriam was one."

Fenwick said, "You didn't like her, but you defended her?"

"There are proper ways to do things. Muriam may have been a back-stabbing, conniving bitch, but I was going to run a perfect convention. If that meant getting in between the loon and the participants, I would. You can't let the loons run around on the loose."

Turner asked, "Does someone have a list of who was in what costume?"

"If they were entering the contest, they would be on a list. I'll get it for you. If you wore a costume, you didn't have to enter the contest. An amazing number don't. They feel that they are in character, and it isn't some competition."

Fenwick said, "When we found Ms. Devers, she was in a Xena, Warrior Princess outfit."

"Muriam? That is hard to believe. She was pretty strait-laced. Isn't that kind of young for her? Why would she be in such an outfit?"

"We're trying to find out," Fenwick said.

"Could she and Foublin have been having an affair?" Turner asked.

"I certainly never heard anything like that. I met Foublin for the first time here at the convention. I thought he was a perfectly nice man. Wasn't he considerably younger than Muriam? Or course, almost everybody was younger than Muriam."

"Did they know each other before this convention?" Turner asked.

"They may have. At the dinner and dessert get-together last night, they didn't seem close or not close."

Fenwick said, "We heard that there might have been something sinister in Mr. Foublin's past."

"I don't know anything about him having a furtive past."

Turner said, "We heard some negative things about her writing group."

"Pah. Her little stable of no-talent hacks. She had pretty boys around her all the time. I don't think she ever did anything with them. Back when I was her editor, she'd flirt with studly young men, but when she went to her hotel room, she was always alone. I'm not sure whether she wasn't paying them enough, or she or they weren't interested enough. It was a standing joke among those in the know. Writing group? Ha!"

"They did write books," Turner said.

"Not a one of them deserved to be published. Not a one. She got a few of them into print over the years. She got them some attention. They made some sales. That doesn't make talent or a meaningful relationship or even a quickie. Her having that group just doesn't make a lot of sense."

Turner said, "You mentioned there was a faction that wanted someone other than Foublin as the fan guest of honor. What was the problem there?"

"I never could figure that out. I just put it down that more people knew the Florida gentleman. His name was Bill Lifton. You know how people can form into factions over minor things. I remember them being enthusiastic for their candidate, but I don't remember anyone becoming hostile." She gave them the names of the people on the committee who were pro-Lifton. She sighed. "This convention is going to be a disaster. Poor Oona. She put her heart and soul into it. Sometimes we had to help her out."

"How so?"

"She is a dear and relentlessly cheerful, but the poor thing has trouble organizing herself out of a paper bag. We put her in charge of simple things, getting special guests picked up from the airport. She organized the hospitality suites. She would give authors tours around the city. Do all the little things to keep them happy. We kept her busy with little things. She was happy. Not anymore. She's going to take this hard."

They followed Bentworth out to the hall. Sanchez said, "We've got a lot of angry people downstairs."

"We've got two dead ones up here," Fenwick said.

They instructed Sanchez to bring Darch Hickenberg to the interrogation room.

After Bentworth left, Fenwick said, "If this negative shit keeps up, we're going to be ankle deep in it. We could get herds of people claiming what a shit Devers was and wishing she was dead or even claiming to have murdered her."

"That should make you happy."

"I don't want herds. A small cluster would do nicely."

Drew Molton, the Area Ten commander, turned the corner and strolled toward them. He asked, "What have you got?"

They told him.

Turner said, "We've got to interrogate everyone who used a broadsword as part of his costume. We've got people who could have changed costumes. They could disguise themselves any number of ways."

"I love disguises," Molton said. "I dressed up as Zorro last Halloween."

Fenwick said, "You're not making that up?"

"I have been known to relax and have fun," Molton replied. "It's just you've never seen me kick back."

"Something to look forward to," Fenwick said.

"Better get these interrogations organized," Molton said.

"The killer could be roaming the halls," Fenwick said. "We need enough beat cops to have one at the entrance to every staircase. We need at least one stationed in every elevator."

Molton said, "They've put you in charge of overtime for the police in the City of Chicago? And you've canceled all the crime in the rest of the local district and in Area Ten."

"We don't have enough personnel?" Fenwick asked.

"We do not. The hotel has sixty floors. I passed two banks of elevators with five each. There's got to be at least one service elevator, probably more. We don't have enough people."

"We can't be responsible if there are any more murders," Fenwick said.

"I won't hold you responsible."

"Someone will try to," Fenwick said.

Turner said, "We could get hotel security to get some people in the stairwells."

"Give that a try," Molton said. "I'll leave you to your work."

Turner and Fenwick organized the logistics of surveillance. They talked to Macer, the hotel security person. "Don't they have cameras on all of these floors?" Fenwick asked.

"They have them in the lobby and on the front desk. No hotel has a camera on every floor."

"Don't the modern ones have emergency call buttons on every floor?" Turner asked.

"I think many do. This one has plans to install them."

Turner said, "Did they round up all the people who brought broadswords to the convention?"

"They're waiting for you. Everyone we know of for sure who brought one claims they can account for theirs, except one. We're collecting them now so they can be checked."

Fenwick said, "What if someone starts flailing away?"

Macer said, "Something called the Medieval Consortium says their members all have extensive training in sword fighting. They are monitoring their group."

"That's great," Fenwick said. "Unless one of them is the killer. Are we going to have to duel someone to death? We could do like Indiana Jones in that one movie when he's menaced by a guy with a sword. He just pulls out his gun and shoots him."

Turner said, "I told Sanchez to have several uniforms on guard with these people. My kid will be among them. I'll want him brought up to one of the rooms Murkle has made available to us. Him and the rest of the people I came with."

Macer said, "I've got the list of all the people who were at the convention who were in costumes. It was several thousand out of all these attendees. There were ten in costumes that included broadswords. Your kid wants to talk to you. You might have a problem."

"Is he okay?" Turner asked.

"Yeah, but he's the only one who can't account for his sword."

8

Turner's stomach lurched. The other two looked at him. He said, "We'll deal with it."

Sanchez arrived. He said, "We've got some of the people who brought swords down the hall waiting to talk to you."

Turner wanted to talk to his son first. The rest of the people would have to wait. Brian, Mrs. Talucci, and Jeff met with Paul in a special room the convention people had set aside for them.

Sanchez added, "Guy named Ben Vargas says he knows you." Sanchez betrayed neither sneer nor knowledge that Ben was Turner's lover. Turner told him to send Ben up. He felt no obligation to give Sanchez or anyone else an explanation for Ben's presence.

He met Ben in the hall. Ben carried a gym bag with him. He nodded to the gym bag. "Mrs. Talucci called. She said Brian needed a change of clothes." Paul filled him in.

"Are you okay?" Ben asked.

"Yeah. I won't be going home until this is completely cleared up."

"You have to come home sometime."

"I know."

Together they hurried to check in with the family. Mrs. Talucci, having doffed the top half of her Tribble disguise, was sitting on the couch next to which Jeff had parked his wheelchair. Brian now wore a jacket along with his leather harness, the butt flap, and creaky old sandals.

"Whose jacket?" Turner asked.

"A friend of Mrs. Talucci's had an extra. How she knows who's going to need what when is a mystery." Ben handed Mrs. Talucci a bundle of clothes then gave Brian the gym bag. After Mrs. Talucci returned from the washroom in a bulky sweatshirt and warm-up pants, Brian used the same room and returned quickly in jeans, running shoes, and a white T-shirt. Paul sat next to him on the bed.

Mrs. Talucci said, "Is there anything you can't talk about with us here? Do you want us to leave the room?"

"No, it's okay."

Someone had ordered room service. There were bottles of pop and juice.

Paul said, "I could use some juice." They served themselves from the room service cart. Brian asked for a beer. He was told no. Brian and Jeff had milk. Mrs. Talucci had a small glass of wine.

"Is something wrong, Dad?" Jeff asked.

"I need to talk to Brian," Paul said.

"Can I stay?"

"Yes, if you're very quiet." Paul's tone as much as his words informed the boy that something serious was going on. Mrs. Talucci remained in the background.

"Where's your broadsword?" Paul asked. This was the only one unaccounted for so far. He knew his son wasn't a killer, but he still felt uneasy.

"That's the thing," Brian said. "I don't know. I was talking with this girl." He blushed. "Okay, I was doing more than talking. There was this one corner of the virtual game room that was kind of dark."

Turner watched his son carefully.

"When we came up for air, the sword was gone. It was kind of in the way. It kept clunking against my legs, her legs, a chair, so I kind of loosened it. I put it only a foot away from me on a table."

Paul asked, "About how long was it between when you remember you last had it and when you noticed it was missing?"

Brian turned more red. He muttered, "Half an hour. Maybe a little more. It wasn't the kind of moment you're thinking about timing yourself."

"Where exactly was this?" Paul asked.

Brian gave him the geography of the game room.

"What did you do when you found it was gone?"

"At first I thought it was Jeff playing some kind of game. He's always trying to one-up me. I looked for him first."

"So you began looking about what time?"

"Must have been about ten thirty or eleven."

Before the second body was found, but after the first.

"What did you do then?"

"This is a big convention. I hunted for him for half an hour. I ran into Mrs. Talucci. I was pretty steamed. She made me report it to the convention security people. They told me they had to notify the authorities. I said my dad was a detective on the Chicago police force. I don't think it made much of a difference. They told me I had to wait. I began to hear rumors. A few of the convention organizers were in the security area. Even they weren't sure what was going on. People kept coming in with all of the weirdest stories. They were trying to separate fact from fiction. This whole convention seemed to be about blurring the line between fact and fiction. I asked to talk to you. I didn't get snotty or rude about it. I just asked. I didn't know you were here. They made me wait around forever. I still thought it might be Jeff playing a stupid joke. I guess a missing weapon is a pretty big deal. Then they told me I had to come up here. Officer Sanchez told me on the way up in the elevator that it was your case. Somebody said that some old lady in a Xena costume died. Muriam Devers? She the one Jeff got all hyper about seeing last night?"

"Yeah."

"I didn't meet her. Not really. She was one of the judges of the qualifying category I was in last night. I remember because she had that red feather. She wasn't in a costume then. Wouldn't she be way too old to wear that?"

"Now you're a fashion critic?"

"Wouldn't it be obvious to everybody?"

"Did you talk to her at all?"

"No, but as I walked past the judges' table somebody pinched my butt. I turned around. It could have been that Devers. A lot of hot girls were hanging around. I thought it was kind of odd to get pinched, but I figured it might be one of the cuter ones. I wasn't upset or anything. I just hoped it was who I wanted it to be. Everybody was laughing and having a good time. That Devers did have this stupid grin on her face. I don't mean to be rude, Mrs. Talucci, but she was like, old. It would have been kind of creepy. I guess it was sort of funny. She looked like she'd just gotten away with something. It wasn't a big deal. Girls have grabbed . . ." He blushed.

"Grabbed what?" Jeff asked.

"Hush," Paul said. His younger son subsided. Paul asked, "Was the stone in your hilt different or the same as the other broadswords at the convention?"

"I wasn't paying much attention to other people's swords. Only guys had them. I had my mind on other things."

"You and the young lady didn't take a detour up to her room?"

"If she has a room, she didn't invite me to it. Am I in trouble?"

"No," Turner said.

"Am I going to be here for a while?"

"I'm afraid so."

"How come?"

"The sword sticking out of Muriam Devers had a blue stone surrounded by glittery stuff on the hilt."

"Oh." Brian turned pale.

Paul was relieved that Devers' murder had been reported long before Brian remembered being without his sword, but the sword that killed Foublin had yet to be found. They had to pin the time down on the second murder.

"Who did it?" Jeff asked.

"We don't know."

"It wasn't Brian," Jeff said.

"Your brother is not a murderer."

"I heard him bragging earlier that he'd been propositioned."

"And that's your business because?"

"Well, it's not."

"Precisely."

"Is Brian going to be arrested?" Jeff asked.

"This is not time for eleven-year-olds being overly dramatic," Paul said.

"What's happened?" Brian asked.

"There seem to be some undercurrents of in-fighting among the convention goers. Lots of glitz and glitter and smiles on the surface."

Jeff said, "Dad, you've got to understand how this stuff works."

"Explain it to me."

Jeff spun his wheelchair around. "Okay, here's the deal. There's factions all over the place. Some of it's serious. Some of it's silly. Some people get really hyper. Like in the game rooms. You've got to know what you're doing. People get mad if you're an amateur playing at an advanced table."

"What about these fights between rival conventions?"

"That's mostly adult stuff. I don't get it. Why not just have a good time wherever you are?"

"What can you tell me about Muriam Devers' books?"

"She's got a bunch of different series. One was for kids. The Freddy books and the Harry Potter books are way better. The kids' books have a lot of girl main characters, which is okay, but they didn't seem like any of the girls I know. They were always outspoken, inquisitive, and cute. Then she describes everything about seventeen times. In her latest one set on an alien planet, she was describing the plants on the world she was creating. It went on for three pages. She spent even more time in her adult books describing things. What was the point? She needed an editor."

"What's the deal on this red feather?" Turner asked.

Mrs. Talucci said, "I read that one. It's this ostrich plume that's out of control. It was the only book of hers I read. Here's what I understood. Whoever had the feather in some ancient realm had great powers. I could never figure out if the powers came from the feather or if the feather was a reward for using those powers for good."

"Like *The Fifty-First Dragon*," Jeff said. Paul raised an eyebrow. "This character believed a feather was magical so he could go out and kill dragons. When someone told him it wasn't magical, he no longer felt he had the power to kill dragons when he never did in the first place. It was only a feather. Not magical."

Brian said, "When am I going to be able to go home?"

Paul said, "If you were an actual suspect, you'd probably be able to go home already. You aren't. All the people with broadswords are going to be questioned. Like I said, yours matched the murder weapon."

Brian said, "That can't be good."

Paul said, "We've seen several of them. My guess is there were any number of those kind around the convention. I'm going to make sure no one has even the slightest suspicion about you." He turned to Jeff. "You should probably go home."

"Can't I please stay, Dad?" He rubbed the wheel of his chair. "I'm worried about Brian."

A whine would have brought a reprimand. A child's demand to stay would have elicited a parental rebuke. Concern for his brother was the right altruistic note. And Paul knew the younger brother idolized the older, even if he'd cut out his tongue before he admitted it. He permitted him to stay.

Paul said, "Everybody should just sit tight. It's probably going to be a lot of boring hours before we'll be able to get out of here."

"Am I going to be a suspect?" Brian asked.

"We're not going to worry about that yet. You might as well get comfortable." Paul got up to leave.

Mrs. Talucci and Ben stepped forward. Ben asked, "Is there anything else we can do?"

"Your presence is plenty," Paul said.

Brian walked with his dad to the door. He said, "Am I going to be okay?"

Paul gazed at his son. "Yes."

Brian met his dad's eyes. "You sure?"

"You're going to be okay." He gripped his son's shoulder, the only paternal gesture of intimacy the teenager had permitted the past few years.

Turner left the room. He knew his son was more than strong enough to inflict the kinds of wounds he'd seen. He also knew his son well. Brian was not a killer. Paul knew he was the kind of kid who would be overwhelmed with weeping and guilt if he committed a crime, much less something as horrific as these murders. The last time he'd accidentally hurt his younger brother, two years ago, he'd sobbed with guilt and remorse. Brian had come bounding down the stairs from his room at a clip that an athletic teenager could quickly reach. Jeff had turned into the living room at the last second. Both boys had gone head over heels. Jeff had required a visit to the hospital to check his wrist, which turned out to be severely sprained but not broken. Brian had moped about for days. He'd finally made it up to Jeff by bringing his brother copies of five of the newest video games that the younger boy couldn't afford on his allowance. Then Brian spent hours playing them with his brother. Much as Jeff might wish for independence, time together with his older brother was precious. Besides, Paul loved his son, knew his son. He'd stake his life on the fact that Brian was not a killer. But the boy being connected in an investigation, however peripherally, caused him anxiety. He thought that immediately would be a good time to solve this case.

Turner found Sanchez. He told him to post a uniformed guard on this floor to keep watch. Turner said, "I want the fingerprints from the murder weapon as soon as possible. Get someone to run matches as fast as you can." If necessary, to eliminate his son as a suspect in his boss's eyes, he'd take Brian's fingerprints. He hoped it wouldn't come to that. It seemed likely that they would be on the weapon they had. If forced to take them, he would. And there was always the possibility of the second weapon, which they did not have.

He found Fenwick and told him what Brian had told him.

"Let's go look at the swords we do have," Fenwick said. "Sanchez had the uniforms collect them. The damn things are in the room next to Devers'."

They examined six broadswords. None was covered in blood. A crime lab technician was handling them carefully. Each had a tag with a name, address, and phone number on it. The tech explained, "We got their names from the convention costume register. We've got three from people who weren't wearing them when we went to question them. The swords were in their rooms. We have three from people who were wearing them. We found them at various parts of the convention. So, six swords accounted for. Seven if you count the one in Devers. The convention people said there were officially eight."

Turner said, "And the one that killed Foublin could also be the one sticking in Ms. Devers, or it could be the missing one."

The tech said, "You also supposedly have some unofficial ones. We're still hunting them down. We're going to have a hard time finding who they were, if there were any. Of the people with the weapons, all claim to have alibis. None of the beat cops who talked to them said anybody was suspicious."

Turner said, "Which means that unless they had a second or third sword, theirs was not used in the killing."

Fenwick said, "Any number of the official and unofficial swords could have been used already without the bodies being discovered. In addition, there's no telling how many random broadswords people might have walked into this convention with. This is kind of a strange bunch."

"At least they don't play around at crime scenes every day," the tech said.

"Speak for yourself," Fenwick said.

The tech guy said, "We're going to have to get all of these to the lab. I'll get you a report as soon as I can. I'll get a couple guys in here. Nobody wants to tote these around the convention without some kind of protection." He left.

Fenwick asked, "Do we need to worry about more possible murders?"

Turner said, "Even if we could check every single room in the hotel, it probably wouldn't do much good. People could have stacks of swords in their cars or scattered around the metropolitan area." He examined the swords without picking them up. Five had glittery stuff on the hilt. Two had blue stones. Turner used his hanky to touch the top of one of the swords. "One of these could be Brian's."

Fenwick said, "We'll have to check fingerprints."

Sanchez entered the room. He said, "This Hickenberg guy you wanted me to get? He says he'll meet you in his hotel room, that he is not at your beck and call."

Fenwick said, "I'll do some becking and calling."

9

Darch Hickenberg sat in his hotel suite. He puffed on a large cigar. The atmosphere in the room told Turner this hadn't been the first cigar the author had smoked during his stay. Hickenberg's corpulent mass rested in a swivel chair at a desk. He looked to be in his mid-fifties. His white shirt was half untucked from his blue dress pants. Turner saw a mustard stain on the front of the shirt.

Murky hotel prints on the murky walls of murky flowers. Industrial-strength couches with matching cushions. Tough to sit on. Tough to relax on.

According to Melissa Bentworth, Hickenberg and Devers had a history together. Turner asked, "How long have you known Muriam Devers?"

"There are rumors she's dead."

"She is."

Hickenberg drew a deep breath. "Well. My word. I've known her for thirty years. She was in a writing seminar I was giving in Buffalo one summer. Back in the days when I used to give writing seminars. Who needs the competition, I always say. Giving them seminars just encourages them." He looked like he expected the detectives to pick up on his humor. Or maybe he was deadly serious and was waiting for them to huzzah in praise. They waited silently. Hickenberg resumed, "They don't want to listen to criticism, constructive or otherwise. They want to hear that you're going to give them a leg up and wave your magic writing wand to make them fabulously wealthy and give them the secret computer program that has the books write themselves. At that time her writing needed a lot of work."

Fenwick said, "A lot of people read her books. A lot of kids began to read because of her. Didn't she sort of pave the way for J. K. Rowling?"

"Really, you can't count what Muriam Devers wrote as writing. And reading her! That's not reading."

Turner knew cracks like this inflamed Fenwick's irritation index. As a barely published poet, his partner took umbrage to others' writing being dismissed cavalierly. Turner said, "But she did get published."

"Yes, she found a publisher who happened to like the very things in her work that I disliked the most. I'm afraid she took umbrage at my honesty. She certainly did get published without any seal of approval from me, although back then, I must admit I only had a few books out."

"We were told the two of you didn't get along," Turner said.

"How absurd, but I suppose you're desperately looking for suspects. She might not have gotten along with me, but I didn't care enough to dislike her. I was far more successful than she. I had more books out. More movies made of my works. More foreign rights sales. She had every reason to be jealous of me, not the other way around."

"Was she?" Turner asked.

"I don't know what was in her head. I never gave her much thought. I really seldom saw her after that first seminar. Oh, I'd run across her occasionally at one of these conventions, but it was nothing significant. I was surprised when she got published. Even more so when she became successful. She joined all those silly fan and writer organizations. She was always trying to make them more democratic—or was it less democratic? Who cares, really? Those kinds of people need to get a life. Fighting over commas and semicolons! Who cares whether or not a fan organization is headquartered in New York or Newton, Iowa? I believe she actually wanted to move the headquarters out to the provinces, or was it the other way around? Either way, it was silly."

Turner wasn't sure how he felt now that he knew he was considered to be living in a province. He was sure that this guy was a pompous jerk, but so far he was doing reasonably well on negatives about Devers. Solutions to murders seldom resided in the praise of the departed's friends. Enemies and gossips more often gave better information.

"Did you see her at this convention?" Turner asked.

"I saw more people than I care to imagine. I did not directly speak to her. I spoke to very few people. My circle consists of my agent and several movie producers and my editor. You constantly have these know-nothings from the provinces asking for autographs, giving you ideas you're supposed to use in a book, hanging on your every word. It is so difficult to take these conventions seriously. All these people dressed up in these nonsensical outfits."

"Don't a lot of these people buy your books?" Fenwick asked.

"Fans! Really! Nerds and dweebs! The real reason I come to these conventions is to play poker with some of the other writers. We often play on Friday nights, but we always have a game during the Saturday night banquet. There's always a Saturday night banquet at these things. They've been serving the same chicken since the first convention back in the deeps of time. The poor bird needs to be retired. My friends and I order room service. This whole mess with the murders has interrupted our game. Several of the players thought it would be irreverent for us to play when there had been death. I think that's absurd. There's death every day in the world. The rest of us go on. They were more afraid of losing their money to me than anything else."

Since Hickenberg had launched his literary diatribes, Turner had seen Fenwick's left fist clench and his face get redder. Turner recognized those signs. They usually preceded Fenwick letting someone know they had reached the limits of his temerity index.

Fenwick said, "You've trashed your fans and taken a swipe at your friends. Is there anybody you like besides yourself?"

"Is that comment designed to irritate me so that I will make some kind of emotional mistake in my wrath and admit I'm a killer? That kind of crap died ages ago."

Fenwick said, "I'm trying to tell you that you're an egotistical slob who has no notion of what is good, or polite, who doesn't have a sense of gratitude or perspective about how lucky you are or what an asshole you are."

Hickenberg laughed, "That's a hell of a nerve. I think I'd like to have you in our poker games."

"Cut the crap," Turner said. He was a bit on edge and spoke more sharply. His concern about Brian's connection to the crime had made him uneasy.

Hickenberg said, "I hate these conventions. How's that for cutting through the crap? I've been on dozens of panels at these stupid things. I'm bored at all the panels, and I'm on the damn panels. I'm bored with the questions. I'm bored with the people. The same people go to the same conventions year after year. I don't go to many conventions anymore, but this one was supposed to be big. And it was. I have sold one hell of a lot of books so far, outsold everyone else, so I've been told. I've made two movie deals. I won a lot of money last night. I expected to win more tonight."

"How nice for you," Fenwick said. "Where were you around ten this morning?"

"I was napping here in my room."

"Any witnesses?" Fenwick asked.

"Not a one."

"A morning nap?" Fenwick asked.

"I'm good at napping. I take as many as I can every day. I figure, go with your strength, and napping is something I'm very good at."

Turner was certain they were looking for a big person. He'd tried wielding Brian's sword back at the garage. Hickenberg was big enough. His bulk might give him the heft to impale someone with a sword, but if a victim wanted to avoid Hickenberg's attack or outrun him, it wouldn't be that hard. Foublin had definitely fought back.

"You have any fights with the people here?"

"No. I came to play poker and make deals. I heard rumors about petty disputes. I don't listen to that drivel. I've made my cash."

"What petty disputes?" Fenwick asked.

"Has anything changed in thirty years? I'm sure it's the same old prattle. The national organization isn't sensitive to our needs. What are we getting for our dues. Let's all exchange e-mail addresses. As if I needed more people to write to."

"Do you know of anybody that Devers had problems with?"

"I wouldn't know."

"She was in a writing group," Turner said.

"Those things are so absurd. I certainly never needed a writing group."

"Do you know any of the people in hers?" Turner asked.

"I'm not sure I ever met any of them. I heard about them. Poor old Muriam. She was so desperate for companionship she used her fame to lure younger men into being interested in her."

"You mean sexual liaisons?" Fenwick asked.

"I hope not. She was old enough to be their mother and sometimes grandmother. She just wanted them as part of her circle. She could have pretty young men hanging around, so why shouldn't she? Not that many of us make real money doing this. When we do, why shouldn't we use our money any way we want?"

"You take part in the costume festivities?" Fenwick asked.

Hickenberg looked like he'd been asked to taste his own shit. "Please. That is juvenile nonsense."

"Anybody dress up like your characters?" Turner asked. He thought the character Hickenberg would fit most closely would be Jabba the Hutt.

"I wouldn't want to know. I'm not interested. I write these genre books to make money. I just sit down with an idea or two and they write themselves. They're really very simple. I make tons of money from them. My real work is essays. I publish them constantly."

"Do they write themselves?" Fenwick asked.

"Very much so," Hickenberg replied. "They're quite simple."

Fenwick said, "Ms. Devers was in a Xena, Warrior Princess costume when we found her."

Hickenberg chuckled, "Old Muriam had some life in her. No, I don't know why she would be wearing something so patently outlandish."

"Did you know Dennis Foublin?" Turner asked.

"Oh, yes, everybody did. He wasn't in a Xena costume as well?"

"No. Did he review your work?" Fenwick asked.

"I'm rich. I don't have to read the reviews so I don't."

Fenwick said, "I've been told that when an author says that, he or she is lying through their teeth."

Hickenberg laughed. "Even if I am lying, what difference does it make?"

110

Fenwick said, "Maybe you were angry at a negative review he wrote."

"You can't seriously think that would be a motive for murder."

Fenwick said, "Can you think of someone who would have a motive to murder Mr. Foublin?"

"No."

"We heard there might have been something sinister in his background."

"Well, I suppose you hear lots of things in a murder investigation. That doesn't make them true."

"Have you heard a rumor even close to that?" Turner asked.

"No."

Fenwick asked, "Do you know if Ms. Devers and Mr. Foublin were close?"

"They could have been having a mad, torrid affair for all I know or care. I have no idea. Sex with Muriam Devers sounds like a gross concept to me."

Fenwick said, "We found broken red feathers near both of the corpses."

"Muriam's stupid signature piece of fluff. I'll bet she was heartily sick of the damn things by this point. Once you start a bit of silly kitsch like that, you're stuck with it forever. Every goddamn reporter wants to ask you about it, or wants to have a picture of you with your schtick for their paper. It's pathetic."

Turner asked, "Could the feathers have had some symbolic meaning to someone who was angry?"

"I have no idea. For that seminar thirty years ago she could submit ten pages and an outline. She had the damn feather popping up every five sentences. I told her to get rid of it. I only read that small portion. I never read the whole of any of her works."

"Maybe your analysis was wrong," Fenwick said.

"Everybody's a critic," Hickenberg said.

"Do you know who might have wanted either of these people dead?" Turner asked.

"No. I really didn't concern myself with them. I didn't care."

Turner got no sense of heightened emotion or anxiety at any level. Hickenberg could be a very deadly killer or just some author who, because he'd had books published, had assumed a mantle of ego big enough to cover several continents.

"You didn't know Mr. Foublin at all?" Turner asked.

"Really! An Internet reviewer? How pathetic. These conventions always have some fan guest of honor. It's to make a poor pathetic schlub who doesn't have a life feel better about himself. I'm not interested."

Fenwick said, "Let me get this straight. You're famous and all these people are inferior to you. Their lives are shit, and you can't sneer fast enough."

"Your analysis is very accurate."

"And you're a shit," Fenwick said, "class A, number one shit."

"So what?" Hickenberg said. "I'm rich and famous and you're not."

Fenwick said, "Maybe I should just arrest you on general principles."

"I can see the headlines," Hickenberg said. "Poor, put-upon writer arrested. I'd be the hero of that little short story. You'd be the villain. I know you'd like to exercise your power as a minor public official to make yourself feel better, but really, is there much point?"

Fenwick said, "Why didn't the killer start with you?"

"He didn't have taste or sense enough."

Turner ended the interview. They weren't getting anywhere and while Fenwick's temper had flared up in a few places, Turner didn't think there was much point in waiting for a total explosion.

As a parting shot as the detectives neared the door, Hickenberg said, "You are a not-famous writer."

Fenwick said, "Parting shots are for cowards."

Out in the hall, Turner asked, "You ever read any of his books?"

"No. He mixes that horror crap with gothic romance on alien planets. I know that because I've read reviews of his stuff."

"He our killer?" Turner asked.

"He fits the profile."

"I thought we didn't profile people," Turner said.

"I do. He's an asshole. That meets my criteria for a criminal profile."

"Kind of a broad category," Turner said.

"You could narrow it down to stupid sons-a-bitches. Or you could hope the nerds and dweebs he trashed rose up and murdered him."

"Problem is, he's still alive."

"That's not my fault."

"Who's our killer?" Turner asked.

"Devers was above it all and could afford to twist the world into shapes that pleased her. That she was a backbiting, conniving bitch was concealed from all but a few. Those who had been a victim of her mad desire to have her own way or had been bulldozed by her mad neuroses could have reason to kill her. It's in that small circle of those who had been victims of her viciousness where we need to look for the killer. He or she might not be there, but we gotta start somewhere."

Turner said, "Obvious victims of her machinations make great suspects. Not so obvious victims would make even better suspects. People who have managed to hide their anger would make great suspects. Hiding their anger most likely means we don't know who they are. By hiding they are a step ahead of the others and way ahead of us. We need to find those who have so far hidden their reactions. They've managed to conceal and kill."

Fenwick said, "Unless it's one of the wounded and slashed egos in those we have managed to uncover."

Sanchez dashed down the hall toward them. "It's getting worse. Come on."

10

Turner and Fenwick rushed after him.

"What?" Turner asked as they ran.

Sanchez pointed to the stairwell on their left. "It's another one. One of us."

"You called it in?" Turner asked.

"Yep. We'll have a mob of us here in a few seconds."

Turner could hear Fenwick puffing behind them. Turner banged open the stairwell door. He heard shouts and cries of agony. All three of them pelted down the stairs.

After three flights Turner saw great spots of red spattering the walls. A few more steps and he saw rivulets of blood on the floor. In another second he saw the victim, a beat cop he didn't know who had a broadsword sticking out of his thigh. As Turner bent over, he read the cop's name tag, RIVACHEC. He looked like he might be a day or two out of the academy. Two uniforms stood around him trying to comfort him. Their buddy was conscious and moaning.

One of the uniformed cops said, "We should pull the sword out."

"Stop," Turner ordered. He knew better than to let amateurs deal with a wound of this magnitude. One of the cops was pressing a hotel towel hard against the wound to put pressure on it to try to stop the bleeding. The towel was quickly turning red with blood. When the cop lifted it off the wound for a moment, Turner saw the tip of the sword poking out of the cloth on the back side of the injured cop's leg. The wound was clear through. They all saw it. One of the beat cops, another youngster, began to get hysterical. "We've got to do something. We can't let him bleed to death. Why won't you do anything? Somebody's got to help."

Fenwick put his bulk in front of this kid. He pitched his voice low and menacing. "Shut the fuck up. Your screaming isn't going to stop the flow of blood." He pulled aside another young cop whose pale face was tending to green. "Go puke somewhere else."

Moments later paramedics rushed through the door. Turner got the uniformed officers away from their colleague. Turner said, "I want this place sealed off. Get cops on every landing in every stairwell. I want cops on every floor. Don't forget the maintenance stairs. Be sure there is a cop in every elevator car. Go."

Turner heard one of the paramedics say, "We're going to have to move him with that damn thing in there. Let's get the bleeding stopped and get him the hell out of here."

They worked quickly and efficiently. First they cut off the pants leg so they could see exactly what they needed to do. Pulses of blood still seeped from around the points where the sword went through the thigh. At least the red was only oozing, not fountaining out.

Turner didn't have a ghoulish desire to watch blood and gore, but he was long since used to seeing ghastly wounds and searing agony.

Out of the victim's hearing, Turner asked a paramedic monitoring a machine, "Is he going to make it?"

"I hope so," was the reply. Another paramedic continued

to apply pressure to the leg while a third began speaking into a phone to a hospital. A fourth was setting up an IV.

They applied gauze-pad bandages around the wound. They hooked him up to oxygen. A C-collar was positioned around his neck. Without jostling the sword, they raised his legs and placed a blanket under them. Turner knew they were trying to stop him from going into shock. At moments when he was conscious, Rivachec would moan.

"Can we possibly talk to him?" Turner said. "I wouldn't ask if it wasn't vital. We've got two other dead bodies here."

A paramedic kept working as he spoke, "You can ask him anything you like. We aren't going to stop working for you. We're going to move him as soon as we can." He spoke to one of his colleagues. "We've got to get him out of here as quickly as possible. He's lost too much blood."

Turner would never harass a wounded person like this if he didn't have a killer on the loose. He leaned close to the cop's face. He didn't think the kid shaved more than twice a week. The cop clutched Turner's hand. His eyes looked glazed. "Am I going to be all right?"

Turner said, "Yes. They're doing everything. They're going to move you soon." Rivachec shut his eyes and gulped. His leg moved. He screamed. His grip on Turner's hand was enough to crunch bones. Turner held on. Moments later Rivachec opened his eyes. He was breathing heavily. He fixed his gaze on Turner.

Out of one corner of his eye, Turner saw that the bleeding was much less. They had begun to wrap the sword so it wouldn't do more damage while the young cop was being transported. Turner saw a gurney just beyond the open stairwell door. "What happened?" Turner asked.

Rivachec spoke between gasps. "I didn't see him. The door swung open. It caught me in the back of the head. I fell forwards. I saw this figure all covered, gloves, a hood, all black.

I tried to pull myself up. He started to swing the sword. I tripped, twisted my ankle, and fell. He swung and stuck me. I screamed. I heard the door slam. He didn't take the stairs. I tried to pull the sword out. I must have fainted. I woke up screaming."

"We're going to move him," a paramedic said. They lifted the stretcher. Under the cop was a broken red ostrich feather.

Turner held Rivachec's hand all the way down to the ambulance. Fenwick followed.

The street in front of the hotel was mobbed with cop cars. The earlier rain had turned to a fine mist blown by a high wind. Turner sat in the ambulance for a few moments as the paramedics made preparations for leaving. He murmured softly to the wounded youngster, "You're going to be fine."

"I'm getting sleepy," Rivachec said.

Turner got out of the way so the paramedics could secure the gurney and the sword. As the ambulance pulled away, Fenwick said, "I hope the kid is going to be all right."

The thought, never far from a cop's mind, was that the wounded colleague could have been him. The possibility of violence and danger was part of the job, the remembrance of which came glaringly back at moments of major stress such as this.

Fenwick said, "Let's get the fucker who's doing this."

Turner said, "I'm thinking of Melvin. It wouldn't be much of a stretch to believe that someone in a cult would see it as a badge of honor to kill a cop."

Fenwick said, "We've got no proof he's in a cult. We've got no description from Rivachec."

Turner nodded. He and Fenwick returned to the hotel. They ignored shouts from reporters who were crowded near the entrance.

The beat cops had used the parking garage ticket stub to find Foublin's car. Turner and Fenwick checked it out. They found a broken red ostrich feather on the front seat.

"What the fuck?" Fenwick said.

"Exactly my sentiments."

"The killer knew we'd check the car. The killer planted this shit. We are being fucked with royally."

"These aren't crimes of passion," Turner said. "This is well planned. Did the killer commit one or two murders and rush out to Foublin's car to plant another message? Why all the feathers? One in the room and one in the car? Why stab Rivachec? What threat was he? He didn't say he saw anything." Neither of them had these answers yet.

They'd asked Macer to examine the registration records for anyone who might have checked out since eleven. It would be a list of names to go over. They had no idea what would lead to the killer and they were desperate to solve the case. They stopped in Macer's office. "Any luck?" Fenwick asked.

"No one who was registered at the convention and at the hotel has checked out of the hotel. We've got one hundred and two people who left as a matter of course this afternoon. We've got a wrestling team from the University of Iowa. That was forty people."

Fenwick said, "All those wrestlers who go bonkers over red feathers have got to be watched. I knew they'd start causing trouble."

Macer gave them copies of the lists.

The detectives stopped in a private room where Mrs. Foublin was sitting with several friends. Turner asked, "When was the last time you were out at your car?"

"Thursday when we got here, why?"

"You or your husband didn't go out for any reason?"

"We had no place to go in Chicago but here. What's wrong with the car?"

Turner said, "We've found broken red ostrich feathers at the crime scenes. There was also one in your car."

Mrs. Foublin looked frightened. "Dennis went to the car once, yesterday morning to get some books. That's the only time I know of. This is unbelievable."

Turner said, "We understand he wrote a number of stories about failing marriages."

"Yes," she said. "It became an in-joke. He'd make up creatures around the galaxy and try to give them unique marital problems often caused by their odd physiology. Our marriage was fine. So many people have asked me about it over the years. Why is it important now?"

"We try to cover everything," Turner said.

Fenwick said, "One person we interviewed said there had been hints on the Internet about your husband's past."

"His past?"

"Could someone be angry at something that happened years ago?" Turner asked.

"I can't imagine. He grew up in a boring suburb. Went to a state university. As far as I know, he never quarreled with anyone. Certainly I know nothing about some past problem that would cause murder."

As they returned to the lobby, Fenwick said, "I don't get a sense of marital problems, although I'm not sure why someone would write an intergalactic busted-marriage manual."

"Wasn't a manual," Turner said, "just stories. Maybe our Melvin was adding a whole lot of his own spin to what he was living through. Mrs. Foublin wouldn't be the first clueless spouse."

Fenwick said, "We need to post guards at the entrance to the parking garage. They need to report anything suspicious. If someone's going to try to get an incriminating sword out of here, it would be simplest to put it in their car. It's a little tough to conceal one of those broadswords."

On the far side of the lobby, Turner spotted Ian leaning casually against a pillar. He caught his friend's eye. They met at the police cordon while Fenwick went upstairs. "He's with me," Turner told the uniformed officer on duty. The two of them stepped to one side.

"Hear you've got blood all over the hotel," Ian said.

"Yeah."

"Sort of like the last Mr. Leather convention."

"You don't get this much blood at the leather convention," Turner replied.

"How would you know?" Ian asked.

Turner said, "Sources."

Turner wanted to know more about these people. He said, "You've talked to the different gay groups?"

Ian riffled through his note pad and tapped his laptop computer. "I've got reams of stuff."

"Anybody you'd trust? Anybody who can give me inside information?"

"The gay fantasy writer seemed pretty well grounded." Turner trusted Ian's instincts.

"Can you get him to talk to me?"

"Sure. What can you tell me about what's going on?"

"Nothing useful for a story. No gay angle to the killings or solution."

"How many killings?"

Turner said, "If I tell you the details, I know you'll keep your mouth shut, but there isn't time now to fill you in completely. I could use some help."

Ian nodded and said, "I'll look for him." Turner made sure Sanchez knew Ian so the reporter would have access. Then he returned to the scene of the attack on the young cop. "Poor kid," Fenwick said.

Turner said, "I want to know how the hell the feather got under him. The killer is walking around with a ready supply? How can he not be obvious?"

A crime scene tech said, "We've got a million prints. Who knows if any of them have anything to do with the crime? We're working on it."

The detectives stopped in at the banquet. The room was crammed with people. A vast chatter of buzz filled the room. Turner spotted Oona Murkle at the head table and walked over to her. She was staring vacantly into space. She didn't notice him until he was directly in front of her.

"Detective?" she said. "We decided to go ahead with the banquet. What else could we do? This was going to be the perfect convention. The most perfect ever." She dabbed at her tears.

"Can you or someone show me the virtual reality room?" he asked.

"I can get one of the help." She beckoned over an elderly man with a red armband that said STAFF in yellow letters.

While they waited for him, Oona asked, "Is there a clue?"

"Just checking things out."

They followed their guide down a corridor crowded with people to a set of meeting rooms. He left them at the door. These rooms had collapsible walls so the contours could be changed. About three had been combined for the virtual reality games. The room had soft golden glows emanating from all four corners. There were at least ten stations in the middle of the room where games could be played. The two short sides of the rectangular room were covered with heavy black drapes from floor to ceiling. When they looked behind the one on the north side of the room, there was a metal table and a folding chair. Turner shut off the image of Brian being intimately involved in this setting. The area was almost completely dark. Not the most romantic place for trysting but randy teenagers—or even desperate adults—would find it adequate.

Fenwick said, "Your kid came to the convention to meet girls?"

Turner said, "And was successful to the point of obliviousness. Sometimes he's not as self-aware as I'd like."

Fenwick said, "Probably as good a definition of a teenager as I've heard."

"Someone could easily have taken the sword and gotten out of here. There's enough odd costumes around. What's one more guy with a broadsword? The thief wouldn't look suspicious."

"Not hard to conceal it either," Fenwick said. "Wear a cape. Wrap the material around the weapon. It's concealed."

"Yeah." They returned to the hotel's main entrance. Turner eyed the sea of blue-clad cops and noted the presence of numerous plainclothes detectives. He said, "It's a shame it takes one of us getting hurt to get this kind of attention."

Fenwick said, "They'll spend a ton on this now. Rivachec is lucky he's not dead. They should have listened to us the first time and posted people where we needed them."

Turner said, "It's not the time to be pissed at the brass. We've got to find a killer." But there was a small part of his mind that was relieved. Brian couldn't possibly have attacked Rivachec. His son was in a room with three other people, and there had been a cop posted outside in the corridor.

Turner and Fenwick took the elevator back up to the suite they'd been using to conduct interrogations. Turner said, "The killer could still be in the hotel. He or she could change into any disguise. The killer could be disguised as a cop."

Fenwick asked, "Where's he storing his bloody clothes? Why doesn't somebody see him?"

"If he's changing quickly, he's got to be staying in the hotel. You'd think somebody would notice a person walking around in clothes that were all covered with blood. Although we've seen people ignore an awful lot of odd things. Or he's able to conceal things quickly."

"Is he planning all these?" Fenwick asked.

"It's hard to tell. Devers or Foublin might have seen something happen to the other one. Or the killings might have been random. Maybe the killer came across one of them as he was dashing away from the other murder."

"Kind of heavy to be dashing around carrying a collection of broadswords. Somebody's got to notice these kinds of costumes."

Turner said, "I don't see Melvin Slate, our nut, having the wherewithal to plan this carefully. Unless he's a far better actor than I think he has the ability to be."

Molton showed up. "What the hell is going on?"

They told him.

"Can we seal off all the floors?" Fenwick asked. "And stop the elevators?"

"You've already got people on every floor. We'll get all these stairwell doors open. We've got to solve this as quickly as possible. Ninety-nine point nine percent of the people in this hotel are innocent. Yes, I know, we're going to inconvenience them. We don't want one of them to become the next victim."

Turner said, "Do we need to evacuate the hotel?"

"This complex is huge," Molton said. "We've got thousands of people milling about in the public areas of the hotel. They're spilling into the street and the convention rooms are full. The restaurants in the area are jammed."

"They would be for a convention of this size anyway," Fenwick said.

Molton considered for a few moments. "We've got all the floors and the lobby covered. Our killer hasn't struck people in groups, yet. Nobody's getting up or down the elevators without an escort. We can't make people leave their rooms. We'll have the cops on each floor knock on every door, explain what's happened and suggest that they leave. Or at the very least, that they don't open their doors to strangers."

"Good enough?" Fenwick said.

"It'll have to be," Molton said.

"There's another complication," Turner said. He told him about Brian's problem.

After he finished, all Molton said was, "Let's solve this." He left.

⸜ 11 ⸝

"Who's next?" Fenwick asked. By now the people from their various lists were waiting to be interviewed in suites comped to the convention. Three beat cops were keeping watch over them.

Fenwick looked at his list. He said, "Sandra Berenking?"

A woman in her late fifties or early sixties in a deep blue evening gown was brought into the interrogation room. As she entered, she said, "Is there a serial killer loose in the convention? Each rumor we hear is worse than the last. Are Muriam and Dennis really dead?"

After they sat down, Fenwick said, "I'm afraid so. A Chicago police officer has been attacked as well."

"A police officer. How awful. The poor man and poor, poor Dennis. He was the sweetest, kindest man. We've e-mailed back and forth for years. He went out of his way to try and help people. He reviewed every single one of the books that I was the agent for. He was good to my authors. His reviews were fair. Often my writers needed publicity. He was willing to give space in his web magazine to new writers or those that didn't have million-dollar publicity campaigns behind them. He looked out for the little guy. Not a lot of folks would do that. He was a good man. He'll be missed."

"Did he have any enemies?" Turner asked.

"None that I know of."

Turner asked, "How well did you know Muriam Devers?"

"I was her first publicist at Galactic Books."

Fenwick said, "We talked to a publicist, Pam Granata."

"I was the company publicist. We're assigned numerous authors. Pam was a personal publicist. They are able to give as much time to a single author as they wish. Pam was as much of a rat as Muriam. I did have other authors, that's true. But I put in a lot of hours of overtime on Muriam's first book. I fought hard to get the best publicity for Muriam Devers when she was a nobody who was just having her first book published. I got her an interview in *Publishers Weekly,* and a spot on a national network morning news show. I believed in that book, much good it did me."

"How do you mean?" Turner asked.

"After the first book turned into gold, she turned into a harridan."

Turner said, "We've been told she was a saint."

"She always was to your face. And she was to her fans. She was genuinely sweet to them. She genuinely wanted to make them feel good. People who worked with her were another matter. She'd never, ever confront you to your face. You'd never find out if she was unhappy with you from her. You'd think everything was fine. But then the next day when I'd hear back from higher-ups, that is not what she would have reported. Later I'd find out that my decision or my agreement with Muriam was completely changed. While I worked at Galactic Books, I learned to keep my mouth shut. She was the star. I had some status for being in charge of the publicity for that first campaign. She had status because she was making the company very, very rich. Before she came along, Galactic Books was little more than a second-rate SF reprint house. Sure they'd print an occasional hardcover, but the owner went nuts with the cash from her work. The company became so profitable, he sold it for a quarter billion ten years ago. Now it's worth far more."

"Why wouldn't she confront you directly?"

"She'd claim she didn't want to make me angry. She didn't want to upset me. That was bull. She wanted whatever she wanted when she wanted it. If she could use her little-girl, simpering smile, then she'd use that. If she had to be a back-stabbing bitch, she'd do that. She didn't care who she trampled on. She didn't care what she'd agreed to. If something came along that was more favorable to her, then she wanted that. She wanted everything that was favorable to her. She was totally unprincipled. She knew to a penny how much her books made. She was intimately involved in every aspect of every decision that would affect her income."

Turner said, "But wouldn't any sensible author want to know all that and show the same concerns?"

"She could afford an army of agents and lawyers to do it for her. That she did it wasn't bad. How she did it may not have been criminal, but it was low, vicious, and mean-spirited."

"What happened to you?"

"I got fired. I found out much later Muriam was behind it. I got the treacly crap to my face all during that time. She told others that I wasn't doing enough for her. I was 'holding back her sales' because of my ineptness. That I didn't understand the genre. Ha! She acted like she was owed the publicity we did for her."

Fenwick asked, "If she was such a jerk, how'd she get the saintly reputation?"

"Hard work on her part and a blizzard of blather from the publicity department. Getting me fired wasn't enough for her. I left and started my own agency. That bitch tried to ruin that as well."

Turner wanted to say, "Don't stop now." Instead he murmured, "What happened?"

"I started in this business as a low-level publicist. After Galactic, I worked for a few companies. Muriam wrecked that. A phone call here. Whispered words there. Jobs dried up. I opened my own office in New York. Me and an answering machine. I'd always wanted to run my own company and work with authors, be an agent who worked *for* authors, who was prompt and returned their calls. I worked hard on building my reputation. Muriam Devers would try and sabotage me. She would try and keep authors from signing with me. She would try and keep people from reviewing my authors' books. Every chance she got, she would disparage my company. For a long time, I took the nobodies other people wouldn't touch. I have a more than respectable list now, some of the top-quality SF and fantasy writers in the business. What skin was it off her nose that these poor struggling authors had an outlet? It wasn't as if people purchasing books by my authors were taking food out of her mouth. What really made her angry is that I was a success. In the past few years several of my authors had cracked the *New York Times* bestseller list. It took me thirty years of hard work to get that far. I'm never going to be able to rival the big agencies, but I'd made a success out of a business that I started from nothing."

Turner said, "I don't get that. She was still angry after thirty years? Why did she care?"

"I don't know. I honestly don't know. I tried to ask her about it once. She denied everything. I knew from people I trusted what she was doing. I knew she was lying. There was nothing I could do about it."

"Who else did she have fights with?" Turner asked.

"I'd hate to implicate other people."

"We have a partial list," Fenwick said. "We've got a number of people who did not like her."

"Well, probably not all of the people who disliked her are at the convention."

"It's a start," Fenwick said.

"Look carefully at that writing group she had. They were a prize bunch."

"How so?" Fenwick asked.

"They were a bunch of back-biting hacks who lived on her fame."

"What difference would that make to anyone besides her?" Fenwick asked.

"This is a gossipy world, a jealous world. Many people are envious of other people's success. They'll do anything to rip and tear. Muriam did. So did her little coterie of evil henchmen, and they were always men. Studly young men."

"Did she have sex with them?" Fenwick asked.

"That was certainly the rumor, but I tend to doubt it. Muriam was a prig in a lot of ways. She'd want the public image without the private commitment. She enjoyed pinching their butts. Everybody would laugh and giggle. I didn't think it was funny. It's been a long time since junior high. Devers loved underage humor. I don't know if her writing group enjoyed the same type of humor or were being paid to enjoy it. If a man did what she did, it would be sexual harassment. I've never heard anybody complain. It's kind of pathetic for anyone to be doing that, much less someone in her eighth decade."

"Where were you between ten and eleven?" Turner asked.

"I had breakfast with several of my authors, then I was giving a seminar on how to write a hook for the opening of a science fiction book."

Turner said, "Do you know anything about the red ostrich feathers connected with Ms. Devers?"

"We made the feathers a cornerstone of the first ad campaign. It helped the whole thing take off. I never got a word of thanks."

Turner said, "She was in a Xena, Warrior Princess outfit when we found her."

Berenking stared at them a moment and then burst into a spate of giggles. Her hand flew to her mouth. "Really?" she asked.

The detectives nodded.

"I'm sorry," she said. "It's just so hard to picture. Muriam didn't do costumes. Not that I ever heard of. To do that kind would just be embarrassing, wouldn't it?"

"Could it have been something sexual?" Fenwick asked.

"Muriam and sex were something else. Her books all had oblique references to sex. In the first one the heroine had lovers several years younger than herself. This notion progressed to the point that in her last book the women's lovers were decades younger."

"Did she take younger lovers in real life?" Fenwick asked.

"Not that I know of. She never brought one around as a date. Not back when I thought of her as a friend. I met her husband. She was still married at the time. He was a perfectly ordinary man. Taught high school."

Fenwick asked, "Could she and Mr. Foublin have been having an affair?"

Berenking considered for a moment then said, "I doubt it. Muriam may have been interested in younger men, but then, by this point, most men were younger than she was."

Zing one in for you, Turner thought.

Fenwick said, "But you still read her books."

"I try to read every fantasy or science fiction book that gets published. Some people think it's an odd habit, but it's better than being a heroin addict. Hers were a requirement. When I gave seminars on writing fantasy, I'd use hers as examples of good and bad things to put in."

As she got up to leave, she asked, "Are we going to be able to go to our rooms soon?"

"We hope so," Turner said.

12

Macer walked in as Berenking walked out. He said, "We've got bloody clothes in a room on one of the top floors."

"No corpse?" Fenwick asked.

"Not yet."

Fenwick said, "I hate it when they take the corpse and leave the bloody clothes. You think they'd have sense enough to take both."

Turner said, "Hell of a hard time carrying around a corpse, the clothes, and the murder weapon."

"A hand cart," Fenwick said. "A wheelbarrow? One of those golf carts, kind of zooming up and down the halls?"

"Is that cop humor?" Macer asked.

"Only in one man's opinion," Turner said.

Out in the hall, Macer used a special key to summon one of the elevators.

They entered a suite on the top floor. Macer said, "The guest says he came back and found this stuff." In a closet in a bedroom they found a heap of clothes covered in blood. There was a brown Speedo swimsuit, a butt flap, and a cape. Brian hadn't worn a cape. And he still had his butt flap and Speedo. Turner doubted if his son had the income or the inclination to buy duplicates of his outfits. Upon seeing the clothes, he was more relieved than anything. There would be less hassle from those who did not know his son about accusing his son. Or accusing the father of trying to cover up for a killer.

There was a broken red ostrich feather on top of the clothes.

"We're sure it's blood?" Fenwick asked.

Turner leaned close and looked carefully. He breathed deeply. It sure smelled like blood. "If it's not, somebody's going to a lot of trouble to make it look like it. And if it's not, we've still got the red feather problem, a heap of stuff where it doesn't belong, or a coincidence beyond all odds."

There was a stir in the hall. Two uniforms brought in a red-faced man at least a hundred pounds overweight. "What's going on?" he demanded.

"Who are you?" Fenwick asked.

"I'm director Samuel Chadwick. Why am I being kept back? This is my room. I found that awful mess. What are those clothes doing in my closet?" He was about five foot eight with a white beard. He wore a black tuxedo, a rainbow bow tie, and a snowy white shirt.

He pointed toward the closet.

"Those weren't there when we left earlier."

"What time did you leave?" Fenwick asked.

"About nine."

"Who is we?" Fenwick asked.

"My lover, Arnold Rackwill, and I."

Rackwill was brought in. He was dressed in an elegantly cut tux. He was thin, blond, and pretty in an if-you-can-afford-him-you-can-have-him kind of way. Rackwill looked confused.

"Who put that there?" Rackwill asked.

"Exactly," Fenwick said.

Chadwick said, "I was with Arnold all day. He was with me. We can vouch for each other."

132

"Which time?" Fenwick asked. "I didn't mention a time."

Rackwill said, "All the time. We attended several convention events. We came back here to change after going out to dinner. This is the closet I use. I know those clothes weren't there before the event."

"Did anybody stop by your room?" Turner asked.

"No," Rackwill said.

Fenwick asked, "Mr. Chadwick, did you happen to look in this closet?"

Chadwick said, "Are you accusing my lover?"

"What I did," Fenwick said, "is ask a question."

Chadwick said, "It sure sounded like an accusation."

Turner said, "Answer the question, please."

Chadwick said, "We were in and out of the different rooms. I didn't inspect anything. I certainly don't remember any bloody clothes. I would have mentioned it then, not waited until now."

"What events did you attend at the convention today?" Fenwick asked.

Chadwick said, "The screenwriters' seminar most of the morning. We were giving tips on what to put in a screenplay that would sell. And these people need a lot of tips." He and Rackwill exchanged a look and smirked. Chadwick continued, "Then we visited the dealers' rooms, ate lunch, then took meetings about movie projects."

"Did either of you come in costume?" Fenwick asked.

"No. We think that's absurd," Chadwick said. "We were here to see if we couldn't make a few movie deals, see what was the latest thing. Sometimes you can get good ideas about what is going to be hot from these conventions."

"What's going to be hot?" Fenwick asked.

"You writing a screenplay?" Chadwick asked.

"Not tonight."

"Sex and violence," Chadwick said. "Things don't change much."

"Were you at the party in Ms. Devers' room last night?" Turner asked.

"Yes. We talked with Muriam about optioning another one of her books. About every third one of hers that becomes a movie becomes a blockbuster. She was due and we wanted what she had."

"Was she interested?" Turner asked.

"Very," Chadwick said. "We'd had lots of success working with her in the past. She's got a production company of her own."

"Anybody else bidding for the rights?" Turner asked.

Rackwill said, "Every other company in the business. Everybody wanted her. She was a known quantity. We had the inside track. She knew us and we'd worked well together before."

Fenwick asked, "Over the years were there people who got angry that they didn't get to make her movies?"

"Hollywood's a cutthroat town," Chadwick said. "And we might have fought amongst ourselves, but Muriam stayed above it all. Her agent let people bid and would take the best offer back to Muriam."

"Anybody bothered by the two thirds of the movies that tanked?" Fenwick asked.

Rackwill said, "Over the past thirty years she's had ten huge blockbusters from her movies. It's one of the best records of success around for an author. They've made lots of movies of Stephen King's stuff, but most of them weren't blockbusters. Sure she's had failures, but her successes far outweighed them. People may not have been sitting at her printer grabbing every sheet of paper that came out, but quite often it was close to that."

"She make people in the industry angry?" Turner asked.

"No," Chadwick said. "She was a delight to deal with. Her agent was professional and helpful. There were no angry negotiations. It was all very matter of fact. Whoever came up with the most money and the best perks got the option."

Rackwill said, "Muriam herself was a joy to be around. She was always pleasant and happy. She always made time to talk to people."

"How long have the two of you known her?" Fenwick asked.

Chadwick said, "For decades she's had yearly retreats at her place in the Rockies, lovely place outside Aspen. I got there as often as I could. Those were meetings for professionals and friends. She and I worked well together. We were friends. We didn't see each other as often as we liked. We weren't friends in that fake Hollywood way, kiss, kiss, fuck off. She was a dear."

"You attend these soirees, Mr. Rackwill?" Fenwick asked.

"Only a few. I met Samuel only five years ago."

"Do you know anything about the people in her writing group?" Turner asked.

"Not really," Chadwick said. "There were these young men who hung around at parties. They seemed to be able to fawn over her without being aware how much they were embarrassing themselves."

"How about you, Mr. Rackwill," Turner asked, "did you know them?"

"No."

Turner eyed him carefully. A short quick answer that set off a cop alarm in the back of his head.

"Did she have fights with anyone?" Fenwick said.

"Lorenzo Cavali," Rackwill said. "He desperately wanted to do her last movie. He bid tons of money for it. Rumor had it there was all kinds of anger on his part."

Turner said, "You said a few moments ago she didn't make anyone angry."

"I said that," Chadwick said. "Cavali was angry. I'm sure he got over it. We all get angry in Hollywood. A deal falls through. The next week you and the same set of angry people are launching a new project together."

"Was Ms. Devers angry?"

"Not that I heard," Rackwill said. "Cavali was. Supposedly he made a fool out of himself in public trying to get the rights to that book."

"Is he at the convention?" Fenwick asked.

"Yes," Chadwick said. "This was the convention to be at this year. The exclusive suites were perks for the players in publishing and film. There were all kinds of possibilities for movies, plays, buying scripts. Big book contracts. It was wonderful. There were screenings of new films. If you could build buzz here, you might go a very long way. It might have been second to Cannes this year. There may be a lot of nuts and hangers-on at these conventions, and there's a lot of silly folderol, but it was a venue that was prized. Everyone in the sci-fi biz was here."

"Anybody else she fight with?" Fenwick asked.

Chadwick said, "I'm not sure she ever fought directly with Cavali. Although I heard he made threats."

"What kind of threats?" Fenwick asked.

"I don't know. It was just a scandal how desperate he was and how angry he was when he didn't get the deal."

"Who did get the deal?" Fenwick asked.

"I did," Chadwick said. "I understand Cavali went nuts when he didn't get the rights. Something about him being nearly broke."

"Who told you this?" Fenwick asked.

"It was on the Hollywood gossip grapevine. Everybody knows everything in that town."

Turner stepped out and asked Macer if he would send his people through the convention looking for Lorenzo Cavali.

When he returned, Fenwick asked, "Did either of you know Dennis Foublin?"

Chadwick said, "We've heard his name as part of the rumors. Who is he?"

Fenwick said, "He ran one of those fan magazines on the

Internet. Lots of science fiction stories, reviews of books and movies."

"Never heard of him," Rackwill said. "Why is he important?"

"He's dead," Fenwick said.

"Did he know Muriam?" Chadwick asked.

"We're checking on all the relationships between all you people," Fenwick said.

Chadwick asked, "Did the same thing happen to Mr. Foublin as did Muriam?"

"They both died," Fenwick said.

"Were they killed in the same way?" Chadwick asked. "There are all kinds of awful rumors."

"We're checking everything," Fenwick said.

Turner asked, "Did Mr. Foublin ever give one of your movies a bad review?"

Chadwick laughed. "I told you. I never heard of him. Reviews don't make a lot of difference to the success of a movie, especially on some silly Internet site."

Fenwick said, "Can't word of mouth on the Internet sell a movie?"

"Yes," Rackwill said, "and most often it is buzz orchestrated by us, fueled by us, and managed by us."

Turner asked, "Do either of you know anything about a red ostrich feather that Ms. Devers carried around?"

"Oh, yes," said Chadwick. "I gave her the idea years ago. I'd read her book. We met at one of her first conventions. I remembered the significance of the feather. I said she ought to carry one around. It would be distinctive. Everyone would know it was her signature thing."

"Do you have one with you?" Turner asked.

"No. It was a great gimmick, but I didn't want them near me. Why is there one on that pile of clothes in the closet?"

Turner said, "Could you examine the clothes and tell us if they are yours? Please don't touch them."

Chadwick and Rackwill leaned in close. They both agreed that they'd never seen the clothes before.

"Could she have been having an affair with Mr. Foublin?"

"I suppose anything is possible," Chadwick said. "I don't picture Muriam having any kind of affair. Then again, I wasn't interested. I met the ex-husband ages ago. I think he was bewildered by all the fame. He seemed so lost and out of his element. He was a school teacher in Centerboro, New York. I believe he retired back there many years ago. I don't know of any affair."

"I don't either," Rackwill added.

Fenwick said, "When we found her, she was in a Xena, Warrior Princess outfit."

"A what?" Chadwick said.

Rackwill added, "That's unbelievable."

"Do either of you know why she would be wearing that costume?" Fenwick asked.

Chadwick shrugged. "Maybe she just felt like it. She had enough money to indulge any whim she had, although I'm not suggesting dressing up was a whim or anything else. I don't ever remember her going in for the costume contests at these conventions. Lots of people wanted her for a judge. She was famous and presumably impartial. Although why people think those are mutually inclusive is beyond me."

"She seldom wore anything but boring outfits," Rackwill said. "I don't believe she'd wear such a thing."

Fenwick said, "Obviously she did since she was caught dead in such a thing."

"Who's going to get that awful mess out of our room?" Rackwill asked.

"We're not staying in this room," Chadwick said.

"You can discuss that with management," Fenwick said.

Rackwill and Chadwick were ushered out the door.

Turner looked back at his notes. "I've got Melissa Bentworth, her first editor at Galactic Books, claiming she gave

Devers the idea about the feathers. And we've got Chadwick claiming the same credit. I wonder which one's lying. Or maybe Devers told them both it was their idea. Stroke both of their egos. How often do you meet someone and strike up a conversation about feathers in a book?"

"I don't," Fenwick said, "which is probably another of my many personality defects. Leaving aside our feather fetish for the moment, we've got people who were her buddies in Aspen. I wonder how many of them are at the convention?"

"More than I'd care to admit. If there were bidding wars for her movies, why weren't there bidding wars for her books? Or maybe there were and we've got people angry about that."

"We'll have to ask," Fenwick said.

Turner said, "Rackwill's answer to knowing members of the writing group was short and to the point."

Fenwick nodded. "Made me suspicious, too. We'll have to try and find out if he was lying, and if it has any connection to the murders."

"We've got the feather anomaly again. What's the killer trying to tell us?"

Fenwick said, "Maybe it means that the next person who claims to have given Devers the idea in the first place, is the killer."

"One can only hope."

13

Macer brought Lorenzo Cavali to the interrogation suite. Cavali was in his early thirties. He had red hair and wore a *Star Trek* outfit. Turner thought it might have been in the officers' colors. He wasn't sure. The tight-fitting spandex clung to a well-muscled body. He was maybe six one with broad shoulders.

Cavali said, "What's happening?"

Fenwick said, "Muriam Devers and Dennis Foublin are dead. A Chicago cop has been wounded."

"This is awful," Cavali said. "What on earth is going on? There's all kinds of rumors swirling through the convention. One is that somebody is decapitating people, one on each floor."

Fenwick said, "You find any headless bodies or random heads, you let us know."

Cavali gazed at Fenwick carefully. He looked like he wasn't sure if the detective was kidding or not.

"How well did you know Ms. Devers?"

"I worked with Muriam. I didn't know Foublin. I don't believe I know any Chicago police officers."

Fenwick said, "We heard you were bidding on the rights

to her last book and that you were angry about not getting them."

"Who told you that? I know who told you. Chadwick. He's here. He'd do anything to discredit me."

"Why would he do that?" Turner asked.

"He's a no-talent hack. He's a has-been. I'm in the new wave of directors. He needed Muriam Devers more than I did."

"How come you didn't get the rights to her last book?" Fenwick asked.

"I was stupid. I was late with my bid. Her agent, Agnes Demint, is real particular. I didn't think one day was that big of a deal. Obviously to Agnes it was. I tried to get in touch with Muriam. I couldn't get through to her."

"Chadwick said you threatened Ms. Devers."

"I got angry when I didn't get the rights. I could use a hit. Okay. Muriam wasn't money in the bank, but she was the closest thing to it. Chadwick was never true to her characters or her stories. Most directors weren't. I was willing to make a movie that would be faithful to the letter and spirit of her works. That would be the first time that would happen. I was a genuine fan of her books. I wasn't some fly-by-night moron who was just looking for a buck. I've been a fan of her books since I was a kid."

"Did she know this?" Turner asked.

"I'm not sure. I seldom actually talked to her."

"What threat did you make?" Turner asked.

"I was in her agent's office when she gave me the news. I've found things out since then. Muriam was not a nice person. She was a certifiable bitch. She was never going to give me the rights in the first place. I found that out months later. I could have been the first one in with my bid, and it wouldn't have made any difference. Chadwick offered her more money and a better deal than I could. I was led to believe mine was the highest bid. I tried to make sure of that. I got hoodwinked. By her agent who had been told to lie to me by Muriam herself."

"Who told you this?" Fenwick asked.

"I'm not stupid. I pieced things together."

"Who told you?" Fenwick repeated.

"It's not one person telling you something. You find out little things from ex-employees, from friends in the industry that might have worked with you before and then become part of another corporation. There is some loyalty in Hollywood, although not much. Muriam was vicious and her viciousness went back a long way."

"How long?" Fenwick asked.

"The director on the very first movie being made from her work was a new guy. He was working very hard to make it in Hollywood. It was his first big break. She got him fired. He never worked in movies in this country again. He went to Europe and India to work in the industries there."

"What was their fight about?" Turner asked.

"I heard it wasn't a fight. I heard that she went behind his back in the most sneaky and underhanded way. She wanted to preserve her image as Ms. All-Holy Good and Pure, but she wanted him out. I heard that he refused to listen to her complaints and problems. Instead of talking to him, like a normal adult, she pulled strings behind the scenes."

"She had that kind of clout?" Fenwick asked.

"I'm sure that was part of the reason she had to work behind the scenes. Normally she wouldn't have. Not on a first movie."

Fenwick asked, "Don't most authors with movie deals just take the money and run?"

"Depends on how big a deal you are and how much ego you've got and how your contract reads. Muriam wanted to run things. She was a micromanager. Did you ever hear her speak in public? She tried to come across as this soft-spoken Madonna. Hah. She was a bitch incarnate."

Turner said, "Mr. Cavali, you still haven't told us about your threat."

142

"It was silly. It was stupid. I made all kinds of threats I couldn't back up. That I would stop the funding for her next movie. That I would put a halt to production on her next project."

"Could you do either of those things?" Turner asked.

"No." He sighed. "Not even close to it. I like to think I'm a player. On a really good day, sometimes I am."

"Did you know what her costume was for the convention?"

"Costume? As far as I know she always appeared elegantly dressed. You know how these conventions have costume fanatics. Those people have no lives. Well, Muriam just laughed at them behind their backs."

"You're in a costume," Fenwick observed.

Cavali blushed. "I usually don't. I guess most of this dressing up is pretty harmless. It seems like a lot because this convention is so huge. What did somebody say, a hundred thousand people? I'm here to try to make money. This outfit is connected to my latest project."

Fenwick said, "We found her dressed in a Xena, Warrior Princess outfit."

"Is that significant?" Cavali asked.

"We're trying to find out," Fenwick said.

"I never saw her in a costume. You'll have to ask other folks about that. Xena? I find that hard to believe. Muriam was very conservative. She was always in fashion but never ahead of it. She wore sensible, nondescript clothes every time I met her. Maybe she was into some kinky stuff."

"Maybe," Fenwick said.

"Do you know anything about the members of her writing group?" Turner asked.

"Not really. Just the usual ribald jokes and rumors. They were a bunch of young studs, and she was their literary Mrs. Robinson. I have no idea if they were having sex. I don't know any of those people."

"Did you ever get invited to the parties in Aspen?"

"No. Us younger people seldom were. She had an 'in crowd' that she invited all the time. The whole Aspen thing was really a joke. The rich go to Aspen to party, and Muriam wanted to think she was one of them. I heard she got shut out of lots of social functions. She may have had as much or even more money than some of them, but I don't think she was ever really one of the stars of the circuit. She had a home there, but I heard she was never really accepted."

"Did you resent not being invited?" Turner asked.

"You can't resent something you don't want or need. The real reason why I didn't get the movie rights was because she double-crossed me. That's how I lost out on the bidding. I was led to believe I'd be the one to get the rights. She backed out. I was never given an explanation about why. I've always believed Chadwick was behind it. He's been a bigger jerk since he's been living with that Rackwill guy, who is a rat."

"How so?" Turner asked.

"If there's a conflict or disagreement, he's always willing to throw gasoline on the flames."

Fenwick asked, "Did you know Dennis Foublin?"

"He was the fan guest of honor at this convention, wasn't he? I saw that in the program. I didn't know him."

Turner asked, "You know anything about red ostrich feathers connected with Ms. Devers?"

"I saw her with them. She carried the damn things everywhere. She insisted they be in the movies of her books as well. I suppose she may have slept with them or taken a shit with them. I always thought it was one of the silliest affectations. She could have burned all the red feathers on the planet and still sold a ton of books. It was dumb."

"Where were you between ten and eleven today?" Fenwick asked.

"I was addressing a seminar on the director's vision for popular heroes."

"What's the director's vision for popular heroes?" Fen-wick asked.

"Sex sells."

Perhaps a bit of a narrow vision, Turner thought. Cavali left.

14

Sanchez entered again.

Fenwick said, "I hope you're showing up here with some kind of solution."

"Nope," Sanchez said. "We've got more problems."

They followed him down the corridor to the stairs. It was easier than trying to summon an elevator. Since the elevators were on lockdown, they would have needed a special key to summon one of them. Fortunately for Fenwick's bulk, they were walking downstairs. At each landing was a cop. They weren't going to be able to keep up this kind of intensive presence for long. Other crimes were still being committed in the city. Turner knew they'd have the help longer than usual because of the injury to the officer, but the extra help was a finite thing.

They walked down to the seventeenth floor. Sanchez said, "One of the hotel guests used this excuse to get to his room. He said his kid needed his inhaler." He led them to the bathroom. The shower stall was covered in blood.

"I think this is real blood again," Turner said.

Fenwick said, "We better get the Crime Lab personnel in here quick. We've got a Hollywood crowd here. Maybe they could fake this stuff pretty convincingly. Hell, some of these people dedicate their lives to making fake things look real."

Turner said, "We could try and find some Hollywood type to do that trick of sticking their finger in the questionable substance and then tasting it." No cop Turner knew, including the dumbest rookie, ever put an unknown substance from a crime scene in his mouth. Turner had seen an awful lot of real blood in an awful lot of contexts. This looked real to him.

"Whose room was this?" Turner asked.

"They've got the guy next door." He glanced at his notebook. "Guy named Donald Diekman and his family were staying in the room. He says he doesn't know a thing."

Turner and Fenwick strode next door. Diekman wore chain mail that reached to his knees, brown leather pants underneath, and a pointy peasant's helmet. He was a beefy guy.

"What's going on?" he asked. "Why is there blood in our room? There's all kind of crazy rumors going on downstairs. Did someone get in our room? Is someone trying to kill us? Did somebody die in our room? All our clothes and things are in there. Are we going to be able to get in and get them?"

"What time did you leave your room?" Fenwick asked.

"A little after one. We've been gone all day. Mostly we were playing wizards' chess in one of the ballrooms. My wife and kids love the game."

"Did people have broadswords?"

"Yeah. Bunch of different people. One of the first rumors I heard was that someone stole a sword and chopped somebody's hand off. Now supposedly there's a serial killer running around with a broadsword. I've heard about sixteen different rumors. Why don't they just announce what is going on? Nobody can get into their rooms. People are starting to get pretty angry."

Fenwick asked, "You ever have run-ins with the Chicago cops?"

"I got a ticket on Lake Shore Drive once. Does that count? What's that got to do with anything?"

"Did you deserve the ticket?" Fenwick asked.

"Pretty much."

"Did you notice anyone hanging around your room?"

"No. Our room was fine when I left. I showered this morning. Neither my wife nor I have been up here. The kids don't even have keys so they couldn't have gotten in."

"Have you had a chance to examine your belongings?" Turner asked.

"I glanced. Everything looks like it's where we left it."

"Did you know Dennis Foublin?" Turner asked.

"Yes. He was a good friend." Diekman looked from one detective to the other. "What's happened?"

Turner told him the news. Diekman sat down on the bed with a thump. He put his elbows on his knees and put his head in his hands. "This can't be true."

"I'm sorry. It is."

"What happened? Wait. Someone confiscated our swords. He was killed with a sword. My god, that's barbaric. Poor Dennis. He was such a good guy."

"He gave a lot of positive reviews," Fenwick said.

"His reviews were always thoughtful and fair-minded. I helped him maintain his web site. I even wrote some reviews for the comic book section. He was second only to me in the SF world in knowledge about comics, although he knew way more than I did about science fiction and fantasy novels."

"Anybody ever get angry about his reviews?" Fenwick asked.

"Oh, people always get angry. Sometimes it was funny. Dennis would mention something in his review and a writer in his or her next book would try and dig back at Dennis."

"Nobody had fights about this?" Fenwick asked.

"It was all very proper, English-department professorial. Nobody in a college gets homicidal."

148

Fenwick said, "I heard departments in colleges can be breeding grounds for double-dealing, hostility, and homicide."

"That's not what he was like." Diekman began to cry. "He was such a good guy."

When Diekman was calmer, Turner asked, "Where'd you guys meet?"

"We were working in the same coffee shop at the University of Minnesota."

"He ever have fights with anybody?" Turner asked.

"Nobody I know of."

Turner said, "We heard a rumor that he might have had something sinister in his background."

"Not that I know of."

"What do you know about his connection with Muriam Devers?" Fenwick asked.

"Muriam is mostly harmless. As far as I know, they got along."

"She used red feathers as part of her schtick," Fenwick commented.

"Yeah. I only knew her slightly, but every time I saw her on the television talk shows, she had that stupid feather."

"Did you know the members of her writing group?" Turner asked.

"I heard they thought of themselves as some kind of an SF mafia."

"How so?" Turner asked.

"Well, they kind of presumed to power. Like, they knew somebody rich, so they should be listened to and catered to for no apparent merit of their own."

"And were they catered to?" Turner asked.

"In their imagination, they certainly were. I suppose there are always those who think by sucking up, they'll get ahead. I suppose some people were nice to them because they were close to Muriam. Maybe a few thought they were genuinely good people. I thought they were mostly harmless."

"But you didn't know them personally?"

"If I ever met them connected with Muriam, I certainly don't remember them. You meet an awful lot of people at conventions. Who remembers them all?"

He knew nothing else helpful. He left.

Turner said, "The killer planned this extremely carefully. This is not random. This is made to keep us looking, to keep us confused. Are these people all connected in some way?"

"I don't believe all the people we've talked to are killers," Fenwick said. "Unless there's some vast conspiracy going on. We've got no proof any of these folks conspired together. Some of them knew one another, but not all of them knew everybody."

"My worry is that we're going to find more corpses as people are allowed into their rooms."

Fenwick said, "There aren't going to be any new corpses up here. Everyone at the convention is downstairs."

"Unless they've been napping in their rooms or reading in their rooms or sitting and brooding in their rooms."

Fenwick said, "People come to conventions to sit and do nothing?"

"Plus we could have old corpses," Turner said. "That's what I'm worried about. With perfect planning or incredible luck, he could have left a heap of dead bodies."

"Dead bodies in a heap?" Fenwick said. "Not a pretty thought."

"The killer would have had lots of opportunities to find victims. He could have been at work for hours before the first body was found. He could have been skipping down the corridors flinging bloody clues in every nearby receptacle."

Fenwick said, "I want to see a killer skipping. I want to testify to that fact in court."

Turner asked, "Was he tossing his signature blood or feathers before he even committed the first murder? I can't imagine a purpose for leaving the bloody clothing around unless the killer was trying to screw with the investigation."

"He could have all kinds of different reasons," Fenwick said.

"He could be changing disguises even as we speak," Turner said. "We've got to get the timing down on this. At the least I'd say this certainly looks like a very angry killer."

Fenwick said, "He wouldn't be able to swing a broadsword around anymore. Anybody sees someone with one of those, it'd be confiscated."

Turner said, "The killer doesn't have to stick with doing people in with a broadsword."

"Awfully clumsy way to kill someone," Fenwick said.

"If he did all this planting of clues before the killing, then it's obvious that it was all well thought out. Was the killer taking a chance by doing this running around while the convention was in full swing? How would he know all these people were not in their rooms? He could find the ones who were giving talks or on panels but not the majority of people."

"Maybe he didn't," Fenwick said. "Maybe he knocked on a few doors or called the rooms ahead of time. If he was staying at the hotel, he'd have access to a phone in his room. He could call randomly from there."

"We still don't know how the killer got into all these rooms."

"Unless the people knew the killer and let him in."

For now they had lots of questions and not a lot of answers. They called for the next person to be interrogated.

15

Agnes Demint, Devers' agent, was next to be interviewed. She was dressed in an elegant pantsuit of pink velvet. Turner guessed she was in her forties. Her makeup looked like it had been applied with a trowel. From the amount of blush, it looked as if she might have simply plunged her face into a vat of the stuff. She shook their hands.

"This is awful," she murmured. She had a low, throaty voice.

Turner said, "We appreciate everyone's willingness to talk to us at such an awful time."

"I'll do anything I can to help find out who did this."

"We've heard different accounts of how Muriam got along with people."

"Fans loved her. She loved them. She wasn't faking it. She genuinely loved being with them. She always had patience with them."

Fenwick said, "We heard it was a different story with some of the people she worked with."

"I suppose there are always malcontents. Most of the people she worked with loved her. I did. She was a dream."

"How did you become her agent?" Fenwick asked.

"I worked with her at one of the larger agencies for about ten years. Then one day she came to me with an offer. I could probably have made a living on just her account, but I'm not stupid. You can't let your whole career rest on keeping one account. This business is too changeable for that. But I took her on as my first client. Many people followed in her wake. I'm eternally grateful to her."

"Who was her agent before?" Fenwick asked.

"Devers started with our agency."

"Why'd she want to leave?" Fenwick asked. "And why'd she pick you?"

"I'm not sure about the leaving part," Demint said. "She said she picked me because I was one of the few people who made comments about her books that made sense."

"She needed praise?" Fenwick asked.

"I praised and I panned as the situation warranted. She liked having someone be honest with her about her work."

Fenwick asked, "What exactly was your role in her career?"

"Agents do any number of things. I read her manuscripts or movie scripts. Sometimes I sent them back with suggestions. Not that often in the beginning, even more rarely in the last few years."

"Did she make changes willingly?" Fenwick asked.

"I rarely asked for an out-and-out change. Mostly I made suggestions. She could follow them or not. I wasn't her editor."

"What else did you do?" Fenwick asked.

"Mostly I negotiated. The negotiations for Muriam were fairly simple. Muriam never got involved. She had everyone talk to me. That's what I'm here for. People could be angry with me, not her. When there was bidding in Hollywood for her books, I'd get all the bids. I opened them. I informed all the others of the highest bid. It was like a high-class auction, very civilized. They were offering tons of money. Movie deals. Those kinds of things."

"How much money are we talking about?" Turner asked.

"Millions."

"Enough to kill for," Turner said.

Demint said, "Muriam would never hurt anyone."

"Wasn't the agency hurt when she left them?" Fenwick asked.

"It is still a huge agency. They have tons of successful clients."

"What was the advantage of having you, on your own?" Fenwick asked.

"I believe she felt more in control. That it was more of a personal touch with just me."

Fenwick said, "If I had a client doing million-dollar deals and I was an agency, I'd give her all kinds of control."

Demint said, "She wanted me."

"And nobody got angry at the negotiations?" Fenwick asked. "She didn't try double-dealing beyond anyone's back?"

"Really! Muriam was not like that."

Fenwick said, "We heard she got the director on her first film fired."

"I don't know about that. Nobody said anything to me. I know the directors changed. I heard it was the studio's decision. Nobody ever told me anything different."

"Did she get along with her editors?"

"She never said a bad word about them to me."

Fenwick said, "One or two of them seemed less than enthralled."

"She was good to me. I made a lot of money from her."

"Do you have any accounts that bring in more money?" Fenwick asked.

"No. A few are beginning to come close, but you've got to remember, Muriam was unique. She was in the stratosphere compared to most writers. She was among the elite in terms of income. I believe she was closing in on Oprah last year."

Fenwick asked, "Did she have enemies of any kind? Anyone you can think of who might have a grudge?"

"Absolutely not."

Fenwick asked, "Can you tell us about Ms. Devers and those feathers?"

"Why on Earth would you be interested in that?"

"It might be important," Fenwick replied.

"Well, it was just this cute thing. Such a great idea. We were going to launch a red feather line of perfume next spring. Are you saying this is a clue? What is going on?"

"We're trying to find out," Fenwick said.

Turner asked, "Did you know the members of her writing group?"

"Writing? Ha! Buffoons. I heard the rumors of why she hung around with them. I tried to ask her about it once. She just laughed and said she enjoyed having a writing group. I don't know if she was using them for sex. I suppose a lot of people would have. She managed to pick some of the hottest young men."

"Did you have a sexual relationship with any of them?"

"I think they're cute. I prefer real men, not gym bunnies full of themselves. Muriam would promise to have her agent read their stuff. I'm her agent, and she never gave me any of their stuff."

"How do you know she promised them?"

"One of them made the mistake of asking me if I'd got around to reading his manuscript. He told me that Muriam had promised to send it to me with her recommendation."

"Who was that?"

"David Hutter."

"What happened to him?"

"I mentioned what he said to Muriam. He was out of the writing group pretty damn fast."

"Muriam lied to these people?"

"I think some people took what she said and made more of it than there was to be made of it."

Fenwick said, "Hutter misunderstood Ms. Devers' intentions?"

"To put it mildly. Muriam had no need to make such promises. As far as I know, she never did. She never passed anything along to me."

"Could she have passed manuscripts along to other people without your knowledge?" Fenwick asked.

"Certainly, but why would she?"

Could be all kinds of reasons, Turner thought. "Is Mr. Hutter at the convention?" he asked.

"I haven't seen him."

Turner asked, "Did you know Dennis Foublin?"

"I'm afraid I didn't. There are so many things to take care of on a much greater scale than one reviewer on the Internet. Those Internet people certainly think they have a lot of influence, but they certainly don't. Muriam Devers didn't make a penny less on a movie deal if some idiot on the Internet didn't like her books."

"Did she have any problems with anyone at the convention?"

"Well, there was the loon."

"Who was that?"

"The loon. There's always at least one at these things. He was terribly thin with tufts of blond hair. He wore these raggedy, ill-fitting clothes. I don't know his name."

Sounded like Melvin Slate to Turner. "What happened?" Turner asked.

"I had to get in between them. He came up to her just before the signing this morning. I'm always on the alert when I'm with her. All too often, fans don't have a sense of proportion, although Muriam was always sweet with them. She was actually talking with him. He kept getting into her personal space, and she kept backing away. It happened twice, and

I stepped in. It wasn't a major deal. It was the only negative thing I can think of."

Turner said, "We found her in a Xena, Warrior Princess outfit."

"A what? I find that hard to believe. Muriam was not a costume person. I can't believe that."

"It's true," Fenwick said.

"Well, perhaps I didn't know her as well as I thought."

She and her lack of knowledge left.

⟪ 16 ⟫

A beat cop, Ann Hesketh, walked up to them in the corridor. "You better see this," she said.

"Now what?" Fenwick said.

They took the service elevator to a deserted corridor on the sixth floor. Hesketh said, "This floor is mostly for private meetings for hotel staff or sometimes VIPs. According to security, no one was scheduled to be meeting on this floor at this time. There are no private rooms on this floor. The room next to this was used by somebody named Louis Eitel. It was a meeting of some Hollywood types."

Eitel was the name they'd gotten from Cavali as the director who'd been fired from Muriam's first movie.

The head of security, Brandon Macer, met them outside a service room. Bins of dirty sheets crammed most of the room from wall to wall. Next to a window someone had written on the wall in three-inch-high letters using blood or red paint, "I'm not done yet."

Fenwick said to Macer, "Would you find all the hotel personnel who had access to this area?"

Macer said, "I'm on it already."

He and Hesketh left. Turner and Fenwick examined each

bit of writing. Turner said, "I don't see a fingerprint anywhere on this. It doesn't look like brush strokes. It might have been done with gloves or any rag or piece of cloth."

"We've seen lots of evidence of excellent planning." Fenwick peered closely at the writing. "Can we now say that the handwriting is . . ."

"Stop," Turner said. "You may not know this but there is a quota of ghastly humor and stupid puns. You have reached your limit. If you exceed your limit, the sky will fall and aliens will invade the Earth."

"I have that kind of power?" Fenwick asked.

"You could try it and see what happens."

"Let me get back to you on that." Fenwick asked, "Do aliens commit more or less crimes than earthlings? More important, if both those things happen will I still be able to get chocolate?"

"One more pun and I will cut off your supply of chocolate permanently."

"That's cruel. That's real horror. That's torture. I will do my best to give it a rest."

"No dopey rhymes, either." Turner sighed. "Your humor *is* crap, but that's not the major thing. I'm really tensed up about Brian's connection with this. I know it's a peripheral connection, but I'm worried."

"Any father would be," Fenwick said. "He's not a killer."

"I know," Turner said. "He'd be bawling his eyes out if he did anything remotely like this. It's just a familial complication I am not happy to have. If I have to, I'll stay all night to get this settled."

"I shall suspend attempts at humor for the duration."

Turner smiled. "I appreciate the effort."

They examined the rest of the service area. If there were telltale fingerprints, they were not readily visible. Nor were there any other smears of blood.

"No feather," Fenwick said.

Turner moved the last bin of clothes away from the service elevator door. "Yeah," he said softly. "It's here." The broken feather was on the floor directly in front of the elevator doors.

Fenwick joined him. He looked from the writing to the feather. He said, "How come it's this far away?"

Turner shrugged. "It's a feather. Maybe it moved in the wind. Or maybe it's some kind of message in a symbolic language that exists only in the killer's mind." Turner spoke into his communicator, "Would you find out if Commander Molton is in the building? If he is, ask him to come to the sixth floor. If he's not here, ask him to come back to the hotel." He also requested the Crime Lab people to work on this room as soon as they were done with the last.

They retreated to the hall.

"What's up?" Macer asked.

"He could be disguised as anything," Turner said. "He could be a dangerous alien or a Chicago cop. If that last is true, he's got more nerve than most killers I've ever seen."

Fenwick said, "However he looks, he's dicking us around. We're running awfully fast, but not getting anywhere. Alice would be proud."

Macer said, "Maybe he wrote this before he began the killing."

"The time sequence is going to be tricky," Turner said. "Some of these he could have prepared beforehand, others later. He certainly wants us confused."

Macer said, "Maybe he's trying to scare someone. Maybe he's trying to get even with someone. Maybe he hasn't hit his real target yet."

"Who's the target?" Fenwick asked. "Why expend your energy on the two who are dead if they weren't the ones you wanted dead? The two deaths have to be connected. There can't be two random murders with broadswords going on at the same time, and then two killers spending the time toting blood from place to place. Nothing has odds that long against it happening and not being connected. A copycat would have to be copying awful fast."

Turner said, "I agree on there not being a copycat. But our guy doesn't have to be rushing around. He could have planted a number of these things any time during the day."

Fenwick asked, "Say he knows somebody's convention schedule. What happens if somebody gets a headache and decides to take a nap? Or what if some hotel worker drops by here unexpectedly?"

"Maybe it was random," Turner said. "Maybe Devers and Foublin were simply at the wrong place at the wrong time."

Macer said, "Nobody's scheduled to be working on this area of this floor again until the morning."

"The killer knows all this?" Fenwick asked.

Macer said, "It's possible, not probable. Then again I never thought it would be possible that we'd have corpses with swords stuck through them."

"Unless it's a hotel worker," Turner said, "who would have a plausible reason for being in various places. Or someone disguised as a hotel worker who could get into a lot of places. We'll have to get all the times of the movements of all the people during the day down on a chart."

Fenwick said, "We're not going to be able to do that for everyone at the convention."

"For now it'll have to be the people we've talked to," Turner said. They used paper from their regulation blue folders to begin making the charts. After fifteen minutes they looked at their handiwork. Fenwick said, "Doesn't tell us much yet."

"If ever," Turner said. "We'll have to add each person or event as we go along."

The elevator opened. Molton walked off, spotted them, and hurried over.

Turner explained the latest.

Molton said, "It would make sense if he was disguised as

a cop or a hotel worker. He could get around easily. Although at the moment, nobody can get up here except us."

Turner said, "He'd have to be hiding bloody clothes."

Fenwick asked, "Why bother to hide bloody clothes? He's gotten away with everything so far."

Turner said, "Getting away might be important to the killer, but he must be making some kind of point with all this crap. He could have gone and come back as himself or in another disguise."

"We better make sure that no one in the hotel is alone," Macer said.

"How?" Fenwick asked. "Somebody told us there's a hundred thousand people at this convention. They might not all be staying at this hotel, but they'd have access. And that doesn't count all the people staying at the hotel not connected with the convention or people simply walking in off the street to eat in one of the restaurants or to meet a friend."

Molton said, "We'll put guards on all the entrances and exits. This is a nightmare. We've got to find this guy."

"We've got to start letting people into their rooms," Macer said.

Turner agreed. "We're getting nowhere keeping them out. As long as we've got enough personnel, why don't we assemble the hotel guests and make an announcement. We don't have to have all the conventioneers. Just the ones staying at the hotel. We can check their keys and identification. Who's going to want to leave a corpse or bloody clothes unreported?"

Fenwick said, "Unless it's the killer. This gives him a chance to get his stuff and get away."

Molton said, "We can monitor anybody that tries to check out."

"What if they just leave?" Fenwick asked.

Turner said, "The killer could have done that any time earlier. This killer isn't stupid. He knows we're watching."

"Maybe it would make him less cautious, not more," Fenwick said.

Oona Murkle, Melissa Bentworth, and the convention organizers worked with the hotel people and the police to assemble as many of the guests as possible. Uniformed cops talked to any hotel employee who had any access to this floor. The officers reported back that all the employees had identification. All of them said they'd seen nothing out of the ordinary.

The police assembled the guests in one of the ballrooms. Molton used a microphone to address the crowd of about two thousand. He finished, "We'll have an officer at the entrance to each stairwell on every floor as well as one stationed next to the elevators. Report even the slightest thing to them."

Molton headed off to organize cops and hotel security, to ensure the safety of the public. Turner and Fenwick returned to the suite to continue their questioning.

In the hall, Fenwick said, "Are these randomly scattered clues connected to the victims or is the murderer just dicking us around?"

"Or trying to confuse us," Turner said, "or scare us. Or scare someone. It doesn't have to be directed at us. I've got a better question. Presumably there is a pattern or at least some connection between Devers and Foublin. The question is, is the killer leaving these as a message to people? If so, what message is it, and is it going to be connected to all the people Devers screwed? That doesn't make a lot of sense. You'd think the people who were screwed would have the most reason to kill Devers. Why leave bloody clothes?"

"Divert suspicion?"

"But it doesn't divert suspicion," Turner said. "So far these people don't seem to be the killers. And some actually liked her or claimed to at any rate. Not all the ones she did mean stuff to are getting stacks of bloody clothes in their rooms."

"There's gotta be some connection," Fenwick said. "Nobody does this kind of planning without a definite purpose."

"The people whose rooms have had this stuff in them must be connected, but not in a lethal way, yet. I always presume the criminals of Chicago are logical beyond imagining."

Fenwick said, "That sounds like the start of a sarcastic comment. Now, just stop that. You're starting to get out of control or worse, trying to sound like me."

"Just because I'm getting in a few good lines."

17

Louis Eitel looked like a taller, thinner Einstein, except Eitel was having an even worse hair day than Einstein in a high gale.

"What's going on?" he demanded.

Fenwick said, "We're trying to figure out if you're a murderer."

Turner knew it was seldom a good idea to begin aggressively with Fenwick.

"How dare you? Do I have to talk to you?"

Turner said, "We need as much background as we can on Muriam Devers and Dennis Foublin. We need to understand."

"Devers! Devers was the bitch from hell. Devers was evil incarnate."

Turner resisted the impulse to say, "Try to hold back." He did say, "We heard she got you fired from her first movie."

"How that bitch had that goody-two-shoes reputation, I will never understand. She could manipulate and destroy with the best of them."

"How'd she get you fired?" Turner asked.

"I was just starting out thirty years ago. I wrote and directed all of my movies. I had several art house successes and one action adventure that had taken off. I was on my way.

I was signed to do her first movie. I was working on the script. I always take great care with everything I do. I was going to make her script better. That woman can barely write."

"She's sold a lot of books," Fenwick said.

"There's a lot of crap and dreck published every year. So what? I wanted to portray realistic characters making adult decisions. She had some boob consulting an intergalactic psychic. Nobody in the book said it was moronic to base one's adult decisions on the blather of a psychic. And then there was that whole red feather schtick. She insisted the damn feather be in every scene with her main character, Althea Morris. I asked her if the character had it with her every waking moment. She said she did. I asked if she had it with her when she took a piss. Devers got all insulted. Nobody ever goes to the bathroom in her books."

"When you're doing intergalactic travel, do you have time to go to the bathroom?" Fenwick asked.

Eitel glared. "The point is, her stuff was drivel. She never said a word to me. She just smiled and smiled. I walked in one day, and I was off the picture. She is a shit. I would have made something of the movie."

"Wasn't it a big success?" Fenwick asked.

"I'd have made it bigger."

Good to be confident, Turner thought.

Turner repeated his question. "How'd she get you fired?"

"She talked to the producers and the studio executives. She had a million-dollar deal. I didn't. They'd wrapped up deals on two of her series. She told them she'd sell them elsewhere if I was still on the picture."

"Did she have a contract?"

"She had an excellent contract. One of the perks her lawyer put in had to do with directors of her movies. She was in and I was out. I was buried for years. I've had to work overseas. Only when I was lucky enough to have an independent

166

film hit it big in the European market last year did I get back in and then just slightly. I'm still just getting back onto the studio movie-making wheel. Getting me fired off one film is one thing. Making sure I got no other offers was another."

"She had that much clout?" Turner asked.

"The studio executives who wanted to keep her happy had that much clout. Maybe it's the same thing. The effect on my career was the same."

"Where were you this morning?" Fenwick asked.

"I had breakfast away from the convention at Ann Sathers on Broadway with several representatives from the city of Chicago. I was working on setting up production here for my next movie. I didn't get back until two."

"We found her in a Xena, Warrior Princess costume."

"Huh. She do that a lot?"

"Not that we can tell."

"She was kind of a prig when I talked to her."

"Do you know Samuel Chadwick and Lorenzo Cavali?"

"Yes. Cavali could be good some day. Like the rest of us Chadwick's had some hits and some misses. Chadwick was one of the inner circle. I heard he went to Devers' Aspen parties once a year. Cavali wasn't as in as he'd like to be. He will be. The kid has talent."

"Did you know her writing group?"

"I vaguely recall hearing talk about them once."

"Did you know Dennis Foublin?"

"No."

"Have you been to your room this afternoon or evening?"

"I stopped in about five. Everything seemed normal. Should I have found something?"

"We aren't sure," Turner said.

Eitel left.

"That much dislike adds tons of zest to the investigation," Fenwick said.

"It's late," Turner said. "We've got a killer on the loose, and we're not going to be able to go home until he's caught or we can assure everyone that they're safe."

"That won't be until we've got the killer." They added Eitel's data to their charts.

◣ 18 ◢

Ralph Marwood, a member of Muriam Devers' writing group, was the next person on the list. He looked to be in his early thirties. He was in a pirate costume with a gauzy, billowy shirt, tight pants, a bandana tied back, an enormous earring in his right ear, and dabs of red on his face and chest, presumably to add a bloody image to his pirate persona.

Marwood said, "They took my scimitar. What's going on? Muriam and I were very close. Is she really . . ." His voice trailed off.

"She was murdered," Fenwick said. Marwood sat down. A codpiece covered his crotch—at least Turner assumed it was a codpiece. If it was the real thing, the guy was a record breaker. He had broad shoulders and big muscles. Big enough to wield the heaviest broadsword. A costume with blood on it for a logical reason would be a good cover for strolling about with the bloody residue of a maniac's madness cleverly in full view. It would take a killer with a hell of a nerve to be doing that. Turner had seen killers with that much nerve.

"You were in her writing group," Turner said.

"Yes, there were four of us. Peter and Gerald are here at the convention. Larry couldn't make it."

"Tell me about this writing group," Turner said.

"Muriam started it years ago. The members have changed. I think in the thirty years since she was first published there were at least twenty people in total, maybe a few more. I met Muriam at a convention just like this one. She invited me to join."

"How did the others become members of the group?" Turner asked.

"Same way I did. Of course, we all lived in New York. It would be tough to have a group if you didn't live in close proximity to each other. We'd get together every two weeks to read our material out loud to each other."

Fenwick asked, "How'd you guys get picked for the group?"

"She read our stuff and liked it."

Fenwick said, "According to what we heard, the men in the group were a bunch of no-talent hacks who were trying to cash in on her fame."

"That's outrageous. Who told you that? Wait. I know who did. Pam Granata. That bitch agent of hers. You've heard the Jennifer Theory of the company publicity agents in New York?"

"No," Fenwick said.

"That the secret truth is there is only one agent in New York for all the companies. Her name is Jennifer. She sits at a switchboard in some publisher's dungeon. All the calls to all the companies are automatically switched to her. She knows nothing and does nothing. They pay her to answer the phone and be cheerful twenty-four hours a day. She is to respond with mindless cheer at all times. I was told Granata was that mindless jerk years ago. She hated us."

"Why?"

"She worked for Devers, but was never able to be her friend. We were her friends."

"Proximity to fame makes you friends?"

"We were real friends. Granata was a bitch."

Fenwick said, "We heard Devers liked to pinch the butts

of studly young men. That being a young, good-looking male was her requirement for inviting someone into the group."

"She never said that."

"It's not hard to figure out," Fenwick said.

"She was a friend," Marwood insisted.

Fenwick said, "There seems to be a sex angle to her death. She was in a Xena, Warrior Princess outfit when we found her. That implies something unusual was going on. The link to it being something sexual isn't a very big leap. She ever pinch your butt?"

"At the first convention where we met in Portland, I was in a jungle costume. My first book was set in the Amazon. I work out. Why not do what I could to advertise my book? She said she was interested."

Fenwick asked, "In your butt or your book?"

Marwood blushed. "I suppose it was a little of both."

Fenwick asked, "Did she pinch everybody in her writing group's butt?"

Marwood smiled. "We never discussed it. Who would admit that somebody as old as your grandmother was pinching your butt?"

Fenwick said, "Or that any of you would be willing to sell your soul to get noticed, published, pinched, or rich, or famous."

"It wasn't like that," Marwood said.

"What was it like?" Fenwick asked.

"Well, we'd meet and have wine and cheese at her place. We always met at her place. Ours weren't as nice. You wouldn't invite the Vanderbilts to visit the plebeians."

"There were no women in the writing group besides Ms. Devers?" Turner asked.

"Not while I was part of it."

Fenwick said, "We heard that you were unhappy with Muriam."

"Who told you that?"

"We've talked to a lot of people today," Fenwick said. "It's getting late. Why don't you save yourself and us a lot of time and tell us what the deal was? Were all four of you guys in the writing group young and studly?"

"Well, sort of, yes, I guess."

"All of you straight?" Fenwick asked.

"I am. I never asked the other guys. They never came on to me. We never discussed it."

"You never discussed who you were dating? You never mentioned your private lives in a friendly setting?"

"Well, okay. I'm straight. The other three guys aren't."

Turner said, "Muriam didn't mind?"

"She didn't care. She just wanted an audience to listen to her latest deathless prose. We were there to praise her. If you raised the slightest criticism, you risked being banished. It wasn't a revolving door being in the group, but you got the idea right away. Her stuff was perfect and could only be more perfect."

Fenwick asked, "Did you guys ever even get to read your stuff?"

"She might have fifty pages to read. We might bring five or ten."

Fenwick said, "Nobody noticed the discrepancy?"

"The only one worth noticing was Muriam. If she didn't notice, you didn't notice. She seldom made many comments about our stuff. It was more like she wanted to get ours out of the way. She knew she had to give us a little more than the glory of basking in her glow. We didn't get much more than that."

"You got careers out of it," Turner said.

"Some of us did. I hadn't yet. I've been in the group three years. I was still being published by a small press. Three books. No movie deals. No big-time publisher showing the slightest interest."

"Did she get sex?" Fenwick asked.

"She didn't actually want anybody to perform sex. At least, she never asked me. The other guys never said anything. Sometimes she liked to dress up. She liked to have an audience. At those times it was an audience of one. She'd sit around in a costume. They were kind of strange. Xena, Catwoman, and Supergirl were the only ones I saw."

"So what happened?" Fenwick asked.

"Not much. She would sit or walk around a little bit or serve tea while dressed up. Mostly she and I would chat and gossip, or rather she would declaim and I'd listen. There were probably others before me. If so, I don't know them. Neither Peter, Larry, nor Gerald ever said they were asked to come over to watch her. They may have been. I don't know. It wasn't a lot of fun to watch, but I liked being part of her literary circle. I liked the blurbs she offered to write for me."

"You sold your soul for your art," Fenwick said.

"If you want to be famous and rich, you better be ready to."

"I can't believe all writers are that way," Fenwick said.

"Look, it's a competitive business. Every agent gives you this lecture about how tough the market is. They want to keep your expectations down so they can take their percent if you ever make it, and they have an excuse when they call and report their latest failure, or an excuse when they never call. Yes, the other guys in the group were competitive. We all were. So what? All businesses are competitive."

"Did it lead to murder?" Fenwick asked.

"I didn't kill anybody."

"Do you think your buddies in the group would?"

"I'd be interested in hearing their answers to your questions."

He knew no more. He left.

As they added his information to their charts, Fenwick said, "He sure looked strong enough to wield a broadsword. He was snarky enough to be a suspect on my list."

"I can see the headlines," Turner responded. "Suspect Snarky. Arrest imminent. Film at ten. Or better yet, we could set up a 'Fenwick's Scale of Snarkiness.'" It would be right up there with Maslow's hierarchy and Piaget's stages of growth."

"But could they match my sense of humor?"

"I hope not."

▄ 19 ▄

Gerald Granville was the next one from the writing group. Granville wore tight blue jeans and a black muscle T-shirt. Turner thought he might be in his early thirties.

He kept a carefully sculpted two-day growth of beard on his handsome face. He could be the action adventure star of any number of muscle-drenched Hollywood films.

Fenwick asked, "We understand you were in Muriam Devers' writing group."

"I can't believe she's dead. We've been friends since I was in my teens. She judged an SF writing competition in my school district. I won. She came to my school and presented me the award. I got published in a science fiction journal during my senior year in high school because of her. I got fame and started making money with my writing very early."

"We heard she liked to pinch butts," Fenwick said.

"I didn't care if she pinched mine. She had access to it any time she wanted."

"You sound more like a slut than a friend," Fenwick said.

"Who cares? She pinched my butt once when I was twenty-three in a large convention hall in New Orleans. She was having a good time. So was I. So were a lot of people. The pinch didn't harm me or her or anyone else. Who cares?"

"We've been told that the members of her writing group were a kind of mafia for her."

"Envious people will say all kinds of things. They were jealous of our relationship with Muriam. They wanted what we had, and they couldn't have it. They didn't have talent."

"Do you have talent," Fenwick asked, "or a good connection who happened to think you were a stud?"

"I won that story contest fair and square. I didn't meet her until the day I got the award. She encouraged me. We corresponded. We began meeting again at conventions after I graduated from college."

"How did the members of the writing group get along?" Fenwick asked.

"I saw Ralph Marwood leaving to be questioned by the police. I know he tried to tell you I'm gay. He'd try and implicate me in anything. I'd been in the writing group longest. He was the newest member. He was the most insecure."

"How would telling us you are gay implicate you in anything?" Turner asked.

Granville looked confused.

"Why was he the most insecure?" Fenwick asked.

"His writing wasn't that good. Several times Muriam had to call him on it. It was as if he wasn't paying attention to the most obvious details."

Fenwick said, "We heard there was a fairly inequitable distribution of time at your writing group."

"Some of us needed more help than others. Muriam got the lion's share of the attention. It was her group. She formed it. She invited people to join. We were her inner circle. She could trust us. Because we were loyal to her and to each other didn't mean we were some kind of mafia. People become friends. They support each other. Those aren't crimes. We were close and helped each other. Publishing can be a cutthroat world.

Some conventions give out awards and people vote for them. Sometimes we campaigned for her. There's no rule that says you can't."

"Did Ms. Devers have any enemies?"

"I'll say. She didn't trust her publishers. She thought they were all money grubbers who would desert her ship if sales ever started to taper off."

Fenwick said, "Everybody connected with her publisher that we interviewed said she was a saint."

"She *was* a saint, to their faces. That's how you have to be in this business. Nobody in their right mind mouths off to an editor. She thought the Hollywood movie people were slime."

Fenwick said, "I thought she invited at least some of them to her place in Colorado every winter."

"She invited those who she thought could be of use to her. She knew every line of every contract she ever signed. She got a percent of the gross on her latest movies. That pissed Hollywood off."

"Anyone in particular?" Fenwick asked.

"It would take me awhile to make a list."

"We spoke with Samuel Chadwick, Arnold Rackwill, Lorenzo Cavali, and Louis Eitel."

"Samuel and his paid-for boyfriend? Ha! Those two always claimed to be best friends with Muriam. Muriam used them to get what she wanted. She laughed at them behind their backs. Chadwick wasn't very good at his job. Rackwill was actually the most competent one, and he has to be very careful that Chadwick doesn't notice how bright he is. Chadwick is not interested in being shown up by some paid-for semi-protégé."

"How well did you know Mr. Rackwill?" Turner asked.

"Not well at all." He spoke with a snap and a hint of a snarl that reawakened Turner's suspicion of Rackwill having some connection with the writing group.

Turner took a gamble. "Was it a one-night stand, a brief affair, or a relationship?"

Granville glared at him, finally lowered his eyes. "One night at a convention."

"He cheated on Chadwick with you."

"I'd hardly call it cheating. It was over in less than fifteen minutes. We never saw each other again. I was trying to sleep with him to help get a book sold to the movies. It didn't get sold. He didn't get any more sex. Are you saying Chadwick or Rackwill would kill Devers and Foublin to get back at me?"

"Just asking questions," Turner said.

"Did she have problems with Cavali and Eitel?" Fenwick asked.

"It was more like she was oblivious to problems."

"We heard she had specific problems with Lorenzo Cavali."

"He had a problem with her. I'm talking more interpersonal stuff. Chadwick used to go to her parties in Aspen every winter. He'd stay at least a week. She may have laughed at him behind his back; but, at the same time, he and his crowd were roaring with laughter behind her back. She thought of herself as this benevolent eccentric, pleasing her fans and producing great art. Hell, it was genre art. So is mine. Chadwick never got snooty to her face. Sometimes they'd all gather down at the local bars and make fun of her pretensions and all that incessant cheerfulness. I was there a few times."

"You were in her writing group," Fenwick said, "and you were part of the group making fun of her."

"Because she was a friend doesn't mean I didn't see her failings."

Turner said, "Recognizing someone's failings and being part of running her down sound like two different things to me."

"Hey, I'm trying to help you guys. Why are you getting all huffy with me?"

Turner said, "We just need to understand the dynamics of all these people."

"Well, I guess."

"Do you know anything about Ms. Devers wearing a Xena, Warrior Princess outfit?" Turner asked.

"A what?" He looked genuinely astonished.

"Did she have such a costume?" Fenwick asked.

"I have no idea."

"She was found dead in it," Turner said.

Granville gaped. "That's unbelievable. Wasn't she a little old for that kind of thing?"

Fenwick said, "You never saw or heard her speak of dressing up or wanting to put on a show?"

"Never."

"We have the impression from people we've talked to that she liked to model costumes for her writing group."

"She never did for me. She never remotely hinted at it. Sexual liaisons were not Muriam's problem. She pinched a few butts. That's all the contact I ever had with her. More would have been kind of sick."

"Who were her other enemies?"

"Melissa Bentworth, her first editor at Galactic Books? She was a piece of work. She absolutely bullied, mistreated, or ignored her authors. She is a lazy-ass thing."

"They had fights?"

"Muriam never fought. She worked behind the scenes to make sure her version of the truth won in the end. She was always willing to put herself out for the little guy. She helped me make my first sale and get published."

"Who's your publisher?" Fenwick asked.

"Intergalactic Express, they're a new imprint. They publish experimental SF and fantasy. They've got some of the best young authors working today."

"Would she fear competition from a new press?"

"No. She didn't need to fear anyone. Nobody could write like her."

Turner said, "We heard David Hutter got tossed out of the writing group."

"Hutter? He was stupid. He didn't have a brain."

Fenwick asked, "Did Ms. Devers promise to get him a reading from her agent?"

"Muriam didn't need to promise anything. She never did that kind of thing. Your work had to stand on its own merit."

"Unless she pinched your butt," Fenwick said.

"You guys are making too much out of the butt pinching. It was just a joke. Harmless."

Turner said, "Agnes Demint didn't think you guys in the writing group were harmless."

"Agnes is a certifiable bitch. She thought she was a big deal. She certainly acted like she was a big deal. Muriam mostly laughed at her behind her back."

"Then why keep her as an agent?" Turner asked.

"She had her uses. She did as she was told. She didn't get in Muriam's way."

"Anybody else who would be on a list of enemies and would be at the convention?"

"I don't know who is at the convention. We got a little booklet in our packets, but I never looked at it."

Fenwick asked, "Where were you from ten to eleven today?"

"I didn't kill her. I've got an alibi. From nine to noon I was giving a seminar on writing experimental science fiction. I saw Muriam after breakfast. After her nine o'clock signing, she was going to her room. We were with several other people who saw her go." He gave them the names. "When I got out of the seminar, I joined the gathering throngs exchanging rumors. Then I was called up here. I didn't do it."

Turner asked, "Did you know Dennis Foublin?"

"We e-mailed each other a few times. I'd only met him once at a party. We talked for all of five minutes."

"You know anyone who would want to kill him?"

"I barely knew him to talk to him."

He left.

Fenwick said, "I wish I could put him at the top of my suspect list." They scribbled on their charts as they talked.

"Why?"

"He was close to the deceased, but he seemed kind of snarky about almost everybody else. That is going to be my new favorite word."

"What?"

"Snarky."

"Hate to see you without a new favorite word," Turner said. "Wordless in Chicago? Doesn't have quite the ring you need."

"So who do you think did it?"

"Granville is certainly the right build. He denied being approached by Muriam for her little costume shows. He could be a clueless dolt who didn't recognize the come-ons. Although someone that good-looking has to be used to people coming on to him."

"Maybe Marwood lied to us. He's the only one who's mentioned the shows so far."

"Well, she was in the costume. Something had to be up. His is the only explanation we've gotten up to this point."

Fenwick looked at his charted diagram of the rooms and floors where they had bloody clothes, feathers, suspects, killings, and the attack on the cop. "This tells me nothing."

"So far," Turner said. They always made diagrams. Sometimes they helped. Sometimes they didn't. The detectives believed that the time they didn't do it would be the time it would have made a difference.

20

On their list from Oona Murkle they found David Hutter's name. They sent for him.

David Hutter was a huge bear of a man in a medieval monk's robe. He wore a great white beard and tonsured hair. He had a deep baritone voice. Turner thought he either needed to bathe more often or use more deodorant.

Fenwick said, "We heard you had some problems with Muriam Devers."

"Doesn't mean I killed her. All kinds of people have all kinds of problems with all kinds of people. Doesn't make them killers."

"Yes," Fenwick said, "but most people we have problems with don't end up dead. Your problem person did."

"Did she really get run through with a broadsword?"

"You have any fights with her?"

"You didn't answer my question."

Fenwick said, "It's late. I'm on overtime. I'd love to see my family sometime this weekend. I'm sure I represent all that is evil in government with my officiousness."

"Why not just answer?" Hutter said.

Turner wasn't sure the guy was wrong. Sometimes it would

be easier just to answer the question instead of trying to bash the person with banter.

Turner said, "She got run through with a broadsword. You have the heft to be on the list of people able to easily wield a sword that heavy. Did you have fights with her?"

If Hutter thought they were playing good cop/bad cop, Turner wasn't going to disabuse him of the notion. "Yes, we had fights. I dared to criticize her. I dared to say what I think. Not just about what she wrote but about what everybody wrote. I was honest."

"Did you give honest positive comments or honest negative comments?" Turner asked.

"Both. Always both. Devers wouldn't listen to me. She never listened to anybody."

"Who would have a reason to kill her?" Fenwick asked.

"I'm not sure. She was a back-stabber. She was quite willing to ruin anybody's career or reputation. Trampling the downtrodden was a skill she had in abundance."

"How did Muriam Devers notice you?"

"I was at a convention about fifteen years ago. That was also fifty pounds ago and before I let my beard grow. She pinched my butt. It was a great joke. Everybody laughed. I got to join her writing group."

"How come you got thrown out?"

"When I met her, I was in awe. I wanted to be an author, a published author. That has been my goal since I was twelve. I wanted to see my words in print. She took an interest in me. An author I'd admired, whose books I'd loved. I was thrilled. I was willing to do anything for her. Very quickly I learned that I should never have put her on such a pedestal. I was young and stupid. For ten years I was young and stupid. That's a lot of stupidity. For a long time I didn't want to believe what I knew to be true, that she was a shit. When I finally admitted it to myself, I began to be less subservient than I was supposed to be, plus I started to gain weight.

Look at all the guys in her group. They had to be studly and stay that way."

"Could she really have been that blatant?" Fenwick asked.

"Sure," Hutter said, "why not? She was rich. Personal writing groups don't have governmental regulations on who can or cannot be in them. She could afford to be anything she wanted."

"What exactly did she do that you had to be subservient about?"

"You laughed at her jokes or you were frozen out. You listened to her criticism, and you changed what she suggested you change in your manuscript or you lost favor. And then there was that sucaryl-drenched reputation. It takes a hell of a lot of energy and careful planning to maintain the façade and be vicious to people at the same time. Like, we were supposed to be the ones who spread vicious rumors at conventions or on the Internet about other people."

Turner asked, "Why would you agree to act for her like that? It might not be criminal, but it was unsavory at the least."

"To get published. To get a better agent. To get a better deal. To make more money."

Fenwick said, "You were willing to sell your soul so you could write about truth and light?"

"I suppose you believe the moronic cliché that all writers are busily producing truth and light for the honor and glory of their craft?"

"Pretty much, yeah," Fenwick said.

"Not likely. It's like any other job. We're in it for the money. And it's a whole lot more like real work than people know. You may not have a water cooler to gather around, but there's gossip and rumors that spread fast. There's infighting and back-stabbing. You have to fight for what is yours."

Turner said, "Maybe it was that way for you and the people in your group. My guess is there are honorable people in the writing profession just like in any other. And dishonest people just like any other. And ambivalent people. The usual gamut."

Fenwick said, "Such fighting doesn't usually involve broadswords stuck through people."

Turner asked, "Who did she make angry enough to do something so violent?"

"Everybody."

"Anybody who specifically fought back?" Turner asked. "Anybody who might get angry enough to kill about it?"

"I never knew any killers, but people lost jobs, prestige, or friends." He told them about Devers' first publicist and first editor. "She pissed off Hollywood people and tried to bring down other authors. She hated Samuel Chadwick and Arnie Rackwill. Samuel because he laughed at her behind her back. He was always trying to lower the price on what she could get. She sneered at him behind his back."

"Do you think any of them would kill someone else?"

"I never would have before today. I don't know. I've heard a famous mystery writer once said that to find the motivation for the murderers they write about, to understand their killers, it was only necessary for a writer to look inside their own souls. We're all capable of great anger. Most of us have enough controls on us to keep our darker impulses in check. I guess anyone could do anything. I don't know of anyone I'd specifically accuse."

"How well do you Arnie Rackwill?"

He sighed. "All this is going to come out. I guess it doesn't really make a difference." He flapped his arms. "I fucked him once. It didn't get me a movie deal. I wasn't angry with him. I guess I'd have slept with any number of people to get a deal."

"Men and women?" Fenwick asked.

"Does it make a difference?" Hutter asked. "A sale is a sale."

Turner said, "She was found in a Xena, Warrior Princess outfit."

"If she trusted you enough, she invited you to her private

soirees, and you'd get to see the show. There were mountains of vanity behind that public image. I suppose we are all different in private, but the difference between her public and private personas seemed more extreme than most. There's a long distance between all that goddamn sweetness and light and her kinky shows."

"What was the show?"

"She'd parade in different outfits, but the Xena was her favorite."

"Wasn't she kind of old for that?" Fenwick asked.

"You think vanity disappears as you get older? You think people don't judge you on how you look because you're older? She had an ego, and it needed to be fed. You didn't feed it, you didn't last in her inner circle. I guess it was a harmless enough thing. I just thought she looked so stupid. I saw the shows for years. Finally, I couldn't hold it in. I laughed. I couldn't stop laughing. She got very offended, and I got booted out of the group."

Turner didn't think it was odd that someone laughing at your private fantasies would be a cause for anger. "Laughing at her sounds kind of cruel," Turner said.

"She set herself above everyone else. She was always better than you. She always got the better contract. The better foreign rights deal. She made money and pots of it, and she let you know it. I have no idea where she spent her millions. I don't care. She was crueler than a playground full of adult bullies. Worse, it was embarrassing to see her be human. She admitted to having needs to people who were essentially work colleagues. Can either of you imagine dressing up in odd costumes in front of the people you work with?"

Turner didn't really want to hear Fenwick's answer to that question. Turner said, "You laughed so she threw you out?"

"Yeah."

"Describe this to me," Turner said. "How did you wind up being the one to watch her?"

"I've talked to people over the years. As far as I can tell, she operated the same way with everyone. You've already discovered the young sexy males, and how she liked to draw them to herself. I know it's hard to believe looking at me, but I was a young sexy male once."

Turner, of course, believed the young part. He wasn't ready to concede that Hutter was sexy once. The general state of the parts of his body Turner could see or smell seemed to need a lot of maintenance.

"Can you give us names please?" Turner asked.

"Over the years she might have had twenty or thirty different guys in the group."

"Did all of them get thrown out because they laughed?"

"I've talked to maybe a quarter of them. Some never got invited to the private showings. Some were never interested. Some saw her for what she was. I guess some were honest people. I don't know which of them are at the convention."

Fenwick asked, "So who was she meeting to do a show for at this convention?"

"I have no idea. I assume one of the people in her writing group. Or it might have been someone whose butt she'd pinched at this convention."

"Would she do a show for someone she just met?" Turner asked.

"Once in a great while."

Turner knew that Brian's butt had been pinched. He couldn't and didn't want to begin to imagine his son agreeing to go to an older woman's room under such odd circumstances, but this was another addition to his unease.

Fenwick asked, "Did you know Dennis Foublin?"

"Sure, I knew Dennis. He was a good guy. We kind of started out together in this business. You know how it is. You get recognized a little on the Internet, in a few little magazines. Fans get interested. I wasn't famous. Denny was cool."

"Do you know if he had any enemies?"

"I can't imagine. Denny was a calm, quiet, pleasant kind of guy. Nobody could get angry at Denny."

"Somebody did," Fenwick said.

"It makes no sense," Hutter said. "There would be no reason to kill him."

"How about something sinister in his background?"

He scratched his head. "That doesn't make any sense. Who said that? Denny was just a regular guy."

"We haven't been able to find any more than a casual connection between him and Ms. Devers."

"She never talked about him while I was around."

Fenwick said, "We need to know your movements this morning."

He gave them his itinerary. He had been part of a panel discussing writing humorous science fiction novels. He claimed to have been in someone's presence the whole day. They would have to check.

He left.

Turner got up and strode toward the window that looked out on the high-rise office building next door. It gleamed with the rain that once again was pouring down. He turned back.

Fenwick said, "There is a pun somewhere in this, something about these people being back-stabbers. A pun waiting to see the light of day."

Turner said, "A pun waiting to die."

Fenwick said, "I got no notion on this guy yet. He's a writer. He tells lies for a living. Many of these people do."

"I imagine they prefer to call it writing novels."

"Either way."

Turner said, "You should be happy at any rate."

"Why?"

"We've got a lot less sweetness and light than we had a several hours ago."

"We haven't had anybody seriously dump on Dennis Foublin yet. Somebody had to not like the guy."

Turner said, "Who was Devers supposed to be meeting to put on her show?"

"She could have been just dressing up for herself, a very private fantasy moment."

"Or someone had an appointment."

They called Sanchez in and asked him about the results of the preliminary interviews with the people on the various lists they'd been given by various suspects.

Sanchez said, "Nobody's reported anything really odd or that they figured you needed to know about."

For the chart they were making, he gave them information on room numbers of the people they'd talked to. Turner and Fenwick would add the room numbers of the places they'd found blood. They also asked him to get Peter Damien who was the only member of the writing group they hadn't talked to yet.

While he was doing that, they met with the CEO of Galactic Books, Murray Keefer. Keefer was in his sixties. He wore an Armani suit with a snowy white shirt and a dark, conservative tie. He reverted to the sweetness and light theme of some of their earlier interviewees.

Fenwick said, "We were told she clawed her way to the top leaving careers and people's lives scattered in her wake."

Keefer said, "Nonsense. Any business has people on their way up and down all the time. People have to work hard to prove themselves. Muriam worked very hard. She was always cheerful and helpful."

"She ever try to get you to fire anyone?" Fenwick asked.

"Never."

"What about her having her publicist fired?"

"I have nothing to do with such low-level staffers. We've had hundreds of those people over the years. Most are sincere enough, but they move on quickly. People don't believe in company loyalty anymore."

Fenwick said, "Can you say Enron?"

Keefer drew himself up a little straighter. He said, "My meetings with Muriam were always pleasant and friendly."

"Even contract negotiations?" Fenwick asked.

"We had lawyers take care of that. I know of no one who would have reason to harm Muriam. I didn't know Dennis Foublin. I don't have much time for the Internet."

He left.

Fenwick said, "The boss is pure."

Turner said, "Of course, she was nice to him. He was signing the paychecks. He's useless."

Sanchez entered with Peter Damien.

▲ 21 ◢

Peter Damien was gorgeous. He had a handsome face, a trim figure, a muscular build, and brown brush-cut hair. Turner thought he might have been in his early twenties. He had on tight, well-worn jeans, a white short-sleeve dress shirt, and running shoes. Turner noted his hands trembled slightly. Too much caffeine, or nerves, or a simple twitch, or a murderer's guilt? They sat.

"What's going on?" Damien asked.

Fenwick said, "We understand Ms. Devers had private little parties where she used to dress up to entertain one, some, or all of the members of her writing group."

A whisper, "Jesus, she was old enough to be my grandmother."

"Did she put on shows for you?" Fenwick asked.

Barely audible, "She hadn't."

"Was she going to?" Fenwick asked.

"Yeah."

"When?" Fenwick asked.

They had to lean close to hear his response. "Today. This morning. Do I need a lawyer?"

"Did you kill her?" Fenwick asked.

A little more vigorous. "No."

"Where were you this morning?" Fenwick asked.

"I went to breakfast. I hovered around her for a while at her signing. She was scheduled for several different ones at different times. I was supposed to wait about an hour and then come to her room."

Fenwick prompted, "What time was this?"

"About ten."

"Did you go?"

"No. I was late. I was talking to an editor from Galactic Books. He was thinking of offering me a deal."

"Which editor?"

"It was a secret deal."

"It wasn't a book deal," Turner guessed.

"Maybe some other things might have come about because of the deal."

Turner said, "You offered sex, money, or what to get published?"

Back to a mutter, "Sex."

This actually made sense to Turner. Peter Damien was an extremely attractive young man.

"How late were you?" Turner asked.

"By the time I was done," he turned red with embarrassment, "making the deal, I was nearly an hour late."

"Ms. Devers wouldn't be angry with that?"

"I hoped not. It was the first time I was invited. It felt really weird."

"How did you know what the invitation meant?" Turner asked.

"Dave Hutter told me. He buttonholed me this morning and made some sarcastic cracks. I was in the writing group to improve my writing. I think it had improved."

Fenwick said, "But you weren't adverse to helping your career along with a little nookie on the side."

"No."

"Did you try to go up to her room?"

"By that time the floor was closed off."

"When did you meet her?"

"Only a few months ago at a convention in Omaha. She pinched my butt. She laughed. I'd never been across the Mississippi River in my life so I thought I'd go. She found out I was from New York, and I got the invitation. I didn't realize when I started that there were odd requirements like watching her dress up. When I got home, I was going to quit the group."

"Watching a dress-up show to improve your career is out, but screwing an editor is okay."

"Muriam was nearly four times my age."

"Which editor?" Fenwick asked.

"Alvin Tilly. He's their newest one."

"How well did you know the other members of the writing group?"

"We'd met six times since I joined the group. We weren't real chummy. We weren't enemies. We were there to work with Muriam."

Fenwick said, "Perhaps we have different definitions of work."

"I know I'm a hypocrite. I wanted to be published. It's been my dream. I had some chances based on my relationship with Muriam. I got to know this editor in the last day or so. I saw my chance. I took it."

"Did you know Dennis Foublin?"

"I visited his web site once in a while. I agreed more than I disagreed with his reviews. I met him last night, and we talked for a few minutes. He was perfectly nice."

They got his room number, and added it and his whereabouts and time frame to the charts.

When he was gone, Fenwick said, "This is kind of a randy bunch."

"My guess is there are as many honorable people in the writing profession as any other. I bet pretty young men like

Peter Damien who have the same scruples and who are willing to take advantage of the same kind of offers exist in any profession."

Fenwick said, "At least we've got an explanation for the Xena stuff. I don't get it."

"I think it's sad," Turner said. "She must have been a lonely old woman."

Fenwick said, "I bet she was a horny rich old babe who was having the time of her life."

"Or that," Turner said.

They found Alvin Tilly. He confirmed Damien's story.

▲ 22 ▲

Sanchez entered with Ian Hume and a portly gentleman in a white beard. He wore a formal dark blue suit, white shirt, and dark blue tie with a hint of a beige stripe in it. The gentleman was Archie Kittleman. Introductions occurred. They all sat.

Kittleman said, "Ian, I don't like this. I've never been involved with the police. I don't know anything about murder."

Ian said, "Relax, Archie. These guys are my friends. I think you might be able to help them."

"I don't see how."

Turner said, "We've had people connected to Muriam Devers and Dennis Foublin to talk to. We need somebody not connected to all of them to give us a realistic perspective."

"I can try. I've been to Foublin's web site, but I've never met him. I was introduced to Devers once about ten years ago. She said hello, I said hello. That was the extent of our conversation. I'm sure she wouldn't remember me."

Turner said, "You only met her once, but what do you know about Muriam Devers—rumors, gossip, stray facts? We're looking for anything."

"Among the gay people in the SF world it was assumed that her writing group guys were all gay."

"Were they?" Turner asked.

"I know at least one of them was."

"How did you learn that?" Turner asked.

Kittleman looked from Ian to Turner to Fenwick. "Ahem."

Ian said, "It's perfectly safe."

Turner said, "We need information. I have no desire to bring trouble to you."

"The young man, David Hutter, seemed interested in furthering his career. At one time he seemed to think that I might be of some use to him. I thought he might be of some use to me in furthering my interest in studly young men. I'd just had the first volume of my trilogy published. His interest lasted about as long as he thought I could help his career. To be honest, my interest in him didn't last much beyond my first orgasm with him. He wasn't very good in bed."

"How well did you get to know Hutter?" Turner asked.

"Well enough to know he was a money-grubbing shit. He wanted cab fare after we were done that first night. It was embarrassing."

Fenwick said, "We found Ms. Dever in a Xena, Warrior Princess outfit. We were told she put on private shows for people whose butts she pinched. Would she do this for a group of gay guys? Wouldn't she want straight guys?"

"I don't know," Kittleman said. "I don't know anything about Xena or any other kinds of outfits. It sounds odd to me. Wasn't she a bit old for that?"

Turner said, "I'm not sure our imaginations or fantasies have an age limit."

Kittleman asked, "How does her writing group being made up of gay men help in solving the murder?"

"We don't know," Turner said. "Right now I need information. I don't know these people or this world."

"It's closed world," Kittleman said. "In many ways it's like a small town. The million-selling authors are like the rich people who live up the hill who you don't see much, but everybody gossips about. It's also true that everybody knows everybody else's business. And if they don't know everybody else's business, they want to know about it, or they make stuff up about it, or they pass along rumors with lots of embellishment."

"Seems pretty normal to me," Fenwick said.

"Exactly," Kittleman replied. "Although it can approach the incestuous."

"How so?" Turner asked.

"A lot of times these writers only see each other at conventions. Your basic writer is working by him or herself. They might call or e-mail each other, but actual face-to-face get-togethers are rare. How many SF writers live in Chicago? Only a few. There aren't that many SF books published every year. So when these authors show up at a convention, they gossip and talk and reminisce about other conventions where they gossiped, talked, and reminisced."

"What fights do they have?" Fenwick asked.

"There were endemic fights. At the conventions themselves there's all kinds of silly nonsense. Mildly famous mid-list authors expect to be lionized. First-time authors with one-hit wonders expect their paths to be strewn with rushes. They aren't all like that, but you get a lot of ego. Like the panels at these conventions. Some people want to pick the panel they will be on and pick the people they will be on with. Then there are those who are not famous enough who want to be assigned to prime panels with even more famous authors to assure themselves of some kind of audience. Then there are the assholes who call at the last minute and beg to be on prize panels."

"There are prize panels?" Fenwick asked. "Who honestly cares?"

"Some of these people care very much. You'd have to ask them why they care so much. There are myriad SF and fantasy organizations. At any one time half of them are fighting over whether their mission should be to serve established writers or whether they should have outreach to people who are trying to break into the profession, or should they serve only fans. Should they concentrate on agents and editors or some other stratum of the hangers-on? You get that in a lot of the genre groups."

"Why fight about that?" Fenwick asked.

"The fight isn't necessarily about the exact subject. Often it's about who has power and influence. Sometimes it's old guard versus new. Or sometimes a rich, new author wants to throw his or her weight around. Or a first-time author who thinks his ten-thousand-dollar advance entitles him to honor and glory beyond imagining. Or sometimes it's someone who thinks he or she is a tenured university professor who can straighten out all the peons."

"Did Devers or Foublin fit those descriptions?"

"Foublin always leaned toward the snotty-professor end of the spectrum. His bestseller list was a joke."

"Did people really take it seriously?" Fenwick asked.

"Well, not like it was *Publishers Weekly* or the *New York Times,* but he was listened to by some dolts."

"What was wrong with the list?" Fenwick asked.

"You had to be paying close attention to what he listed to figure out what was wrong. I didn't notice until somebody pointed it out to me. It was most often in what he didn't write. Like, if he put that your book was a sure-fire bestseller, then, sure fire, it was on his list. It might not make anybody else's list, but it was on his. He claimed to be in contact with more stores than anyone else. I think he just made his list up."

"Did people get mad about that?" Turner asked. "Anybody try to point it out to him, get even?"

"He had clout. You didn't mess with clout. The vast majority of people thought he was this saintly guy. Everybody always claims writers are grousing about being mistreated.

When you actually are mistreated, then it's very much the boy who bitched problem. If you're always a victim then when you really are a victim, nobody can tell the difference. There were no confrontations where people threw drinks, if that's what you mean. In this world you followed the rules or you went nowhere. It took me ten years to get the first volume of my space opera published."

"Because it had gay characters?" Ian asked.

"It's a hard world to break into, period. It probably didn't help that the characters were gay. Although Foublin was a homophobic son of a bitch."

"He was?" Ian asked. "You have proof?" His pencil came out.

"I didn't think this was a newspaper interview," Kittleman said.

"It's not," Turner said. Ian subsided.

Kittleman said, "The proof was in what he left out. I went back through the logs of his web magazine. No book with gay characters, not a one, ever got reviewed. No openly gay authors ever got reviewed. My first book came out ten years ago. The second volume five years ago. The silence in general was deafening, but many small magazines and web sites at least mentioned my work. There were more SF and fantasy bookstores back then. Most of the owners were incredibly kind. Foublin wasn't cruel. He was silent, which can be the most damning thing of all."

Fenwick said, "He was one guy with a web site."

"Who I resented for his homophobia. Look back through all his work. There aren't a lot of gay characters in science fiction and fantasy. If you read Foublin, you wouldn't know there were any."

"Were there angry gay authors who wanted to take him on?"

"There aren't enough of us around to take anyone on. It was just something we noticed. I wouldn't have known

Foublin to talk to. I know of him. Some of us were suspicious about reviews that appeared on the bigger web sites. The gay authors thought that sometimes homophobic creeps would write nasty reviews just to bring down the average the site gave you."

"Would Foublin do this?" Turner asked.

"I have no proof, only suspicions."

Turner said, "We were told some people claimed he had trouble getting his facts precisely right."

"It was a constant problem. One writer had a particular kind of poison figure prominently in his book as well as right in the title. Foublin screwed it up and said the dénouement hinged on someone being strangled. How can a conscientious reviewer screw up so completely?"

"Oona Murkle said his getting facts wrong was an accusation from a faction that was disgruntled and that it wasn't a big deal."

"Poor Oona. She really is a nice person. She bit off way more than she could chew when she began organizing the drive to get the convention to Chicago. She's a very well-meaning, very sweet fan, a nice old lady. She's been around since dirt. She's familiar with everybody and such a help, but I'm not sure she has any real friends in the SF world. She's kind of sad. She's the one who doesn't get things right."

"How's that?" Fenwick asked.

"Oona is a dear. She had sense to turn over this operation to a committee a year ago. She'd been trying to do it all herself. It takes an army of volunteers to make a convention this big work. Here's one example. She had the notion that it was necessary to hide all the panel assignments from the people on the panels. How absurd. People want to know what they're doing. Some, although a very few, want to actually prepare for their panels."

"Don't they always prepare something?" Turner asked.

Kittleman looked amused. "Far too many of the panelists think because they've made a movie deal, had a book published, or had their name in the paper, that makes them an expert on whatever panel they are on. Whether or not they even know anything about the panel topic."

Fenwick said, "They don't match expertise to the panel you're on?"

"Usually. Not always. You might be on panel about dogs in SF and your books might have had one dog in one obscure chapter. She was lucky she got Devers and that movie premiere early on. Oona is a dear, but I'm afraid she's also a dope."

"How so?"

"She's an awful writer. She's been trying to get published for years. She writes these one-thousand-page epics. Word is, the dialogue is endless, the plots convoluted, the characters wooden. She keeps sending them out, bless her heart."

"How do you know about her writing?" Fenwick asked.

"She tried to publish it on the Internet. There's a scam. It's so feeble and pathetic. All those wannabes putting out these thousands of pages that no one is ever going to want to read."

"No one ever called Foublin on his imprecision?" Fenwick asked.

"A few people tried to, but most of the people would rush to defend him."

"Is this infighting really serious?" Fenwick asked.

"In an incestuous, college-English-department kind of way, yeah. People can get worked up about little stuff."

"But enough for murder?" Fenwick asked.

"Obviously somebody was upset enough about something," Kittleman replied.

"Were the fights about who was in charge serious?" Fenwick asked.

"To those involved, yes."

"We got a lot of sweetness and light about Devers," Fenwick said.

"That's Oona and her crowd. They are always cheerful. They worked hard setting up this convention. I'll give them that. They busted their butts to make this thing the biggest and best."

"Who was Foublin an old-fashioned nasty professor to?" Fenwick asked.

"He had a way of condescending, as if you weren't quite clean enough. His reviews never got nasty, but if you paid attention long enough, you could tell which ones he didn't like."

"How so?" Turner asked.

"If he didn't like your book, all he would do is summarize the plot and not mention one thing remotely approaching an opinion."

"Isn't that good?" Fenwick asked. "At least you get mentioned."

"But he never mentioned any gay writer."

"What about these Hollywood people?" Turner asked. "Samuel Chadwick, Arnold Rackwill, Lorenzo Cavali, and Louis Eitel."

Kittleman waved a dismissive hand. "Who really cares about that Hollywood crowd?"

"You got turned down," Fenwick said.

"Yes."

"That bother you?"

"Yes. I'd be happy to take Hollywood money. Anybody would. Anybody who says they wouldn't is lying."

"Did Foublin and Devers have trouble with Hollywood money?" Fenwick asked.

"Foublin never got offered any, that I know of. Devers made a pile."

"Can you tell us anything about the Hollywood crowd?"

"From what I've heard, Rackwill is a shit. I know for sure he's at the end of his time with Chadwick."

"How's that?" Fenwick asked.

"They met five years ago. Chadwick is notorious for dumping his paid pretty boys after five years. Rackwill's at his limit. Rackwill is such a jerk, I wouldn't put anything past him."

"Including murder?" Fenwick asked.

Kittleman sat up straighter. "I'm not ready to make that kind of accusation."

"Does Rackwill know his time is probably almost up?"

Kittleman said, "Everybody else does. Why wouldn't he? One rumor said Rackwill was screwing at least one of the guys in Devers' writing group. Hell, I was having sex with one of them. I'd have done it with as many of them as I could and just about anybody else if I thought it might get me a deal."

"Isn't that kind of crass?" Turner asked.

"I'd say everybody does it, but they don't. I justify it with my ambition. Sleeping with Hutter didn't hurt anybody. It might have gotten me a deal. It didn't harm the man I was sleeping with."

"Who did Rackwill sleep with?"

"Hutter."

"That cause you problems?" Turner asked.

"If I'd been in a relationship with him, yeah, it would have. But I wasn't. Hutter left the group a month or so after we had sex."

"Did one cause the other?"

"Not that I ever heard of. All gay people are supposed to be in love with Rackwill and Chadwick because they kissed at one of those lesser award shows. You know, on stage after Chadwick won some second-tier award. Now, if you want real emotion, Chadwick and Cavali hate each other. Rackwill is a shit."

"How is Rackwill a shit?"

"If there's double-dealing, Rackwill will be dealing the doubles. He's trouble."

"Why do Chadwick and Cavali hate each other?" Turner asked.

"Business rivals. Who can get a getter deal, a bigger star, all that ego-stabbing which is lifeblood to Hollywood insiders."

"What about Melissa Bentworth and Sandra Berenking, her editor and publicist at Galactic Books?"

"The once and current editor," Kittleman said. "I know Melissa from her helping run this convention. She did everything she could for me when my books came out. Melissa is a hard-working woman. It is not easy running a small press. It is even harder to make a profit with one. She has done so. I heard Devers was pissed about that."

"Why?"

"Muriam was a grudge collector, so I've been told. She carried lots of grudges against anyone who ever said something negative about her books."

"Aren't editors supposed to make criticisms?" Fenwick asked.

"You know that. I know that. Muriam was a hard case."

"What about her current editor?" Turner asked.

"Brianna Perkins is a toady. I heard she might be on her way out. If Muriam was in her corner, then Muriam was her ticket to staying. If Muriam was against her, then Brianna could kiss her job good-bye."

"Authors have that kind of clout?" Fenwick asked.

"If you're making millions for the company, you can have a lot of say in anything."

Turner said, "Who helped you get published?"

"I busted my own butt."

Fenwick said, "Who was upset by Devers throwing her weight around?"

"It was so subtle on Muriam's part or on the part of her agent. That agent is evil incarnate. Maude Protherow would say anything to protect Muriam."

"How's that?" Fenwick asked.

"They'd make deals all right. With networks and shows. Muriam even got to be one of those interviewed before the Academy Awards. Muriam would be real sneaky. She'd let it be known, often through her writing group mafia, that if a show wanted her, then they better not have someone else. If necessary she'd go over, under, around, or through anybody including her publicist to get something that she thought was beneficial to herself."

"Nobody tried to put a stop to this?" Fenwick asked.

"At least one person did," Kittleman said, "otherwise she wouldn't be dead. Muriam hated competition."

Fenwick asked, "Is there someone among authors who does like it?"

"Libertarians think it's the great panacea for our times."

"Good thing somebody's got a handle on the panacea," Fenwick said. "I've been putting up with it not being here for a long time."

Turner said, "One of our sources told us there was some kind of hidden secret in Dennis Foublin's life. That it was mentioned on the Internet, but not explained."

"I've never heard of anything like that."

Fenwick said, "Mr. Kittleman, where were you this morning?"

"I was leading a seminar on how to write the fantasy epic. We were reading passages of wannabes' work out loud to each other. It was fun actually. We worked on the prose, refining, giving details. I didn't kill anybody. Perhaps in my next book I could write a mystery and do in all the people I don't like."

"Lot of those?" Fenwick asked.

"I've got a list," Kittleman said. He left.

The detectives began entering all their data on their charts.

A beat cop entered the suite. "You guys better come quick."

◣ 23 ◢

Sanchez led them to the top floor of the hotel, the most renowned feature of which was the rotating restaurant Chicago At Night. Turner had never been. It was supposed to be extremely exclusive. His sons preferred burgers and fries. He and Ben went out once a year for a special meal at the small Italian restaurant on the far north side of the city where they'd first expressed their love for each other. Chicago At Night was out of their league. As they passed through the crowded dining room, Turner caught a glimpse of the sky-scrapers of the Loop in the distance.

Sanchez led them to a complex of service rooms in the center of the building. Gray cement block walls encased a pair of service elevators, the tops of emergency stairwells, pipes two feet in diameter, and entrances to the roof.

"Is the only entrance through the restaurant?" Turner asked.

"That and the service elevators."

Macer was at the bottom of a set of stairs. At the door to the outside he showed them an open, but intact, lock.

"Someone had a key?" Fenwick said.

Turner leaned down closely. "Not hard to break these.

Screwdriver and a hammer and a fairly hard blow is all you need. He could have used a key or a few simple tools, or the hilt of a broadsword."

Fenwick asked, "This is all the security you had between here and outside?"

"We don't expect an attack from the roof. There's no room for a helicopter landing pad. If somebody is sophisticated and desperate enough to climb to the top of the building and then break back in, more power to them. Climbing these buildings is a stunt tried by very few. Their presence climbing would be noted very early on."

Macer led them outside. The roof was a half-block rectangle. There was a cooling and heating tower in about the middle. The rain had stopped. Water was gathered in gloomy pools at random intervals. Security lights cast feeble light on a fiberglass rooftop sculpture garden. The evenly spaced, clear plastic, multi-hued, twisted geometrical shapes reflected the meager light. Shadows gathered in pools at their bases. Their flashlights seemed to push at the darkness rather than give sufficient illumination. Sounds from far below drifted up. Turner heard a distant siren. If you lived in Chicago, half the time, if you listened carefully you could hear a distant siren. The body was in the darkest shadow of the cooling tower. The blood from the corpse matched the red reflected in the puddles of water dimly lit by the inadequate emergency lights.

The skull of a thin young man had been cloven nearly in two. The body was sprawled amid the folds of a vast black cape. No weapon was immediately visible. The nearly naked corpse was on its stomach. Bits of a leather harness clung to the corpse. Shreds of a brown Speedo flapped in the light breeze. What he could make out in the poor light caused Turner to gasp involuntarily. He rushed forward the last few steps. From closer up, he could make out the face. It was not Brian. He breathed a sigh of relief. It was more of a Roman legionnaire's outfit. Turner stepped on shards of broken spectacles. He crouched down. It was a pair of black horn-rimmed glasses, the left eye of which had been shattered. Very possibly stepped on by the owner or his killer.

Turner said, "It's Melvin Slate."

"Another fucking feather," Fenwick muttered.

Turner spotted the offending plumage three feet past the head. Bits of a broken ostrich feather fluttered in the breeze. "No sword," he commented. On the thumb of the left hand there was no thumb ring. He pointed his flashlight beam. He leaned over until he could see the other thumb. He said, "The other ring is still there."

"Our killer was planting feathers and removing rings?"

Turner said, "When you're a killer using a broadsword, I guess you're entitled to as many eccentricities as you want."

In a short period of time Macer and the Crime Lab people had the scene around the body illuminated, and the detectives, the ME, and tech staffs were bathed in bright white lights.

Turner and Fenwick inspected the area. Before taking each step they examined the ground carefully. They covered the area between the stairs and the body.

"There's blood all over the place up here," Fenwick said. He and Turner were halfway around the roof. Away from the brightness around the body, they used their flashlights. Turner looked back. He could see the body and about half the rooftop. They had keys to everything on the roof that needed a key. The wind up here came in sporadic puffs. A four-foot brick wall topped by four feet of thick Plexiglas around the perimeter kept out the worst of the Chicago winds. Turner understood that in summer diners could eat in the lee of the walls. The second storage space they examined had stacks of chairs, presumably for the restaurant. Fenwick flipped on the light switch. A bare bulb illumined rows of chairs. Under the first few were three more broadswords and a stack of red feathers and a heap of bloody clothes.

Fenwick said, "This case is really starting to have an edge to it."

"Watch it, there's enough swords here to damage even you."

"Here's the answer to some questions," Fenwick said.

"And brings up some more," Turner said. "Is one of these the sword that killed Slate or Foublin?" He leaned close and shone his flashlight on the three of them. They looked pristinely clean. The rest of the room had a thin film of undisturbed dust on every surface. He said, "The killer is a neatnik or none of these have been used."

Fenwick said, "Somebody's going to ask why we didn't look on the roof earlier."

"Nobody thought to look on the roof. Who knew there would be a place up here to hide clues?"

"Is this the killer's stash?" Fenwick asked. "His only stash? Or an elaborate set-up?"

"The killer had to have a stash someplace," Turner said. "Yeah, okay, we've got hundreds of rooms this crap could be in, but the roof is a reasonably logical but very out-of-the-way place." They returned to the corpse scene and mentioned the materials in the storage room so the tech team would know to check it.

"Does this mean there will definitely be no more killings?" Fenwick asked. "And most importantly, why is Melvin Slate dead? He'd be a much better candidate for the killer, if he wasn't a corpse."

"A killer corpse," Turner said. "Now there's a concept waiting to happen or the title of a cheap slasher movie."

Fenwick said, "Slate could have worn that cape to conceal swords and bloody clothes and all kinds of shit."

Turner said, "A logical conclusion is that he was in it with someone and they had a falling out. Maybe he was double-crossed by his accomplice. We've got to find out if we can trace this guy's movements from when he left us to here."

"How'd he get up here?" Fenwick said. "Didn't somebody notice? He breaks a lock. Nobody hears anything?"

Turner climbed the ladder to the top of the cooling tower. The wind was cruel at this height. The front had passed, the rain had stopped, and the wind was in off the lake. He was well beyond the protection of the eight-foot barrier. The view was spectacular. Turner was not afraid of heights, but he had a quick flash of vertigo on the last few steps. He'd never been so open and exposed so high up. Here the wind was untrammeled by the eight-foot barrier. He felt himself buffeted by the gusts. He gripped the rungs tighter. As he neared the top, for an instant he flashed on a killer taking a swipe at his head as it appeared over the edge of the tower. He crammed his flashlight in his belt, steadied himself, then climbed the last few rungs. He peered carefully over the edge onto the top of the tower. No humans. No sword. He saw a black backpack about two feet away. One end flapped in the wind. He wrapped one arm around the ladder and reached for the backpack. He pulled it close, fumbled with it carefully, secured it over his shoulder and climbed back down.

He and Fenwick examined the prize at the foot of the ladder. Inside they found size twenty-eight waist jeans with a belt that dangled a foot beyond the last loop, black high-top tennis shoes, and a ragged and torn T-shirt.

"Slate's," Turner said.

Fenwick said, "He told us he didn't do costumes."

"He lied," Turner said. "He might have said a lot of stuff, but he isn't going to anymore."

They also found a plastic hotel room key.

Fenwick said, "He claimed he wasn't staying at the hotel."

"He lied," Turner said.

"I got that part," Fenwick said.

Wrapped in a grease-stained cloth at the bottom was an electronic device. Turner held it in his plastic covered hand. "A Palm Pilot?"

"Computers are getting too damn small."

Turner unwrapped a set of wires leading from the computer to a plastic card the size of the modern room key.

Turner said, "He was the one who could get into the rooms. He was in on the killings. There were two of them."

"Unless he had one of these and was a petty thief as well as a nerd."

"Neither of us believes in coincidences. This is why he didn't want us to look in his backpack. He had the damn thing with him."

Fenwick said, "He probably had it with him, yeah. Or he was really clever. Or he and his coconspirator traded them off."

"Or the coconspirator has one of his own."

Macer checked the hotel computer and called back up to them with Slate's room number.

After the ME's team finished their investigation, they joined Turner and Fenwick near a sculpture that was a deep blue, six-foot Lucite isosceles triangle whose top point had been twisted into a golden swirl.

The ME said, "Your victim up here fought. A lot."

"Is all the blood his?"

"Can't tell yet. He's got cuts on his arms. He's got blood and bits of stuff under his fingernails. Could be he clawed at the roof in his death agony. Could be he got in a few licks on his killer." He showed them the diagram he'd drawn. Turner and Fenwick took out their preliminary sketches. Photographs were always taken of the scenes, but the detectives always made their own diagrams. "He got bashed in the head about halfway between the cooling tower and the entrance. That's where the blood starts. He did not die right away. The brain is a funny thing. He was bleeding and dying, but he was fighting or at least thrashing and stumbling. They went around the roof."

"He was chasing somebody?" Fenwick asked.

"More staggering and fighting, probably gouging and

scratching. He could have been dodging out of the way. He could have been verging on unconscious. It's hard to tell."

Fenwick said, "We found a heap of swords, and we've got the accounted-for ones downstairs. We still don't know if one, some, or all of the ones in the heap killed one some or all of our victims."

"Can't tell you about any of that yet," the ME said.

"How long has this guy been dead?" Turner asked.

"Less than half an hour. The blood hasn't even begun to dry. Whoever found him probably did so pretty soon after the death."

"Any violence done to the thumb?" Turner asked. "He had rings on both thumbs when we saw him earlier."

The ME had one of his assistants bring over one of the bright lights. He examined the appendage. "I don't see any signs of violence. I'll examine it more closely at the morgue."

Sanchez brought over Purdy Smeedum who spoke with an eastern European accent. "I come to smoke. I see blood. I run downstairs. That's all I know."

"People smoke up here?" Fenwick said.

"All time. Not illegal. Outdoor café open only in summer."

"Who does and how often?"

"Oh. Not too much. On my shift, just me. One break every two hours. Union rules. I come when my shift begins. I come up again a little while ago. I see lock. I see body."

"You have a key?" Fenwick asked.

"Yes. Sometimes I come up here to do work. No problems before this here at work. No problems now? Okay?"

"Macer is your problem with work rule violations," Fenwick said. "We've got corpses to deal with. Did you know Muriam Devers?"

"No. Who she?" He looked in the direction of the corpse. "That not a lady."

"She died earlier," Turner explained. "You know anybody at this convention?"

"No. Lots of conventions. I sweep floors, mop, carry things. I work hard."

They asked about Foublin and Slate. His lack of knowledge seemed genuine.

On the way down to Melvin's room, Fenwick said, "I'll bite. Why is the ring missing?"

"Don't know," Turner said.

"No repartee? No comments?"

"Today it's just frustration."

A NO MAID SERVICE sign hung on the door. Turner and Fenwick used the key to enter Melvin's room. Inside, black fishing net was draped from every wall. A bloody sword transfixing an anvil dominated the center of the room. Whips, chains, and leather harnesses lay strewn in heaps around the floor.

Fenwick flicked the anvil with his glove-clad finger. "Is this real?"

"I hope not."

"How did he get this crap in here?" Fenwick asked.

"Persistence," Turner said. Fenwick glared. Turner said, "It's a big convention center. They've got people toting boxes in all the time. It must have taken him hours to get all this crap up here. He didn't bring it in one load. It might take someone awhile to get all this shit up here, but it could be done, especially if he had help."

Fenwick tapped a plastic bag on the nightstand. "Looks like fake blood."

"We've had plenty enough of the real stuff."

Fenwick asked, "Is this the horror movie suite?"

Turner said, "No, the set for a medieval torture movie."

"They make movies about medieval torture?"

"Not that I'll admit to watching. We've got a lot of movie people here, maybe they helped him."

Next to the anvil in the middle of the floor was a vase filled with red ostrich feathers.

Fenwick said, "An obsessed ostrich feather freak?"

"Or somebody planted them here. They wanted our convention loser to be implicated."

"Hard not to be implicated with all this shit in here."

"Guilt by medieval weirdness?"

"Works for me," Fenwick said.

On the desk were two laptop computers plugged into the wall. The one on the left was dense with single spaced prose. Turner examined the words. They told of a tumescent plant on the planet Zarth. He scrolled up and down for a few moments. The other computer seemed to be filled with electronic games. Turner examined the desktop and the documents folder. Nothing leapt out at him. He said, "We'll have to get these to the tech guys. Nothing looks suspicious right up front."

"Wouldn't be a mystery if it did," Fenwick replied.

They opened three large suitcases. They were filled with costumes. Some Turner didn't recognize. He assumed they were for characters in books or movies he'd never seen or read. Some were obvious, a Chicago cop's leather jacket, a fireman's heavy coat, a starship captain's spandex shirt.

Turner held up a number of items. "With a little imagination, he could have been about anyone."

Fenwick asked, "Did he plan the costumes because he needed them for the murder, or was this his run-of-the-mill convention attire?"

Turner shrugged. "I dunno."

Near the bottom they found a black cape with an enormous black hood and a set of gloves. The front of the cape and the gloves were splotched with dark stains. "Blood," Turner said. "He wore these when he attacked Rivachec. Maybe some of the others as well."

In the bathroom they found more bloody clothes. Turner said, "I bet the blood on all of these matches Devers' or

Foublin's or Rivachec's or maybe even Slate's. We've got bloody clothes all over the place. Did whoever kill Slate stash them there? If the killer had time to get back down here after he murdered Slate. Where were the guards for this floor?"

Fenwick said, "His room is the first one in from the service elevator. You wait for the guard to turn his back for a second, then you rush in here. In and out in a couple seconds. We should have had guards in all the elevators from the beginning."

"If we're stopping people down below, why would we need to have them?"

Fenwick said, "I suppose. Did he kill all of them? He attacked a cop? He was that organized? Maybe whoever killed Slate was that organized."

"I'm not sure I'm worried about organizational abilities, yet," Turner said. "I'm more worried that the real killer planted all this stuff."

"Maybe Slate was just a dumb, nerdy loser," Fenwick said.

"Yes," Turner said, "but he's also a dead, dumb, nerdy loser. Maybe he was pretty smart or thought he was. Half the criminals in the town think they're geniuses. Maybe he outsmarted himself. You heard the ME. Slate fought. He didn't commit suicide. Remember, there was no sword near the body."

"Maybe he just flung it over the side or it was one of the three we found."

Turner said, "Right, the killer totes around stacks of bloody clothes hither and yon, but says, 'You know, I need to tidy up this sword a bit.' He leaves it with his other stack or, I don't know, maybe he flings the damn sword off the roof."

"Doesn't sound logical," Fenwick admitted.

Turner said, "And if it was flung over the roof, we have more problems. I don't know a lot of people who, when they see a broadsword crash down beside them just say, 'Oh, look Hazel, it's a broadsword that just fell out of the sky and almost killed one of us—let's ignore it and go about our business.'"

Fenwick said, "There's a lot of top of building around up there where it could be lying in the dark. It could have been thrown off and be on a ledge."

"And how likely do we think that is?" Turner asked.

"Not very," Fenwick admitted.

"Although we'll have to look," Turner said.

Fenwick said, "Or maybe as he was twitching around before his body shut down, he flung the thing over the edge to throw us off the correct scent."

"There's a gag waiting to cash in on far-fetched Fenwick flights of fancy, but I can't quite pull it off."

"Okay," Fenwick said, "I'm not trying to come up with impossible scenarios. I'm just saying there's objections. We always discuss objections."

Turner said, "Sorry, I'm getting snarky because of my kid. I was scared for a few seconds up there."

"Yeah, Slate looked like a scrawny nerd when we interviewed him. Sorry. A few bits of leather and him being thin and it being in deep shadow."

"I knew Brian wouldn't leave that room. For a few moments my fears overcame my logic."

"You okay?"

"I'll be a hell of a lot better when we've solved this."

"Why'd this guy lie to us about staying here?" Fenwick asked.

"We were threatening to look in his backpack. I imagine he didn't want his room investigated."

"He's the killer?" Fenwick asked.

"It's got a certain symmetry," Turner said, "up to a point. He's the resident loon. He's the killer. The only problem is, he's dead."

Fenwick said, "Some sainted savior in attempt to attain perfect symmetry whacked him one."

"Great," Turner said. "And why hasn't our sainted savior come forth?"

"That's the thing with sainted saviors," Fenwick said. "They're shy."

"Bullshit," Turner said.

"It's the sainted saviors' code," Fenwick said. "Like the code of the west. The bad guy always gets it in the end. The good guy rides into the sunset. And he only kisses his horse."

"You sure you got the code right?"

"I could be off slightly."

Turner said, "If Slate's the killer, why is he dead? If he's not the killer, why is he dead? His death means we've got somebody still loose in the hotel who could have even more stacks of swords."

"Maybe they're multiplying," Fenwick said. "Breeding."

Turner said, "Phallic symbols of the world unite."

"Somehow I think that should be my line."

On their charts they saw that Slate's room was on the sixth floor, the lowest that had rooms for the public. It was at the major junction of the two corridors. Next to his room were the swinging doors behind which were the pop machines and the service elevator.

They called down to Sanchez. No one had stopped people from going up to the restaurant. It was a public place and had separate elevators from the rest of the building.

They found car keys and the stub for the parking garage. They trudged down to the attendants on duty. Two uniformed cops watched the people in line. There was a huge line to retrieve their cars. Turner and Fenwick stepped to one of the attendants who was standing idly waiting. Turner figured hotels must hire at least one guy to stand idly around the parking garage so people in line could get irritated that someone was just standing around idly waiting.

Fenwick presented him the card and said, "We need to go see this car."

"You gotta get in line." Delivered with an irritated snarl from a flunky who didn't bother to look up. Fenwick took out his badge and got into the personal space of the rude attendant. The man backed away. Fenwick pushed the personal space with the man backpedaling until they were out of sight of the people in line. Then he took the guy by the lapels and said, "You are going to lead us to this car, and now is going to be a good time to do it. Then you're going to come back down here and look like you're working very, very hard to please all those people in line."

The attendant quickly led them to a rickety elevator. They ascended three floors. The parking garage looked like all parking garages. Cement, cold, oil spots in empty spaces, tire-blackened center strips, water dripping in odd places, and the butt ends of lots of cars. Slate's vehicle was a dented and rust-encrusted dark blue van at least twenty years old. It must have barely fit under the height restrictions for the garage. The back seat was folded down. Inside was a car-top luggage carrier. Turner said, "He'd have to go to the trouble of unhooking this thing before he could get it into the parking garage."

"A dedicated and determined killer," Fenwick said. "The very best kind."

Under an army blanket they found three more broadswords.

Fenwick said, "I know a clue when I see one."

Turner said, "Yeah, but it doesn't prove anything. Maybe we could open a used broadsword shop, but it's not helpful. The questions still are is the loon the killer or is the loon in cahoots with the killer?"

"Nobody says 'cahoots' anymore," Fenwick said.

"I do. Did."

"Well, don't."

They put on their plastic gloves and began to remove merchandise from the rear of the van. They found broken red ostrich feathers under the front seat.

"Killer could have planted this stuff," Turner said. "It could be part of the pattern of feathers and death, although we've got seven here. Looks more like a killer's connection rather than a killer's signature."

"Unless he was practicing," Fenwick said.

"How hard can it be to break a feather?" Turner asked.

"Something went wrong?" Fenwick suggested, "or it could be one big set up. This could have all been done hours before."

"The problem is setting the clothes in the rooms or the halls or in these cars, assumes somebody is not going to find them until after bodies start to fall."

"I dunno," Fenwick said. "You'd think somebody would report bloody clothes. I'm not so sure about the feather problem. Dead bodies, sure somebody's gonna blab, or scream, definitely get upset. This feather crap would be out of context, but not in the same league. So far we've got nobody who found stuff before our first corpse."

"Which doesn't mean it wasn't there," Turner said. "I just don't think there's enough time for our killer to get around to all these places."

"Unless somebody knew the schedules of all these people," Fenwick said. "Not hard to look in the convention program. At least some of these people would be out of their rooms at particular times."

"We've got too many people stationed throughout the hotel for it to have happened recently."

"Between our arrival and Rivachec's wounding he had at least an hour. Probably more."

"It wasn't that long ago when we interviewed Melvin Slate," Turner pointed out.

"Slate know something about the killer or was in it with the killer."

Turner said, "Gotta be. He saw something or knew something. Slate didn't strike me as the kind of guy to go rushing to the police."

Fenwick said, "Maybe he knew something earlier when

we were questioning him. Maybe if I hadn't been so snarky we'd have gotten what he knew."

"Would you be you if you weren't snarky?" Turner asked.

"I'd be me, but maybe we'd be more effective."

"I couldn't get it out of him either," Turner said. "When we find the killer we'll get the time line. It's not your fault if he's dead."

"Yeah," Fenwick said. "It may not be, but I'm not feeling real good about it right now."

Turner called the ME's office. His question of could there have been more than one killer was met with uncertainty. The ME said, "In each of the rooms we have evidence of all kinds of people, any one or two or more of whom could have been the killer. We have no notion of anyone else's identity. So far we only have blood from the dead people. We don't have the stuff from up on the roof processed. I'm not even sure it's here yet."

"Could you get that taken care of as quickly as possible?" Turner asked. "We might have a killer on the loose."

"Do what I can."

They summoned Oona Murkle, Melissa Bentworth, and the other convention organizers. They told them about Melvin Slate's death. There were some tears. Turner didn't think it was because they knew him—perhaps it was a mixture of sadness for any loss, but also watching what they had worked to produce turn to ashes.

Oona said, "This is too awful. I know he wasn't famous, but most of the people here aren't. Every life is valuable. How awful? Did the same thing happen to him that happened to . . . ?"

"Yes," Turner said.

"This is terrible. Terrible. This is only getting worse. What's happening? What's gone wrong? Yesterday at this time this was a perfect convention. Oh my, oh my." Her hand trembled as she dabbed a tissue at her eyes. "I've worked so hard to make this a perfect experience for everyone. We've done everything. All those volunteers. The committee in charge. It's been so wonderful." She gulped, then gasped, then whimpered, then cried softly for a few moments. She and Bentworth comforted each other for several minutes. The other organizers looked shocked and stunned.

After the tears had stopped, Turner asked, "Ms. Murkle, can you and the others give us a little more help?"

"I don't know. I'm so upset."

"If you could try," Turner said.

She, Melissa, and the others all nodded.

"Do you know anybody who might have known Melvin Slate?" Fenwick asked.

No one did. "I'll check with all the volunteers," Oona said.

"We'll send a uniformed officer with you," Fenwick said.

"Certainly. If you think that will help. Someone must have known him. He couldn't be here all by himself."

Yeah, he could, Turner thought. They'd sent beat cops to all the people in the ballroom who were waiting to go up to their rooms to see if any of them knew Melvin Slate.

Murkle and the others left.

When they'd gone, Fenwick went to use the washroom. He came back a moment later. Carrying a broken red ostrich feather. Fenwick brandished the thing above his head and exclaimed, "What the fuck?"

Turner rose, "The killer has been in here since we left to check on Melvin Slate?"

"I never checked the bathroom when we first came in here. Nobody's used it that I know of. It could have been there for hours. Since yesterday. For the past ten years."

"No bloody clothes?" Turner asked.

"No."

"Which means what?" Turner asked.

"I feel left out," Fenwick said. "Everybody else gets clothes and feathers. We only get a fucking feather."

"Some of them got dead and feathers but no clothes."

Fenwick said, "I think I'm going to file a killer harassment complaint."

Turner said, "We already have a department for that. It's called the police."

"Worse luck. I could have been rich."

They talked to Sanchez. He said, "Nobody's guarding this part of the corridor. It's the room where you're doing the interrogations. Who'd think that would need protecting? This is the floor where the first murder took place. There's somebody around the corner in front of the door where your family and friends are and near the room we found the first victim in. I didn't stay here. I followed you guys up to the roof."

"This area was unguarded," Fenwick said, "for as long as we were on the roof and in his room. Somebody has a hell of a lot of access."

But neither Macer nor the convention people knew anyone who had used this room. It was one of the comped rooms that had been set aside for any emergency VIP who might show up.

When the detectives were alone, Turner said, "Could the killer have been trying to get rid of all the cops on this floor in order to get to my family?"

"Why?" Fenwick asked. "Someone who's angry at you? We've only had the run-of-the-mill gang and spouse shootings lately. Could be an old case that someone's angry about, but how would they know that we'd catch this case?"

"If the killer is disguised as a cop, it might give him some access to some of this knowledge."

Fenwick said, "We've got guards here now who are known to us who are not going to fuck up."

Turner nodded. He drew a deep breath. "I want this solved now, tonight."

Fenwick said, "Do we have two killers for sure?"

"Has to be, but the timing is screwed up. It could still be

the killer planting all this stuff hours before. We know when Devers was killed pretty precisely because of the scream. We know when our cop was attacked."

Sanchez brought in a woman who looked to be in her early thirties. She might have been five feet tall and weighed about one hundred five pounds. She wore blue jeans and a dark blue cashmere sweater.

Sanchez said, "This is Nettie Timson. Brandon Mercer sent her up. Ms. Timson knew Melvin Slate." Sanchez left. The three of them sat.

24

Turner said, "You know Melvin Slate?"

"I live in the apartment next door to him and his mother. Is he okay?"

Turner said, "I have difficult news. Melvin is dead."

"Oh, my dear. Oh, my." Her hand flew to her face. "His poor mother. He takes care of her. His brothers and sisters treat Melvin and their mother like dirt. She has no one else. That poor man and his poor mother. What on Earth happened?"

Turner gave her a simple outline.

"How well did you know him?" Turner asked.

"We were neighbors. We watched out for each other. We didn't date. That would be difficult with Melvin."

"Why so?" Turner asked.

"Well, he was kind of a loner, but a sweet guy. A nice guy. He was always willing to help anyone in the building. He was better than the landlord at helping getting things fixed. He'd pester the landlord for you. He'd write letters. He'd even try to fix things sometimes. He wasn't very good at it."

Turner said, "He had kind of a negative reputation at the convention."

"You had to be very patient with Melvin. It took a long

time for him to be comfortable with people. He's very at ease in the apartment house. His parents lived there since before he was born. His dad died twenty years ago. It's been him and his mom since."

"How long have you known him?"

"A little over seven years."

"Do you know anyone who would want to hurt him?"

"No. I can't imagine it. He was sweet. Always sweet."

"He told us he wasn't registered at the hotel," Turner said, "but he was."

"He saved every penny to be able to go to these conventions. He wasn't always able to stay at the major hotels. They were expensive."

Turner asked, "Is there a reason why he would lie to us about where he was staying?"

"I can't imagine him doing that. Melvin just didn't tell lies. You'd think living with his mother, he'd develop some secret life, but he was just a gentle soul."

"What kind of job did he have?"

"He was an assistant manager of a pet store. He was very good with the animals. Very gentle. Not so good with the customers."

"How so?" Turner asked.

"If a customer mistreated an animal, it would upset Melvin. I don't blame him. I know one example that came up every springtime. He thought it was criminal to allow people to buy rabbits and little chicks for Easter. He said they just bought them for their kids who neglected them and hurt them and then abandoned them. So many of the poor things died. I guess he was right."

"Are you registered at the convention?" Turner asked.

"No. It was on CLTV news that Muriam Devers had been killed here at the convention. Melvin's mom called me. She frets and worries. She asked me to come down here. I asked for Melvin at the registration desk. They said people were looking for anyone who knew him. I met this older woman who took me to hotel security."

"We never asked about him at the registration desk," Fenwick said.

"We had no reason to," Turner said.

"How could he have died such a violent death?" Timson asked. "He was so meek and mild. He was always in his room writing away. That's all he did in his spare time, write and go to the library. They couldn't afford the Internet charge at home so he had to go to the library to get on the net. Except for his job, he didn't go out much. Never on a date. Besides work, the library and the grocery store were about the only other places he went."

"What did he write?" Turner asked.

"I only read one short story once. A very short one. I don't read much. It had all kinds of flowery descriptions, and he used a lot of big words. He must have been well educated, very smart, but kind and gentle."

"Did he ever try and get anything published?" Turner asked.

"I don't know."

Turner said, "He wore black and gray thumb rings."

"Yeah, he said he got them at a garage sale out on Montrose. He said he had to take a bus to get to it."

"Sometimes people who wear them are members of some pretty dangerous cults."

"Melvin? A member of a cult? I don't think so. He was so gentle. You should have seen him with his mother. He was wonderfully patient."

Turner asked, "Did red ostrich feathers have any special meaning to him?"

"Not that I know of. I think I saw one when I was in his room once. He was showing me his latest manuscript. He had stacks of unfinished manuscripts."

"Did he ever mention anyone named Dennis Foublin?"

"No. Wasn't that the other person who was on the news?"

"Yes."

"Oh, dear. He's dead also. Oh, dear."

Turner said, "Melvin was dressed in a costume when we found him. Did he wear lots of costumes?"

"I don't know what he did at these conventions. He went to a lot of them. On the weekends he was gone, I always checked in with his mom once or twice."

"What's wrong with her?" Turner asked.

"Cancer. Long, lingering, painful cancer. Melvin is a saint for how he helped her. I felt sorry for both of them."

▲ 25 ▲

As Nettie Timson was leaving, there was a commotion outside their door. Turner heard Sanchez's voice and several
others. The two detectives hurried to the entrance. In the
hall Sanchez had his feet spread, his hands on his hips, and
was facing Darch Hickenberg. The supercilious author was
surrounded by several other beat cops. Hickenberg was
pointing his finger at Sanchez and speaking loudly. "This is an
outrage." He spotted the two detectives and advanced toward them. The uniformed officers moved to bar his way.

Turner and Fenwick stepped forward. "What the hell is
going on?" Fenwick asked.

Hickenberg had on one of the hotel's fuzzy blue bathrobes,
the sides of which were flapping open. Underneath he wore a
pair of purple sweatpants and a black sweatshirt with the logo
of a California winery imprinted on it.

Hickenberg was holding a broken red ostrich feather.

"Where'd you get that?" Fenwick demanded.

Hickenberg said, "I want to know what the hell is going on
around here. Aren't the police doing anything to protect us?"

Turner thwarted any attempt by Fenwick at bombast. He
wasn't in the mood. He needed answers, and he needed them

now. Turner said, "We want to know what is going on as well. Why don't you step in here, and we can discuss it?" But Turner's patience was on a thin edge. Part of him would welcome a Fenwick eruption.

They entered the interrogation suite. Hickenberg took up half the couch. He flung the feather on the coffee table.

Turner asked, "What's happened?"

"About six I decided to see if I couldn't get a poker game started in spite of all this. I figured if a group of us were all together, no one could accuse us of committing a crime. I'd been up in my room all afternoon since before you questioned me. When I wanted to go back to my room, the police wouldn't let me on the elevator until I produced my room key. I didn't realize we wouldn't be let back up. That's an outrage."

"You went to the lobby," Turner prompted.

"I couldn't get anybody on the phone. I thought I'd check around."

"In your bathrobe?" Fenwick asked.

"I tried going to a friend's room. The police stopped me. I was forced to appear in the lobby as you see me. I was the cause of amusement. The police department will pay for this. I started talking to a few people. Everybody was saying there's been more murders, and they weren't being allowed into their rooms or suites without permitting them to be searched. The police were officious about my going, but they were positively obstreperous about my returning. I, however, am not an idiot. If there's a killer on the loose, then absurd as it may seem, I felt my room should be inspected to make sure it was safe. I ascended to the room with two officers. On top of my laptop computer I found that." He pointed to the feather.

Fenwick said, "It wasn't there when you left?"

"Of course it wasn't there. Why do you think I'm so pissed off? Someone was in my room. I demanded to see you two. They said you were up on this floor. What the hell is going on?"

Fenwick said, "You've never had one of these?"

"Never. They're silly affectations."

"No one else has a key to your room?"

"Of course not."

"One of your poker buddies?"

"No."

"Did you get two keys when you checked in?"

"I didn't bother."

Fenwick asked, "You didn't let anyone into your room?"

"Are you implying that I could have missed someone planting one of these stupid feathers?"

Turner recognized the empurpled cheeks of his partner. He decided not to attempt to intervene. He was fed up with Hickenberg as well.

Fenwick said, "I asked a fucking question. It was a simple fucking question. How the fuck would I know what you miss or don't miss? How the fuck would I know how observant you are? How the fuck would I know how stupid you are? You certainly think you're pretty fucking bright, but you're the one in this group who's been tootling around one of the most expensive hotels in Chicago in a fucking bathrobe." Fenwick could speak very fast and very loudly and very articulately when he was really pissed. He was really pissed. Fenwick glared at Hickenberg. "Answer the fucking question or do I need to break it down into words of one syllable?"

Hickenberg actually looked abashed, like a deflated Rush Limbaugh. "I, uh, I didn't let anyone in."

"Fine," Fenwick snapped.

Turner said, "There's got to be a reason why you got one of those feathers. There's got to be some connection between you and Devers and Foublin."

"Was I going to be killed?"

"Hard to say," Turner said. "How long were you downstairs?"

"It wound up being over an hour and a half. I talked to a lot of people. I had to wait quite awhile for the police."

Turner said, "You left before we assigned personnel to each floor. It happened after you left. There's quite a time gap."

Turner didn't mention the notion that Hickenberg himself could in some way be involved. He'd also seen others before try to capitalize on a crime for their own publicity purposes. He didn't see Hickenberg having the wherewithal to be rushing about the hotel planting clues and wielding swords. Although if there were two killers, he could certainly be part of the planning and do some planting of clues.

◣ 26 ◢

Hickenberg got escorted off. Turner said, "The Hickenberg feather might not be as helpful as we'd like. He claims he was gone for an hour and a half, but the big blowhard might have been downstairs for several hours."

"Obstreperous blowhard," Fenwick said.

"That your new favorite word?"

"Only if that fuck is the killer."

"Was somebody trying to kill Hickenberg?" Turner asked.

"Justifiable homicide," Fenwick said, "and this time I'm sticking to my guns, even if he isn't dead yet."

Sanchez reentered, "I've got another one of those losers. Melissa Bentworth pointed him out to me." Sanchez spoke into his communicator and summoned the person to be questioned.

Otto Oxenham was tall and even more emaciated than Melvin Slate. He wore a baggy black T-shirt with a death's head on the front. He wore metal rings on both thumbs. Each ring had alternating flame and pentagram decorations on them. His pants bagged at the waist and knees and hung over his shoes to drag on the floor. He had zits peeking out of his wisps of whiskers on his chin. His prominent nose separated two of the greenest eyes Turner had ever seen. Turner thought he must be wearing contacts. Oxenham looked like he might still be in his teens.

He said, "Is Mel really dead?"

"I'm sorry, yes," Turner said.

"I just don't believe that," Oxenham said. "We were always careful. Always."

"Careful about what?" Turner asked.

"We talked on the Internet a lot. You always have to be careful when you go out. You never know who you're going to meet."

"Anybody specific you had to be careful about?"

"People didn't like us. We didn't dress the same way as others. I'm one of the goths in high school everybody else avoids."

Fenwick said, "If everybody avoided you, who did you have to be careful of?"

"We were hassled in high school. We were hassled at conventions."

"Who would hassle you?"

"Security guards. Uptight people. I always paid my way. I never tried to cheat on getting in. If you pay, why should they hassle you?"

Turner asked, "How long have you known Melvin?"

"Four or five years. We met in a chat room about SF. He was a good writer. We subscribed to several of the same listservs. I read a bunch of his stuff that he sent me on the Internet. I sent him my stuff, too. He gave good criticisms. I could trust him. You can't trust a lot of people in the SF world. He taught me that."

"Why can't you trust them?" Turner asked.

"If you send script proposals to Hollywood, they try to steal your ideas. Same with editors. You send them a proposal or three chapters and an outline and they try and steal them."

234

"Wouldn't they be sued?" Fenwick asked.

"We're all just little guys. They've got big lawyers and big budgets."

"But if that's how they do business," Fenwick said, "wouldn't the more famous and richer authors complain and file suit?"

"They're in it with them. Where do you think all those famous writers get their ideas? From us little guys who are dumb enough to keep sending them stuff."

"Then how did they get to be famous writers?" Fenwick asked.

"It's a conspiracy," Oxenham insisted.

Turner wasn't in much of a mood to hear this debate. He said, "Did you see Melvin at the convention today?"

"A few times. We met in line to get books signed by Deborah Krenck. She is such a good writer. She isn't bogged down in patriarchal linearity."

"What?" Fenwick asked.

Before Oxenham could explain, Turner said, "When was the last time you saw Melvin?"

"We ate sandwiches under an awning across the street in the park for lunch. Neither of us could afford this hotel food. It's way overpriced."

"You knew he was staying at the hotel?"

"Yeah. He had to cut corners pretty much. He didn't have a lot of money."

"Are you staying at the hotel?" Turner asked.

"I take the train down every day from the north suburbs. I'm a senior at New Trier High School."

"Was Melvin going to be wearing a costume?"

"He didn't say anything to me about a costume. We talked about how stupid some of them were."

"We found a lot of them in his room."

"We talked about that. If you were going to do a costume,

you should do it right. We discussed everything. He didn't treat me like a kid. He listened to me. We both had dreams."

"What were those?" Turner asked. He sensed Fenwick's exasperation beginning to rise. Turner figured if he had to listen to debates about paranoia, then Fenwick could listen to a kid's dreams. Besides, Turner was still trying to figure out what made Melvin tick. He'd gotten himself murdered and Turner needed to understand the hidden depths there.

Oxenham said, "He wanted to be a published writer. He'd been trying for years. He was dedicated to his craft. Even if he never got anything published, he still wrote. Every day. He didn't get published because of the people who were out to get him. Authors wouldn't give you their secrets for getting manuscripts finished and getting them published. It was a closed world. We had to fight against that."

"Who specifically?" Turner asked.

"The convention planners. I know I don't dress absolutely perfectly, but you could tell they were always watching you. If you tried to talk to an author, they were always there to try and stop you."

Fenwick said, "Look at yourself. Would you trust someone dressed like you?"

"Is that profiling? Do I have to wear a Brooks Brothers suit to get respect?"

"Did you ever try it?" Fenwick asked.

"You don't wear a Brooks Brothers suit," Oxenham countered.

"I'm not a murder suspect," Fenwick said. "I'm not a corpse."

"Does that mean I am a murder suspect or a corpse?" Oxenham asked.

"Neither yet," Fenwick said.

Turner asked, "Did Melvin say anything about being in danger, being worried about anything specific?"

"We were always careful. We always watched to see who the security guards were. We tried to keep away from them. We tried to watch out for cheaters in the game rooms. We were meeting up with some people late tonight. We were going to go to a fast food place for dinner, although downtown is awfully expensive even at a fast food place. How can they raise their prices when you're only ten miles away from where it's much cheaper?"

Turner asked, "Did he mention going up on the roof?"

Oxenham licked his lips with a thin purple tongue. "You guys don't know about the roof here?"

Turner and Fenwick shook their heads.

"It's like a Chicago legend. There's all these secret places in Chicago. You see newspapers write about them sometimes. Like odd stuff at the tops of buildings. Mel and I went to every place that was in the paper and then we tried to find some of our own. It was fun."

"What was odd about this place?" Turner asked.

"It had that Lucite garden. It was an island of serenity. You didn't have to pay. A lot of tourists hadn't discovered it yet. When they built this hotel, they wanted a spot of peace and serenity."

Turner said, "You wear the same kind of thumb rings as Melvin."

"Yeah, he got his at a garage sale out on Montrose. I had to hunt to find the exact same kind."

"Why did you want the same ones?" Turner asked.

"I thought they were cool."

Fenwick said, "We associate that kind of thing with some pretty sinister cults."

"I'm not a member of a cult."

"One of Melvin's rings is missing."

"I don't have it."

"Why would someone take it?"

"I don't know."

"To prove to a cult leader that the murder had taken place?" Fenwick asked.

Oxenham said, "Why would you need to prove it? Murders make the headlines in this city all the time."

He knew no more. He left.

"Patriarchal linearity?" Fenwick asked.

Turner said, "It means that it tells a story from beginning to end in sequential order."

"Patriarchal linearity?" Fenwick re-asked.

"You could make it your new favorite word, or more accurately favorite phrase."

"How do you know what that means?"

"If you can write poetry, I can read books."

"Show off."

Turner said, "Why isn't this a cult thing?"

Fenwick said, "I just don't take these guys that seriously."

"Slate got himself killed. That's serious."

Fenwick said, "Mostly what I know about that cult crap comes from Carruthers."

"I thought you said you didn't listen to him."

"Maybe I watched you listening to him. The point is, yeah, you hear about some cults require you to kill somebody before you can get in. I don't think that's what is happening here. Oxenham seemed like a reasonably harmless dweeb to me."

"Those are the kind you have to watch out for," Turner said, "the ones who look harmless."

Fenwick said, "I know we're not going to dismiss anything out of hand, but I'm not looking for a cult solution to this."

"Neither am I, but we're not going to make the fatal mistake of omitting a possibility just because it's unlikely."

Fenwick nodded.

Turner said, "I'm going to check on my kids and Ben."

238

⊾ 27 ⊿

Paul walked into the room with his family in it. Brian was lying on the bed, his eyes on the television which was playing softly. When Paul entered, he sat up on the bed and turned off the television. He asked, "What's up, Dad?"

"There have been a few developments." He outlined recent events, omitting gory details. He finished, "You didn't leave the room, did you?"

Ben said, "We've been here all the time. We did get one call that you wanted to talk to Brian, but when he went downstairs you weren't down there. He came right back up."

Paul felt ill. "What time was this?"

"About an hour, maybe an hour and a half ago," Brian said. "Why did you want to talk to me?"

"I didn't."

The room became very silent. Paul could hear the distant sound of water moving in pipes. The wind howled outside the window.

Paul asked, "What did the voice sound like?"

"It was kind of mechanical. It might have been a computer-generated voice. A real sophisticated one. Or someone recording a disguised voice on a computer and playing it back."

"What if you asked it a question?" Jeff, the younger boy asked. "They wouldn't have time to record a new message."

"I didn't think to ask any questions. I figured Dad wanted to talk to me."

Paul said, "From now on, you need to leave with a police escort and then only with a cop I have introduced you to and that you've met through me before."

Turner knew they'd found two high-end laptop computers in Slate's room. Either one would have been capable of playing a recorded voice.

Mrs. Talucci and Myra were not present. Ben said, "It's getting kind of late. Mrs. Talucci was tired. Myra drove her home."

"I thought she never got tired," Fenwick said.

"She's over ninety," Turner said. "She's entitled to be tired any time she wants." He blushed. "Sorry. It's late. I'm fed up and frustrated." He turned to Brian. "How are you holding up?"

Brian said, "Was someone going to try and kill me when I went to talk to you?"

Paul didn't want to lie to his son. He also didn't want to accelerate the boy's fear or his own. He said, "There was another murder about that time. I think the killer may have wanted to try to implicate you."

"But cops watched me get on and off the elevator. Officer Sanchez made sure I wasn't hassled. He can vouch for me."

"So you were pretty safe."

"I did spend some time looking for you. I had to ask around. Nobody knew. You weren't in the lobby. A lot of cops were. I figured if it was important, you'd find me here, so I came back up. Nobody called you?"

"It wasn't officially announced you were here. Did you tell them you were my kid?"

"No."

Paul said, "They might not have understood the urgency. I kept you up here. I kept that information away from the others.

240

I'm afraid that might have put you in danger. The killer is playing with our minds."

"Have you found anything definite?" Brian asked.

"We can't find a sword that we can prove was yours. Once we've got that, we'll get you out of here. We've got one very active killer. He's done a great deal. You'd have had to have left this room a whole lot of times to do a whole lot of crazy stuff."

Brian said, "I only left the once . . ."

Paul stopped him, "You don't need to explain to me. I don't need alibis or excuses from you. You're going to be okay."

"Thanks, Dad," Brian said.

Paul sighed, "Unfortunately, I don't know how much longer it's going to take."

Jeff said, "Ben said I should go home with Myra and Mrs. Talucci. I didn't want to go." Jeff added a tone of petulance that Paul found irritating in anyone.

Paul looked at his younger son. The detective had had a full day of crime and criminals and suspects. He pulled himself together. One of the things he'd been concerned about was his children's relationship with Ben after his lover moved in. Both boys liked Ben. Brian and Ben often kept up a gentle repartee that was comfortable and friendly. Paul seldom had to discipline Brian. Jeff tended to test limits. Why he chose this moment to challenge Ben, he didn't know. Maybe it was like a little kid throwing a tantrum. You pick the worst moment to challenge the adult most greatly.

Paul squatted down next to Jeff's wheelchair. His older son had escaped a possible lethal situation. That fear of loss kept his temper in check. Losing his sons was his greatest fear. He draped his arm over the back of the chair. He gazed at his son and with an effort of supreme patience said, "We talked for a long time about Ben moving in, didn't we?"

Jeff nodded.

"You know what we said about discipline."

"Yeah, but Dad."

"That's enough," Paul said.

"But."

"Enough." His voice reached its deepest thrum. Neither of sons had ever challenged him after that tone was used. "Enough," he said very quietly again. "You know the rules. You obey me. You obey Ben. You listen to your brother. This is a work situation. I'm sorry you boys got involved in this. There's nothing to be done about that. You've helped me with information about the convention. I appreciate that. However, you need to think about better choices in your behavior."

Jeff hung his head. "Sorry, Dad." He twisted his body to look at Ben. "I'm sorry, Ben."

"It's okay," Ben said.

Paul looked at his son's twisted back. The movement had revealed the front of the back of the wheelchair. He spotted a splash of red. "What's this?" he asked. Jeff began to turn. "Hold still," Paul said. Jeff froze. Paul reached behind his boy.

Using a plastic glove, Turner pulled out a broken red feather. Fear for his family welled up inside him, but cold, unreasoning fury took him for a moment.

"Dad?" Jeff asked.

Paul whispered. "You're going to be all right." He was not going to frighten his sons. With a softness more startling than his deep thrum, he asked, "Where did this come from?"

No one had seen it before.

"When were you last out of the chair?" Paul asked.

"I went to the bathroom before we came up here," Jeff said.

Ben asked, "Is that one of the feathers like Ms. Devers had?"

"Yes," Turner said.

"Why would there be one back there?" Jeff asked.

"I don't know," Paul said. But he was afraid he did. His family wouldn't know about the placement of the feathers around the crime scenes. Someone was sending him a message.

Brian asked, "Something's wrong, isn't it, Dad?"

Paul said, "Something is very wrong."

Jeff said, "I don't get it."

Paul said, "There's nothing to get yet. Buck and I need to get back to work right away. No matter what, do not leave this room. I will have armed guards on the doors. They will not let you go."

"If there's a fire, do we leave?" Jeff asked.

"You do what the policeman outside the door tells you."

Turner and Fenwick walked down the small hall to the door. Paul beckoned to Ben. His lover followed him into the corridor.

"What's going on?" Ben asked.

"We've found a broken red feather at each crime scene."

"Jesus Christ," Ben said. "Are you okay?"

"As long as you guys are okay, I'm okay. I've got to work this case." He summoned one of the beat cops. He said, "My son has been threatened by the killer." He showed him the feather. "This is the killer's signature. No one, no one, is to go in or out of this room. We'll send someone to stay with you." He read the name on the man's tag. Turner sent him for Sanchez, whom he knew and trusted implicitly. A few minutes later the beat cop arrived. Turner quickly filled him in.

Sanchez said, "I'll take care of it. Bruno's here. I know he's not a fake cop."

Ben and Paul moved until they turned a corner and were out of sight of the others.

Paul bashed his hand against the corridor wall. His breath came in ragged gasps. "To fuck with my family!" His voice was raw and hoarse. He bashed his hand again. "Nobody fucks with my family. I will not allow it." He slumped against the wall and repeatedly slapped the palm of his hand against it.

"Is there anything I can do?" Ben asked.

"I've got to solve this. It's got to happen soon."

243

"I'll stay with the boys. We'll be all right. You've taken all the precautions you need to. We'll be safe."

Turner swallowed the comment—but you weren't earlier, the killer was inches from all of you. It would do no good to magnify any fear that Ben was feeling. Paul got his breathing under control. He said, "The killer is going to pay for this."

Ben said, "I know you'll do everything possible." Paul pulled Ben into a fierce embrace. They went back to the others in the hall. Bruno, the other beat cop, showed up. Ben went back into the room. Fenwick and Turner left.

When they were finally alone in the interrogation suite, Fenwick said, "Double and triple fuck. Double, double, and triple, triple fuck." One sure sign that Fenwick had reached total fury was when he reached this level of maledictions. Unbeknown to him, he nearly repeated Turner's curse from moments before. Fenwick said, "Nobody goes after our kids, yours or mine. Nobody. Don't worry, we'll take care of this." He put a hand on his friend's shoulder.

Turner said, "We should have hunted through Slate's backpack when we first had a chance. If we'd have done that, then maybe my boys wouldn't be in the middle of this. We're careful about someone's rights, but when it hits home, I know which side I come down on."

"We'd all protect our kids. We couldn't have known. Don't start that 'had I but known' crap. You are not responsible for your kids being in danger."

"I will be until we catch the second killer."

"Is this cult thing more possible now?" Fenwick asked. "Maybe it would be a badge of honor for a cult member to hurt a cop's family as well as a cop."

"A dangerous game that is going to come to an end."

He called Molton and apprised him of this latest development.

"Son of a bitch," Molton said. He promised more cops and his own imminent return to the scene.

"What now?" Fenwick asked.

"We get that chart of all the movements of the people. We figure out who the hell was where when."

They taped a number of eight-and-a-half-by-eleven pieces of paper together so they'd have a large enough chart. Then they put the names of all the people they'd talked to down one side and all the times in fifteen minute intervals since ten that morning along the top.

28

Turner checked the guest list that Macer had provided them against the convention roster that Murkle had provided. Slate's name was on the one for the convention. Turner said, "We wouldn't have found his name. He wasn't registered."

"Whose room was it?"

"We need to find out." They perused the list of comped rooms. "There's one too many rooms," Turner said.

"What?"

Turner showed him.

"Who gave him the room?"

"Had to be one of the convention planners."

They heard what sounded like a fire alarm. They hurried down the corridor to his family's room. The cops and the family were safe inside.

"Is there really a fire?" Jeff asked.

"We'll find out," Paul said.

"Do we have to evacuate?" Jeff asked.

Paul used the phone in the room to call Macer. "Is it a real fire?"

"We've got a lot of smoke in the dealers' room, and we got a second alarm from the top floor near the restaurant."

"Arson?"

"That's my guess. We're evacuating everybody."

Paul hung up. "We're going to leave." They'd have to carry Jeff's wheelchair down all the stairs. They rushed to the emergency exit. There was no smoke up here now, but the elevators had all stopped. There was a knot of people at the stairs. They waited in line. People were grumbling about the need for evacuation. A few had their suitcases, others toilet kits, one his laptop. Most were a bit disheveled and in odd states of dress. It was late and many might have been awakened.

"The wheelchair's going to clog everything," said a newly arrived hotel guest waiting in line behind them.

Fenwick started to say something. Paul put out a hand. "He's right." He picked up his son.

"Hey," Jeff protested.

"I'll carry you," Paul said. "It's the only way." The stairs were filled with people filing orderly down. People murmured and a few even chatted. A few were cranky. No one seemed out of control. Fenwick huffed a lot. Paul knew that if they were going up, his partner would have been in real trouble.

Halfway down they met some firemen coming up. All stood aside to give them quick passage.

Two thirds of the way down Ben asked, "You need some help?"

Paul refused any assistance. No matter how far it was, he would not tire of carrying his son.

At the ground floor, he took his family outside. An army of fire trucks and personnel had been added to the official confusion in the streets outside the hotel. After ensuring Sanchez and another beat cop were guarding his family, Turner and Fenwick made their way toward the battalion chief at the Incident Command Post. Firemen in their black coats and rubber boots hurried about.

Turner said, "The killer's using this."

"Got to be," Fenwick said, "but why?"

"He needs to get something out of the hotel?"

"The incriminating broadsword is my guess," Fenwick said.

"He's dressed as a fireman," Turner said. "That's what this is about. Think about all the costumes in Slate's room. Was there a fireman's disguise?"

"A black rain slicker," Fenwick said. "I thought it was kind of odd."

"The killer planned that well ahead?" Turner asked.

They arrived at the command center. Molton, the battalion chief, and the local police commander were huddled together. Showing their badges, Turner and Fenwick moved past the other personnel and joined the commanders.

Turner explained their theory.

The fire commander said, "The fire in the dealer's room was fairly serious, but the sprinklers worked. They'll lose most everything from fire or water, but it's out. The fire on the top floor was a bunch of linens and things for the restaurant."

"Was it arson?" Turner asked.

"I've examined both sites," the battalion commander said. "We'll have an official investigation, but I've been to enough of these. Unofficially, we've got an arsonist on the loose."

The streets were thronged with guests. "Are they going to be letting people back in soon?" Turner asked.

"It'll be a few hours before we're done checking the whole complex to make sure it's safe for people to go back in."

Turner and Fenwick stepped across the street. They could see Brian, Jeff, Ben, and their police escort about fifty feet away. Jeff waved. Paul waved back. They had propped his younger son on a hotel chair. Brian hovered close by.

Turner saw Oona Murkle moving toward his family. Her matronly bulk proceeded slowly.

"It's another fake," Turner said. "The fire isn't to cover any kind of escape. All the killer has to do is walk out, check out at a normal time if he's a hotel guest. There's no need for this."

"Unless he's planning another killing."

Turner whirled to look for his family. Oona was about five feet away from Jeff. She walked awkwardly. Turner dashed forward. Fenwick followed. Turner heard several people gasp as he leaped forward and tackled Oona Murkle. He felt her bulk fall under him. He heard the clank of metal as she hit the ground. Moving the folds of her billowing nightgown, he saw a broken red feather and a broadsword with flecks of blood on it.

29

"How'd you know it was her?" Molton asked.

"I didn't until the damn sword hit the ground. I was suspicious. Bentworth told us she was in charge of the small stuff. She was the one in charge of the rooms. She'd have had the easiest access to get Slate in."

They took Oona to Area Ten police headquarters to interrogate her.

Turner asked, "Why my family?"

"I saw you last night when your sons did well in those costume competitions. Everybody was happy except me. Everybody cheered and clapped for the poor kid in the wheelchair. Pah. I hated your family on sight. All those clever costumes in that group, and you in that stupid sport coat. You stood out. I asked about you discreetly. I knew who you were. I remembered. I thought your family might come in handy."

"What started all this?" Fenwick asked.

Murkle sighed. "Everybody is always happy at these. I'm up. I'm always up. I'm known as the cheerful one. I'm the one they can successfully shunt aside. Old Oona. Poor Oona. She won't mind, we'll give her all the shit work. Never the honors. Never the recognition. Never a nibble from a publisher. Never a moment's recognition. Nobody ever wanted to make me fan guest of honor. Nobody dreamt of doing something nice for poor old Oona. I saw your older boy necking behind that curtain. I kind of keep a watch on things. I notice things. I'd seen your kids. The older boy was pushing the younger until the older met the young lady. I saw where they were headed. Nobody is supposed to be behind there. I was going to kill Muriam Devers from the start. I had it all planned perfectly. When I saw your kid, I saw my chance. I saw him go back here with that girl. I knew he wasn't supposed to be back here. I followed him. Kids these days. No respect. He unbuckled his sword. He couldn't maneuver with it on. He was occupied with his young lady. I took the sword. It fit in with my schemes."

"How did you plan to get away with a public murder in the street?"

"If I got the chance, I would do what I could to any member of your family. There was a lot of confusion and chaos. There was only one sword with tell-tale blood on it. I know from what I've read, they can find traces on anything. I had to get rid of it. If nothing else the confusion would let me get the thing out of here."

"Why not just put it in your car?"

"Guards were everywhere. You had people watching the exits to the parking garage. I couldn't risk it. It's safer to hide something in as public a way as possible."

"How'd you hook up with Slate?"

"He was a bonus. It didn't hurt that at the last one of these in Chicago I caught him in a room he didn't belong in. He knew how to break into the rooms. He had one of those deals you see in television and the movies. You know, one of those plastic cards connected by wires to a box about as big as a calculator. It had a read out. I have no idea where he got it from. He's been breaking into rooms at conventions for years."

"Why didn't you turn him in?" Fenwick asked. "You couldn't have had any connection to him."

251

"I felt sorry for him when I'd seen him at previous conventions. The poor soul was such a mess. I pitied him. I was kind to him. He was grateful. My pity got me an ally. Then I saw them giving him a hard time at the registration desk at this convention. Something about a late payment. He didn't think what I had planned was going to go nearly as far as I thought, although he was almost as frustrated and angry at some of these people as was I. At first he was just helping me plant the damn feathers and the bloody clothes. He thought we were just going to mess with their minds."

"Slate had been breaking into rooms?" Fenwick asked.

"At numerous conventions. For years. He confessed quite readily to me. Once he knew I wasn't going to turn him in to the police, he seemed quite eager to join in the original mischief. He seemed pleased to actually be treated with respect by anyone. When it escalated, at first he seemed quite eager."

"How did it escalate?"

"We were in Muriam's room. I thought she'd be down at that damn signing forever. She was, but not as long a forever as I thought. When we heard her come in, we hid in the unused bedroom in the suite. She changed into her Xena costume. What a joke that was. I think she was waiting for one of her boy toys for a late-morning assignation. Slate made a noise. She searched and caught us. We had an argument. Slate began swinging around that damn sword. She was going to expose me. She was going to embarrass and humiliate me in front of everyone."

"Why'd you pick her room in the first place?"

"Up to the last minute, she'd been trying to ruin the convention. I'd worked so hard to make it perfect."

"How was she going to ruin it?" Turner asked.

"She didn't really want to show up. She tried to get out of it. She didn't tell any of her lackeys. No one was supposed to know. She made threats to me. I stood my ground. The bitch. On the ride in the from the airport she said she was going to try and get people to not go to the banquet, to not go to the panels, to criticize everything."

"Why?" Turner asked.

"She wasn't getting the kind of attention she felt she deserved. She wasn't enough of a star of the show. She said she had been under the impression she was to be the main attraction. That I'd lied to her. That is absolutely not true. She just wanted to wreck. She had everything and I had nothing. She wouldn't read my manuscript. She wouldn't help me get it published. That's the main thing I've wanted my whole life. She wouldn't do a thing for me after all that I'd done for her for years. She wouldn't help. She wouldn't be faithful."

Fenwick asked, "What was it that you had done that you thought had earned reciprocation on her part?"

"I always tried to help her. I was loyal. Even though her last fifteen books were error-laden drivel, I was supportive. I always gave a hundred ten percent. Do you know how hard it is to be relentlessly cheerful in the face of someone who is so awful to you?"

Turner asked, "Which of you actually killed Ms. Devers?"

"Slate. He was swinging the damn thing to threaten her. He slipped. It was quite sharp. I'd made sure of that. If he hadn't done it, I would have. My, how she screamed. I'll enjoy that scream for a long time."

Turner thought she sounded tougher than a lot of hardened gang bangers he'd dealt with. Her anger and frustration must have built for years. She was also probably nuts. Turner wasn't sure they'd ever have enough forensic evidence to prove which of them did the killing. He was more than willing to listen to Oona Murkle, but he was less than willing to buy her story without a lot of convincing data.

"Why'd you leave the door to Devers' room open?" Turner asked.

"Her scream stunned Slate. I had to practically drag him out of there. He was behind me. There was no time to go back.

Someone could have come around a corner or poked a head out a door at any second."

"Why'd you murder Dennis Foublin?" Turner asked.

"He was a monster."

"How so?"

"He ignored me. Him and Muriam together. They plotted against me."

"You had proof of this."

"People talked."

"Did you ever talk to either of them about what they were trying to do?"

"I didn't have to. I knew what they thought. I saw how they looked at me."

Turner wasn't heavily into the interpretation of random looks from people.

Murkle said, "Foublin wouldn't read my manuscripts. He'd send them back unopened. He never gave me a chance. He could have talked to people. He could have given me a boost on his web site."

"Slate gave us the information that there was something sinister in Foublin's background."

"I told him to tell you that. I thought it would send you off in a wrong direction when investigating."

"Who actually killed Foublin?"

"When we ran out of Muriam's room, we rushed down the stairs. Foublin was entering his room. He saw us. We couldn't be seen together. Slate had blood on his clothes. We got him in his room. Slate held him. Foublin had been mean to Slate at a convention. For a while the first murder seemed to bring something out in him, something cruel. I was a little worried. Foublin was struggling and thrashing. It was lucky that I stuck him instead of Slate."

Fenwick asked, "How come you had an extra feather to leave with Foublin's corpse?"

254

"We were carrying stuff around in Slate's backpack. If you'd have looked in it, you'd have seen broken feathers and bloody clothes. When I brought him to the attention of one of the cops, he didn't have it with him. Some friend came up and brought it to him. Said he'd left it at a table he was sitting at. An unattended backpack? I shuddered. I thought it was hopeless, but it was too late by then. He did well enough. It wasn't your questioning that got to him. I think it was the blood."

"You're the one who brought Slate to our attention," Fenwick said. "Why?"

"It was part of the plan. It would be an obvious red herring. The convention nut."

Turner said, "He was just kind of sad."

"That was the point," she said.

"You left the door to Foublin's room open as well," Turner said.

"That was more by design. The killing had to happen more quickly, but he died without a sound. It was all so quick. We had time to plant the feather and get some bloody clothes. I wanted the corpses found. I wanted there to be uproar. I wanted to watch chaos. I've always lived by the rules and it got me nothing. I wanted the world to revolve around something I did."

"How'd you get so many broadswords?" Turner asked.

"Collected them over the years. I planted some of them on Wednesday. I'd been given a very thorough tour of the hotel. I knew the outdoor café section of the restaurant at the top of the hotel was closed until May. That storage area was unused." Turner remembered the dust.

"Why'd Slate have to die?" Fenwick asked.

"He was losing his nerve. He was the hardest of all because I had to kill him by myself."

Fenwick said, "We have evidence that he might have fought back."

"I got in a good blow from behind. He did a lot of stagger-ing around. I barely got out of there, down to his room with bloody remnants, and back to somewhere safe."

"Why did you put those swords and clothes on the roof?"

"Confusion."

"But how'd you get them up there?"

"Planning. Hard work. No one was expecting something lethal at this convention. I had lots of access from being the liaison with the hotel. Who suspects a matronly woman in her sixties? The stuff on the roof we could get done at three or four in the morning."

"When did you start planting the clothes and feathers in rooms?"

"This morning. I checked people's schedules. We barely got out of the hall after Muriam's death. If we hadn't planted everything before she showed up, I'm not sure we would have made it. Fortunately, I'd planned thoroughly. Slate had helped with all the bloody stuff earlier. It took awhile to get the look and smell right. We did use some real blood from Foublin. Some of the blood was fake. We used some of each to make it more difficult for the police to figure out what was going on. We were lucky to have more time with Foublin. Slate didn't re-ally have the nerve for killing. Once I'd decided to finish off Muriam and use him as a partner, I knew I'd have to eliminate him. It was a risk bringing him to you although you'd have found the loon eventually."

Turner asked, "Weren't you worried he'd break the first time we talked to him?"

"Only a little. At that time he was pretty strong. He began to unravel as more and more cops showed up. When he stabbed the police officer, I think it tipped the scales."

"What happened to his thumb ring?" Turner asked.

"He was always twisting and fiddling with the things. When he got nervous, it got worse. On the roof, before I had to kill him, he was frighteningly nervous. He kept taking them off and putting them back on. He was pacing back and forth, whining and complaining in that high reedy voice. He turned his back on me, and I hit him in the middle of a fidget. After he died, I accidentally kicked the ring. I was lucky to find it. I threw it over the wall. I thought it would help confuse the police."

"We never found it," Fenwick said.

"Why hurt the cop?" Turner asked.

"Slate did that by himself. It was an accident. Slate was going in the door while the cop was coming out. He had a pile of bloody clothes with him at the time. I was behind him."

Turner asked, "Why put his backpack on top of the water tower on the roof?"

"I didn't want to be seen with it. I knew you'd examined it. If I was seen, you might figure out the connection between us. I didn't want to just dump it over the side. I didn't want to hurt an innocent person." She gulped and looked from one to the other of them. "About halfway up the tower, I got a little nervous. I tossed it. Why would anyone think to look up there?"

"Why plant all the stupid feathers?" Fenwick asked.

"It was her symbol. Fine. It could symbolize her death. Stupid fucking Ramble bird."

Turner wasn't agape at the epithet. He'd seen ghastly murder done. A little old lady with a foul mouth wasn't going to even register on his alarm scale.

Murkle was continuing. "I also wanted to plant them everywhere. I had access to all the registration records. I knew enough people. I had enough feathers. I put them in the rooms of the rude or inconsiderate. Everyone who'd ever been supercilious at a convention. Anyone who'd made my work harder with some stupid, petty request. Everybody had to have some stupid, petty request that had to be met or they wouldn't come to the convention. I wish I could have crushed them to death with all the minutiae of their silly, silly requests. The writer Hickenberg was a mean man. I figured I might not be able to kill them all, but I could scare them. They would remember me. I might not be able to get my fiction published, but I could make a headline. Someone would notice my work besides these drones and hacks who plan these conventions."

Fenwick asked, "Why the feather in our bathroom?"

"I knew I wouldn't be physically able to assault you, but I thought I'd scare or confuse you. I slipped the feather into your son's wheelchair. The one in the bathroom was a follow up. I just wish I'd had some bloody clothes."

"Why would the feathers be frightening to other people?" Fenwick asked.

"Maybe they wouldn't be, but I'd understand them. She stole my idea. I had ostrich feathers in several of my books."

"She read your unpublished works?"

"Way back when, I met her at a convention. She agreed to read a manuscript of mine. It had red feathers. I never got published. She did. Her first book was filled with the damn things. Every time I saw her carrying one of those damn things, every single time, I wanted to strangle her."

"Why give Slate one of the hospitality suites?"

"We had to have some place as a central location."

"It gave us a hint that you were involved in something not right."

"Ha," she said. "You're not so bright. You all kept trying to think of some connection between all the people who got feathers or bloody clothes. It was simplicity itself. They were the ones who I arranged rides for from the airport. The first one I picked up was Muriam. She was mean to me. She was rude. She had no reason to be a snot. She'd sneered at me since reading that first book of mine. I confronted her about the feathers. She denied ever having read my manuscript. Just out and out denied it. I can take a lot. I've put up with a lot in my life. That was too much. To deny reality? That drives me insane. That was when I snapped. I knew I had to do something. That was Wednesday when she came in early for the convention. Slate and I had already made plans for mischief. It wasn't hard to accelerate."

She was taken away.

Fenwick said, "I understand the desire to be published. I'd give a lot to see my stuff make it into a book."

"You're not willing to kill for it?"

"Not tonight. We've got a mountain of paperwork, and I'm bushed."

30

Paul Turner arrived home very late. Brian was on the couch. Jeff had his head on his brother's shoulder and was fast asleep. Ben was on the other end of the couch. They were watching *Midnight*, a black-and-white movie starring Claudette Colbert. Afraid of awakening his brother, Brian sat up only slightly. He whispered, "Is everything going to be okay?"

"Yeah."

Paul ruffled his older boy's hair. "Everything's fine."

Ben stood up and moved next to him. Paul put his arm around him.

"Was it really that old lady?" Brian asked.

"The older woman and a partner in crime."

"Why?" Brian asked.

"Because people have disappointments all the time. Because sometimes disappointment hurts too much."

"Why us?" Brian asked.

"Random chance," Turner said.

Brian digested this bit of reality.

Jeff awakened and said, "I lost my costume."

Paul said, "After all that's happened, would you really want to go to another SF costume event?"

"Why not? Bad things happened, sure, but they weren't our fault. You solved the case."

"You could have been hurt."

"But I've got you guys to protect me."

And Turner wanted to protect them and keep them safe forever. Later, he let Ben wrap his arms around him, and for a little while he felt protected as well.